MOUSE

THE STAR CRUSHER

BY JAKE PARKER

graphix

AN IMPRINT OF

SCHOLASTIC

New York   Toronto   London   Auckland   Sydney   Mexico City   New Delhi   Hong Kong

OFFICIAL
GSA
DOCUMENT

FOR
EYES
ONLY

ACKNOWLEDGMENTS

Big galactic thanks to Anthony Wu, Jason Caffoe, Kohl Glass, Katie Smith, Tom Saville, Mike Lee, Dave Strick, and Phil Falco for giving their time and talents to the creation of this book. And a stellar thank-you to Judy Hansen, Sheila Keenan, and David Saylor for your faith in me. Most importantly, thanks to my wife, Alison, for her whip cracking, her wrangling of kids, and her patience. This book would still be fiddling around in the recesses of my imagination if not for her.

ISBN: 978-0-545-11714-2 (hardcover)
ISBN: 978-0-545-11715-9 (paperback)

Library of Congress Cataloging-in-Publication Data Available

15 14   17 18/0

First edition, January 2010
Edited by Sheila Keenan
Creative Director: David Saylor
Book design by Phil Falco
Printed in the U.S.A.   40

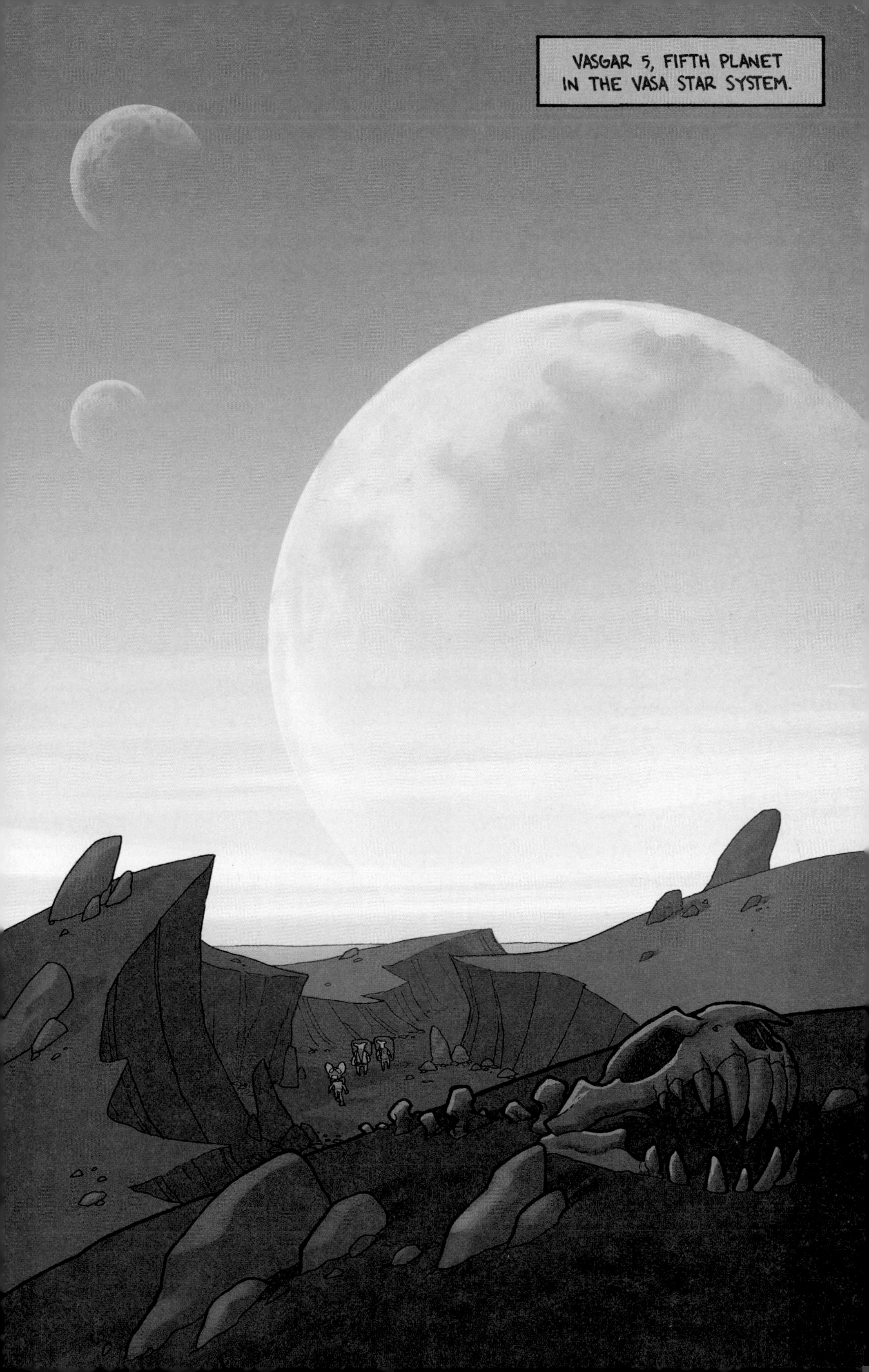
VASGAR 5, FIFTH PLANET IN THE VASA STAR SYSTEM.

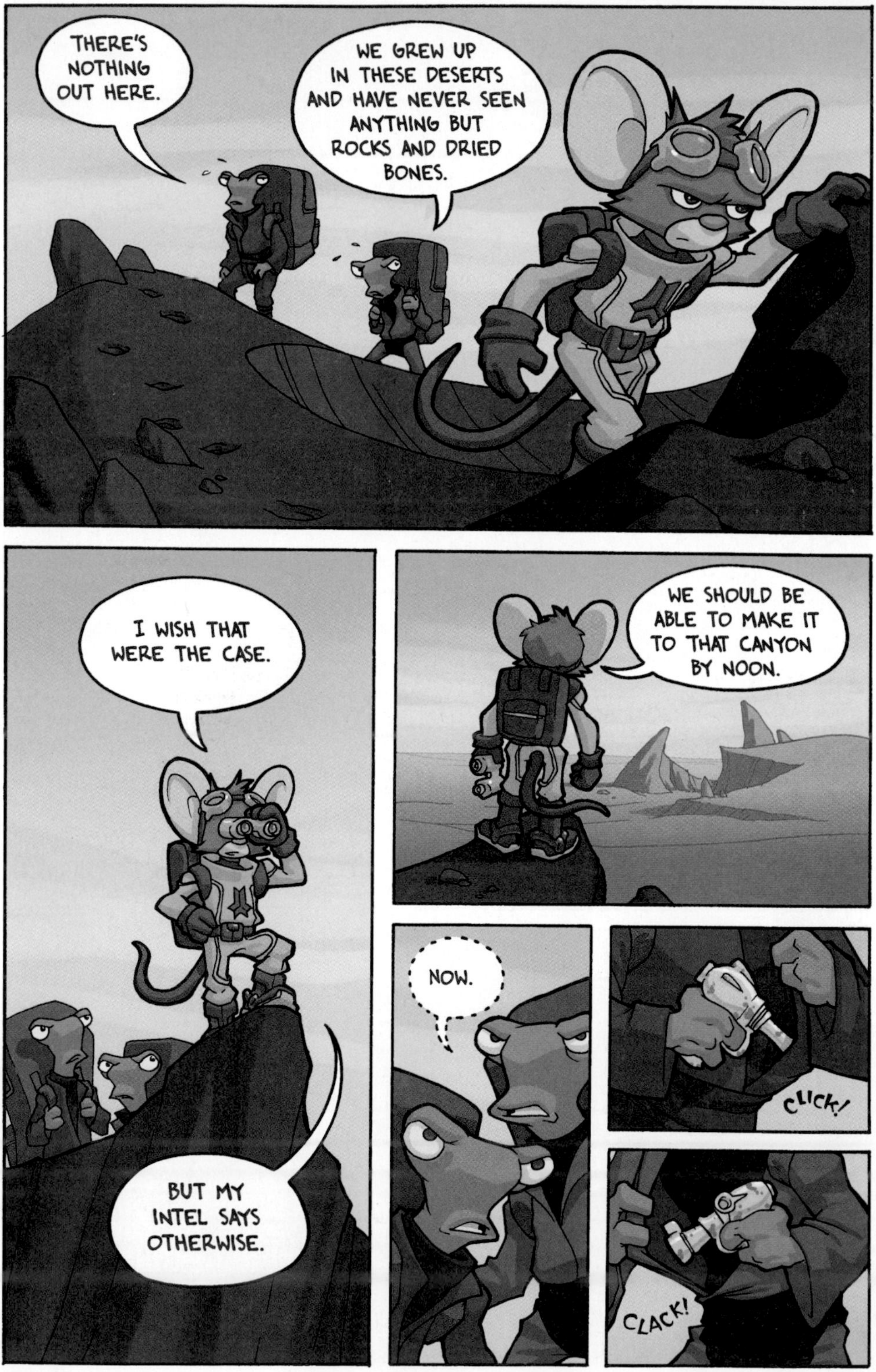
THERE'S NOTHING OUT HERE.
WE GREW UP IN THESE DESERTS AND HAVE NEVER SEEN ANYTHING BUT ROCKS AND DRIED BONES.
I WISH THAT WERE THE CASE.
BUT MY INTEL SAYS OTHERWISE.
WE SHOULD BE ABLE TO MAKE IT TO THAT CANYON BY NOON.
NOW.
CLICK!
CLACK!

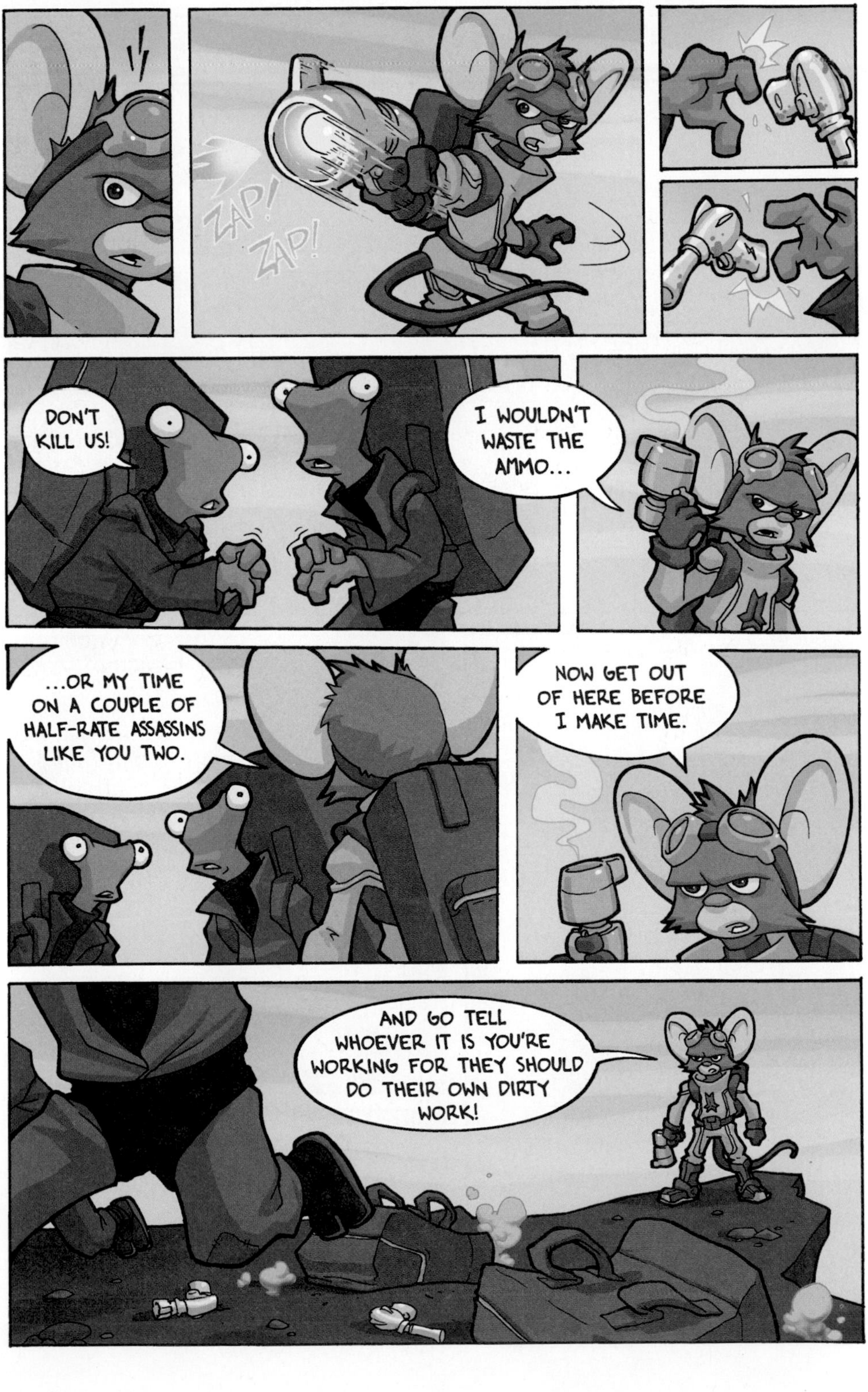
ZAP! ZAP!
DON'T KILL US!
I WOULDN'T WASTE THE AMMO...
...OR MY TIME ON A COUPLE OF HALF-RATE ASSASSINS LIKE YOU TWO.
NOW GET OUT OF HERE BEFORE I MAKE TIME.
AND GO TELL WHOEVER IT IS YOU'RE WORKING FOR THEY SHOULD DO THEIR OWN DIRTY WORK!

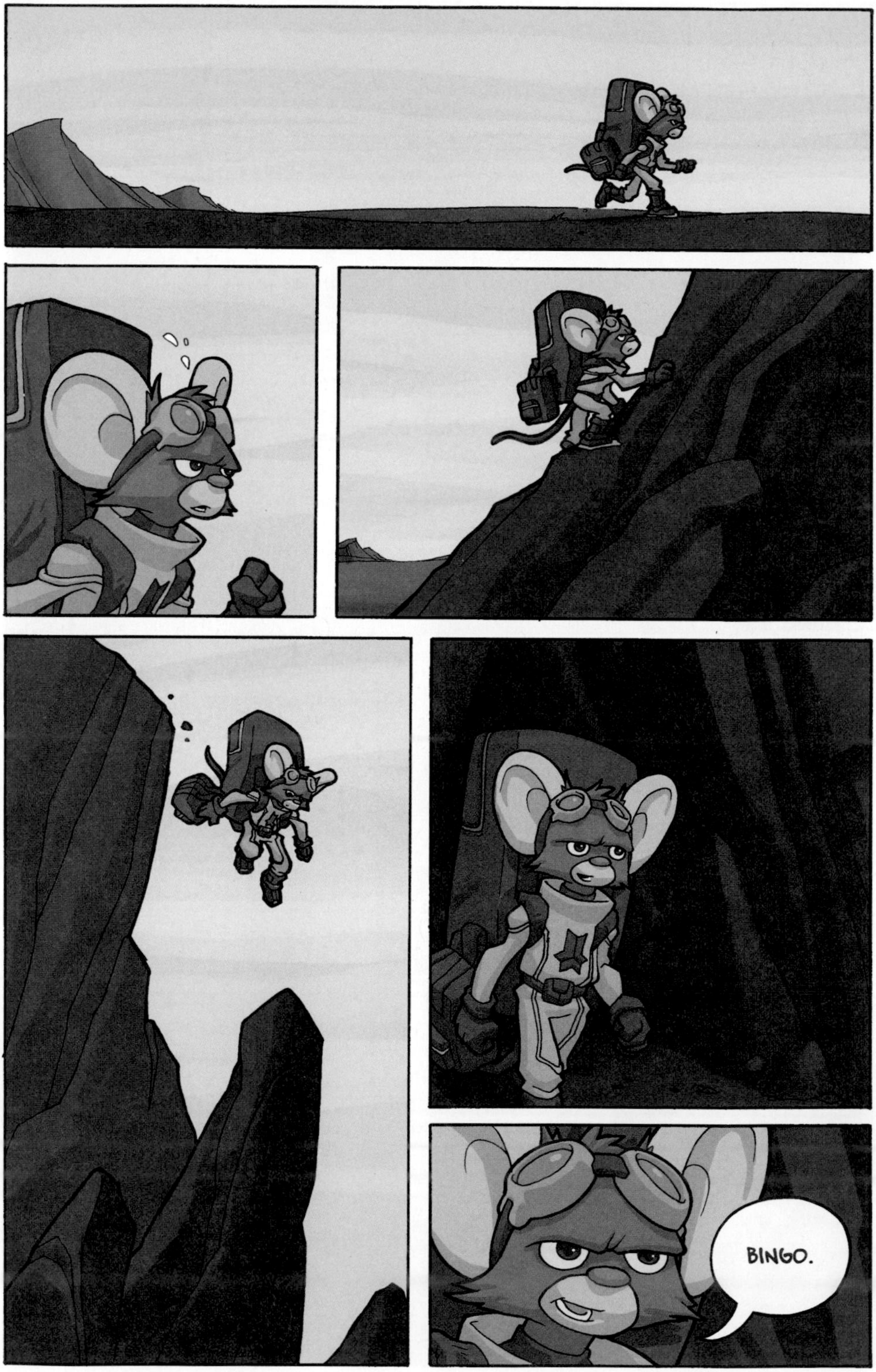
BINGO.

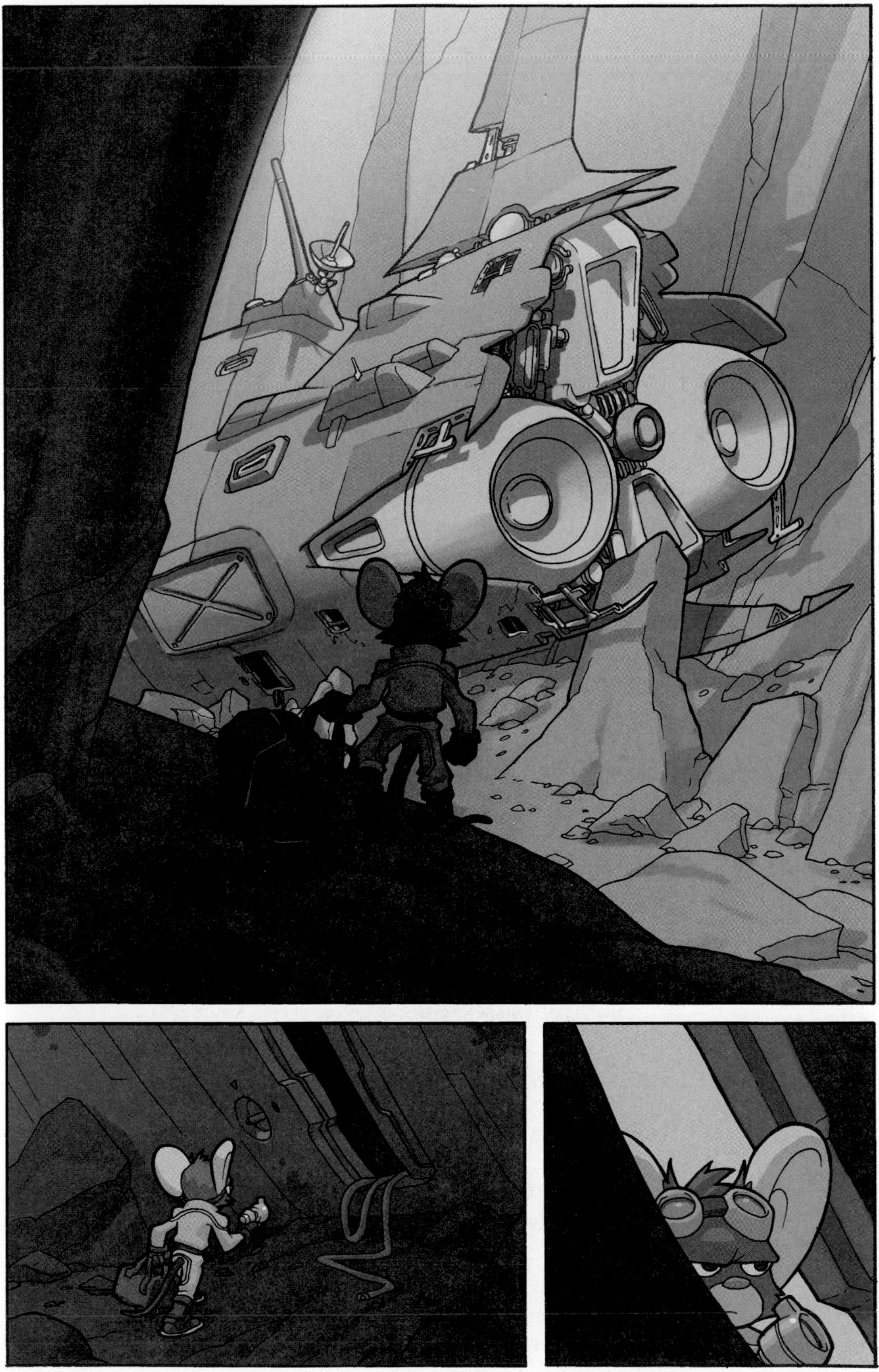

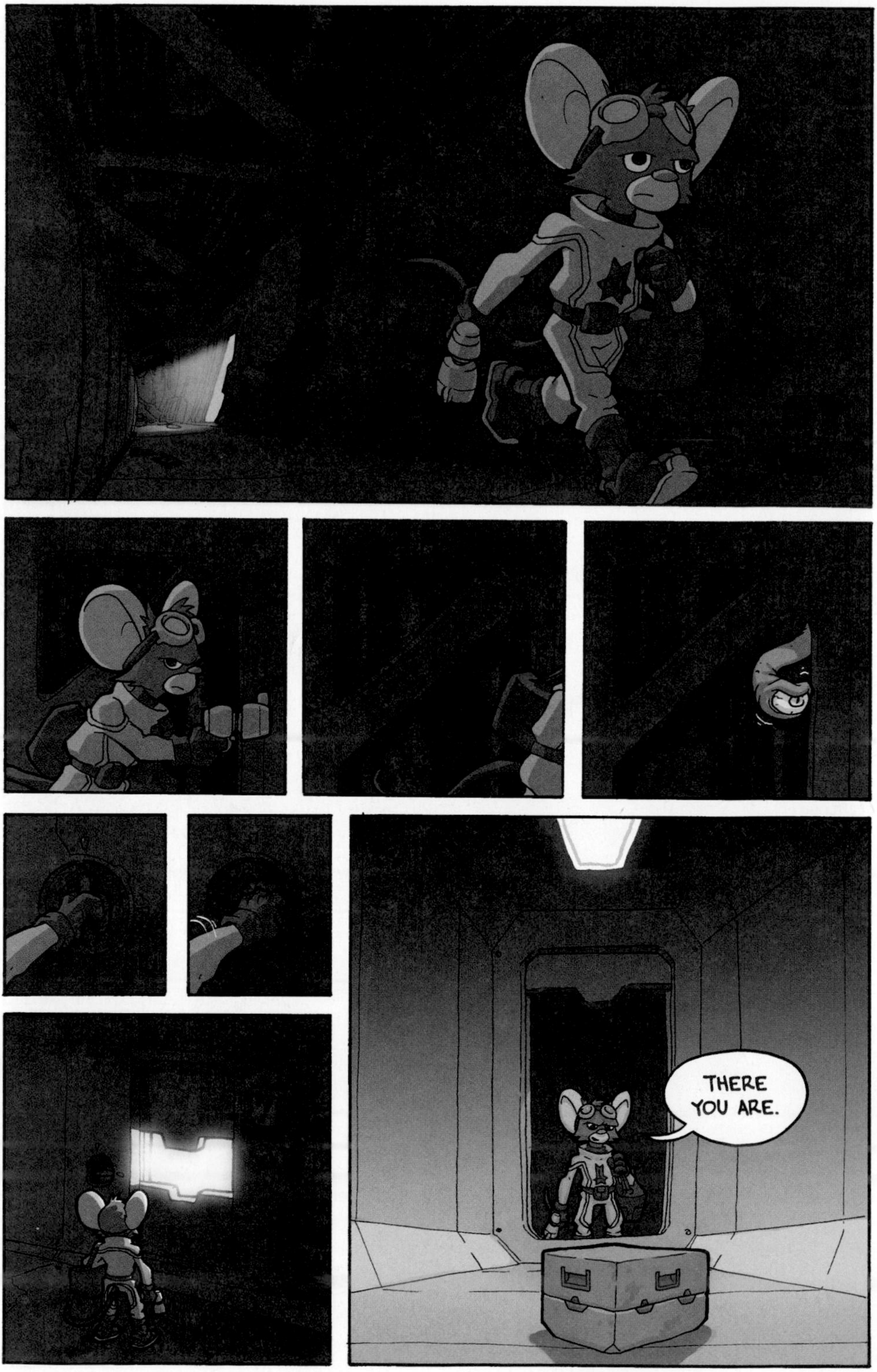
THERE YOU ARE.

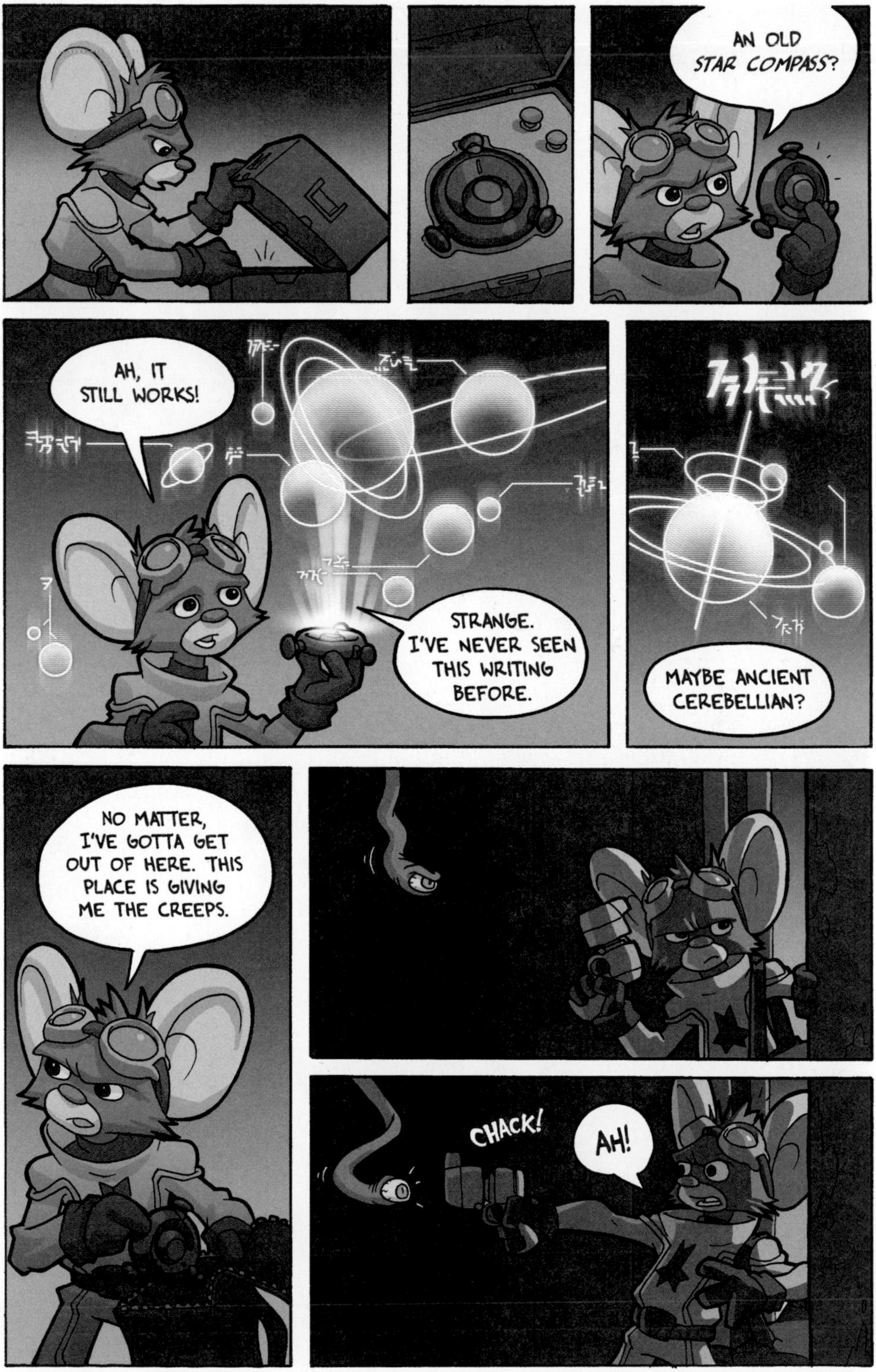
AN OLD STAR COMPASS?
AH, IT STILL WORKS!
STRANGE. I'VE NEVER SEEN THIS WRITING BEFORE.
MAYBE ANCIENT CEREBELLIAN?
NO MATTER, I'VE GOTTA GET OUT OF HERE. THIS PLACE IS GIVING ME THE CREEPS.
CHACK!
AH!

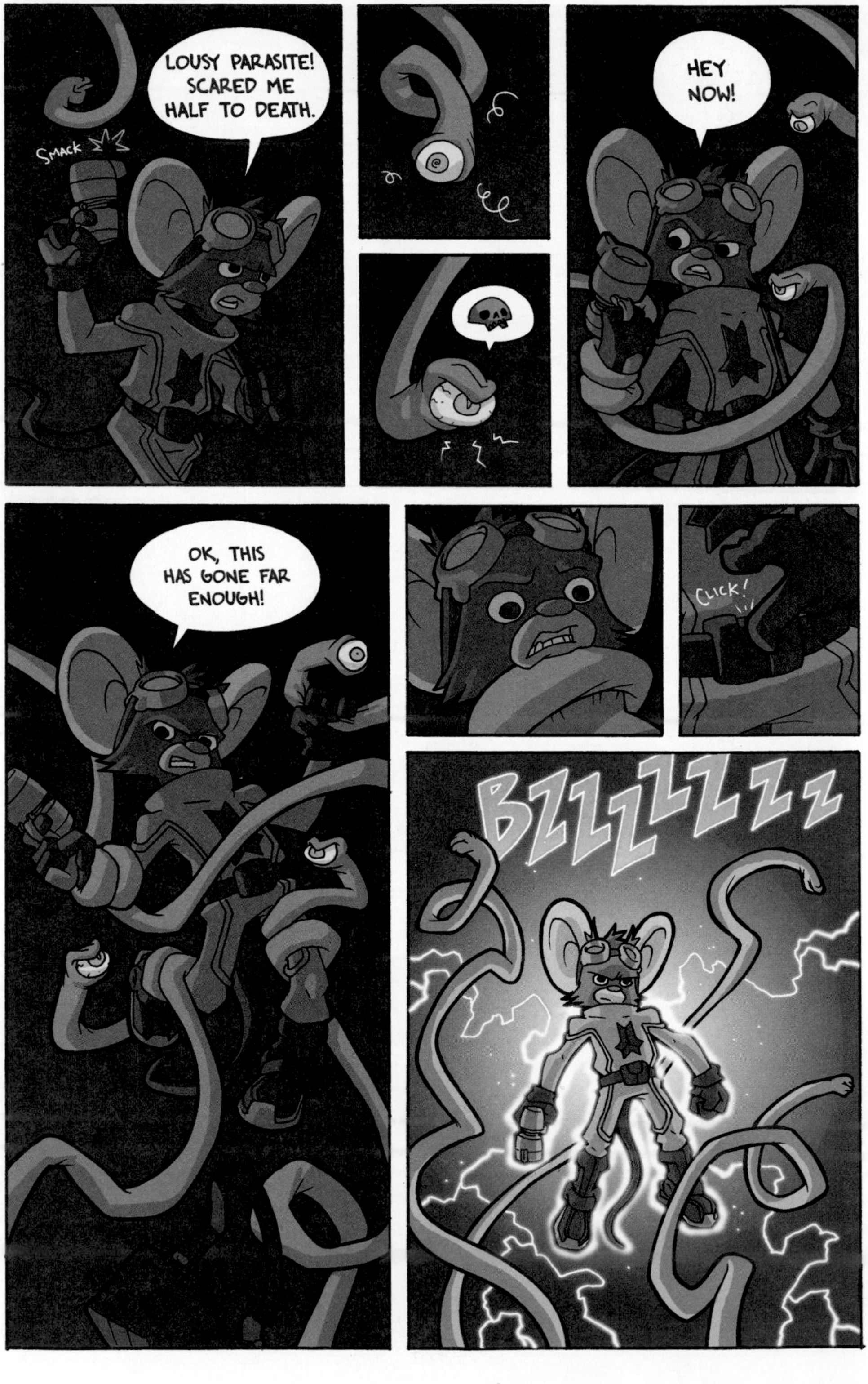
LOUSY PARASITE! SCARED ME HALF TO DEATH.
SMACK
HEY NOW!
OK, THIS HAS GONE FAR ENOUGH!
CLICK!
BZZZZZZZ

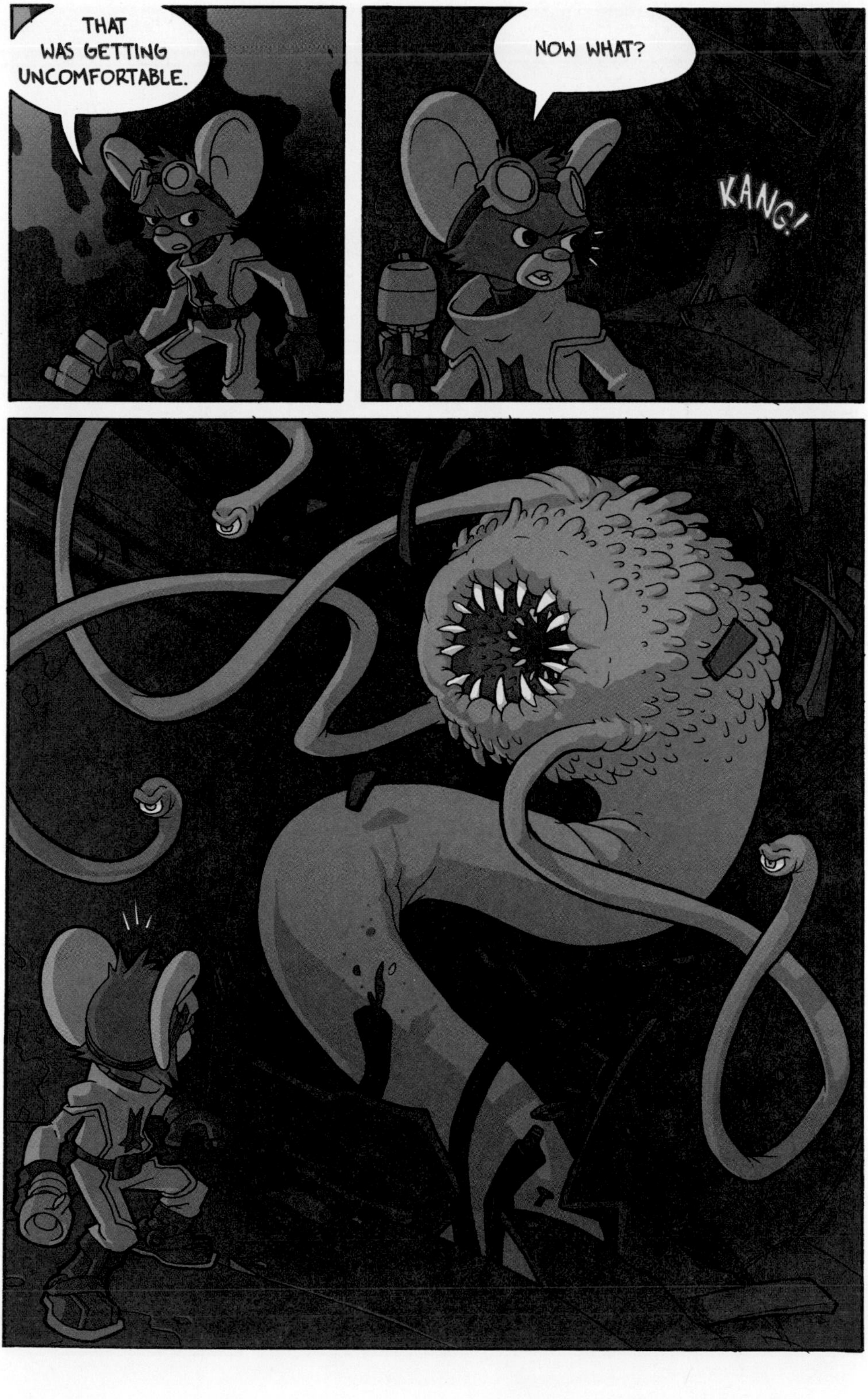
THAT WAS GETTING UNCOMFORTABLE.
NOW WHAT?
KANG!

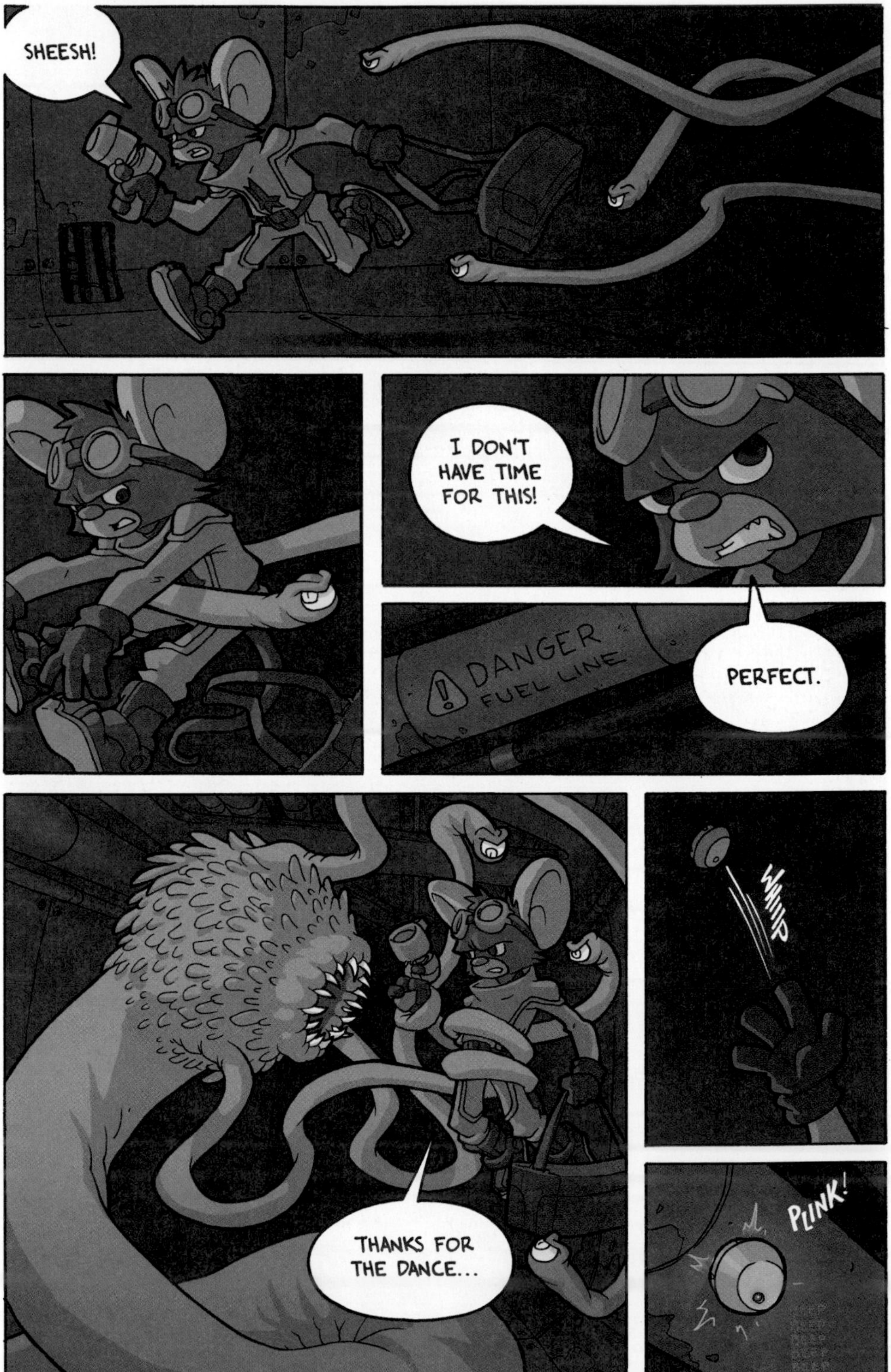
SHEESH!
I DON'T HAVE TIME FOR THIS!
DANGER FUEL LINE
PERFECT.
WHIP
THANKS FOR THE DANCE...
PLINK!

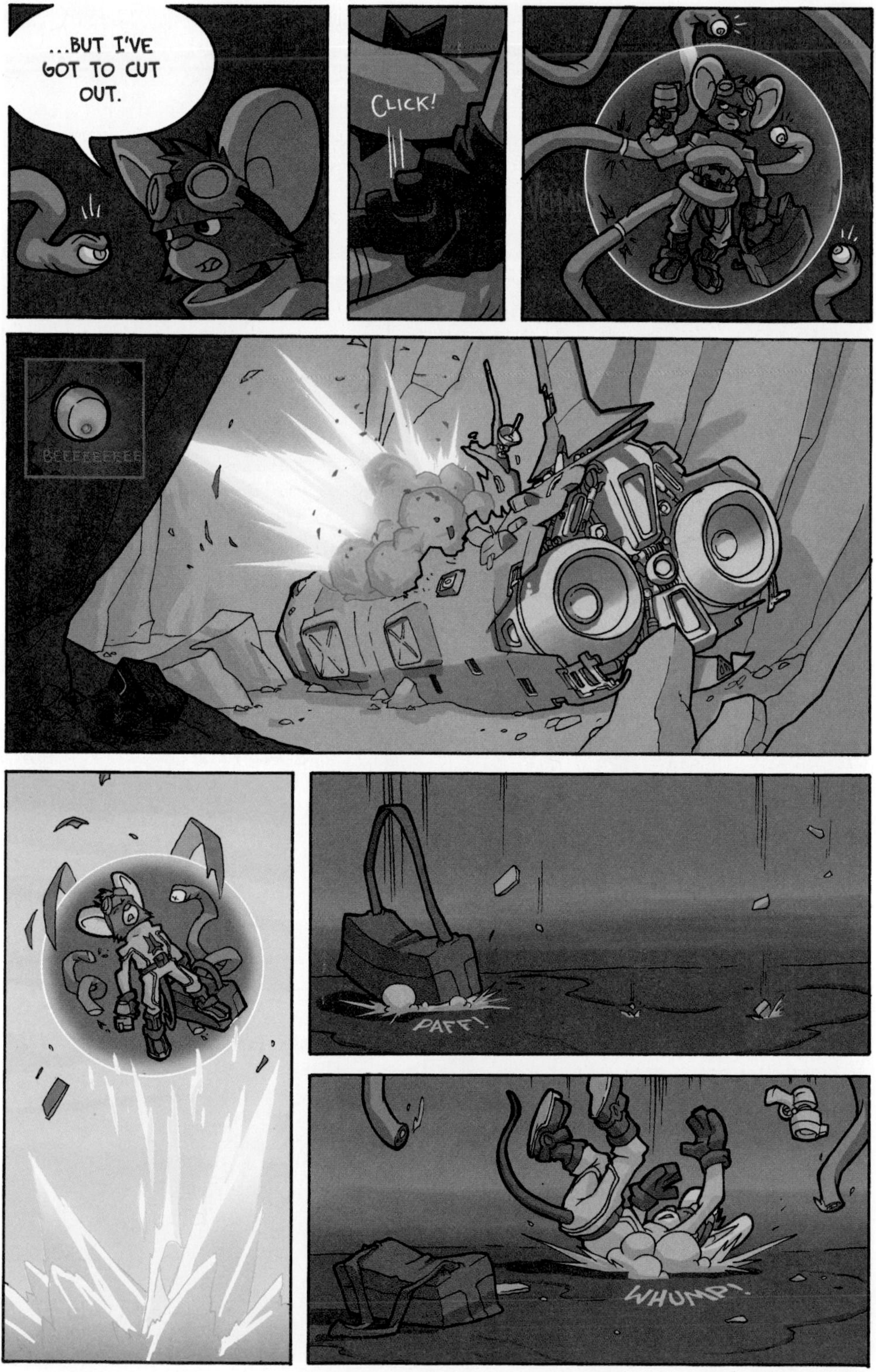
...BUT I'VE GOT TO CUT OUT.
CLICK!
BEEEEEEEEEE
PAFF!
WHUMP!

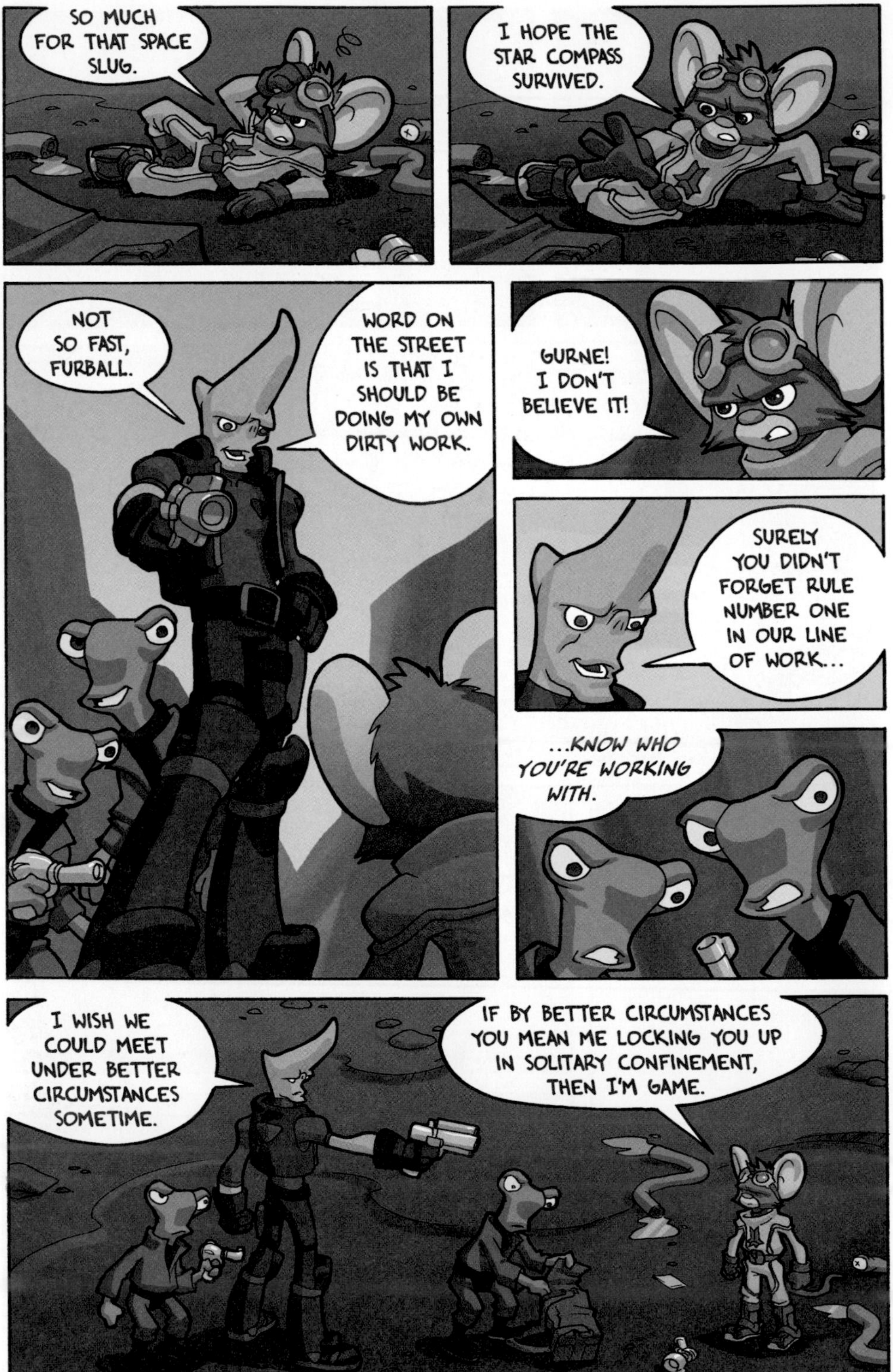
SO MUCH FOR THAT SPACE SLUG.
I HOPE THE STAR COMPASS SURVIVED.
NOT SO FAST, FURBALL.
WORD ON THE STREET IS THAT I SHOULD BE DOING MY OWN DIRTY WORK.
GURNE! I DON'T BELIEVE IT!
SURELY YOU DIDN'T FORGET RULE NUMBER ONE IN OUR LINE OF WORK...
...KNOW WHO YOU'RE WORKING WITH.
I WISH WE COULD MEET UNDER BETTER CIRCUMSTANCES SOMETIME.
IF BY BETTER CIRCUMSTANCES YOU MEAN ME LOCKING YOU UP IN SOLITARY CONFINEMENT, THEN I'M GAME.

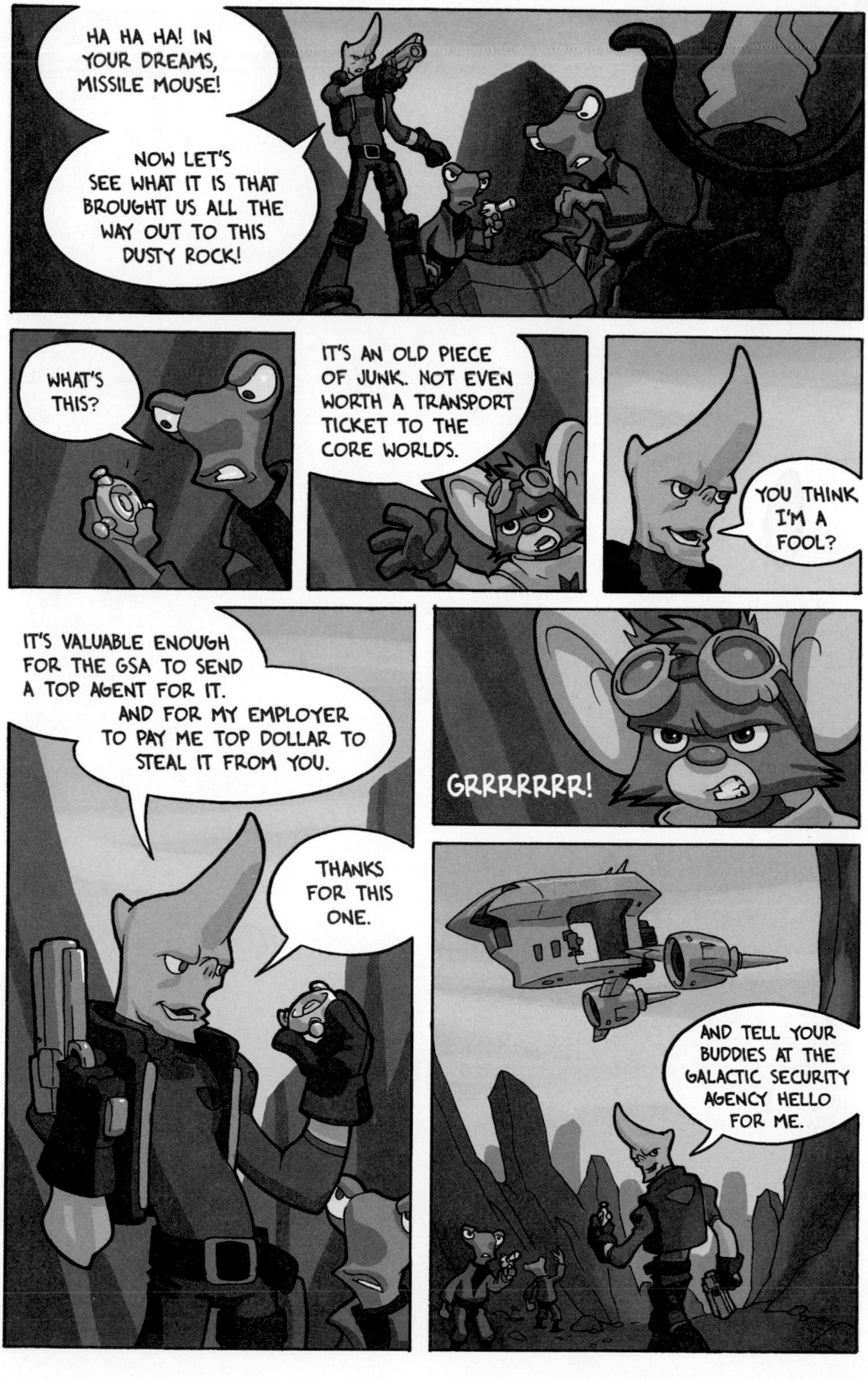
HA HA HA! IN YOUR DREAMS, MISSILE MOUSE!
NOW LET'S SEE WHAT IT IS THAT BROUGHT US ALL THE WAY OUT TO THIS DUSTY ROCK!
WHAT'S THIS?
IT'S AN OLD PIECE OF JUNK. NOT EVEN WORTH A TRANSPORT TICKET TO THE CORE WORLDS.
YOU THINK I'M A FOOL?
IT'S VALUABLE ENOUGH FOR THE GSA TO SEND A TOP AGENT FOR IT.
AND FOR MY EMPLOYER TO PAY ME TOP DOLLAR TO STEAL IT FROM YOU.
THANKS FOR THIS ONE.
GRRRRRRR!
AND TELL YOUR BUDDIES AT THE GALACTIC SECURITY AGENCY HELLO FOR ME.

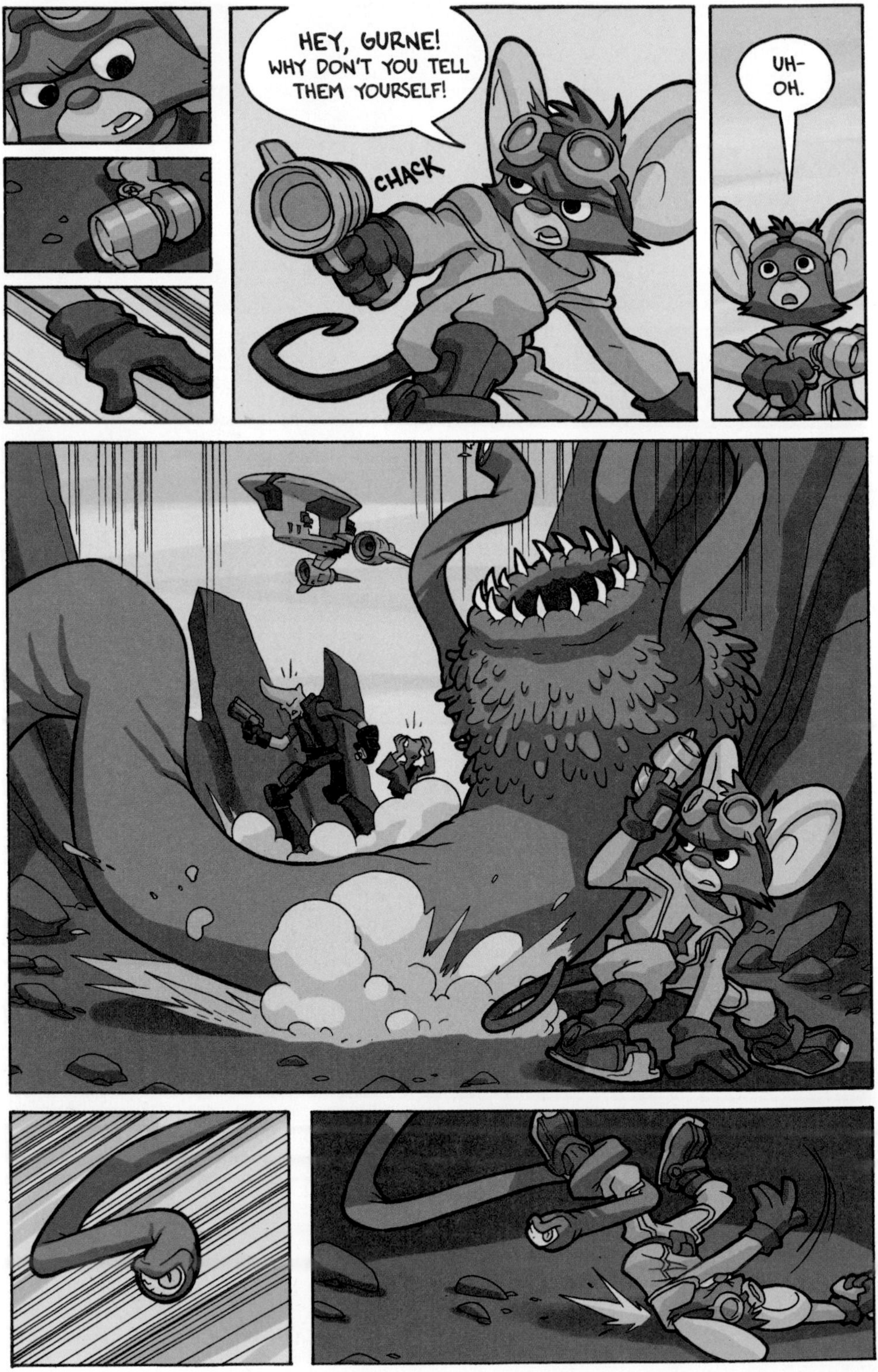
HEY, GURNE!
WHY DON'T YOU TELL THEM YOURSELF!
CHACK
UH-OH.

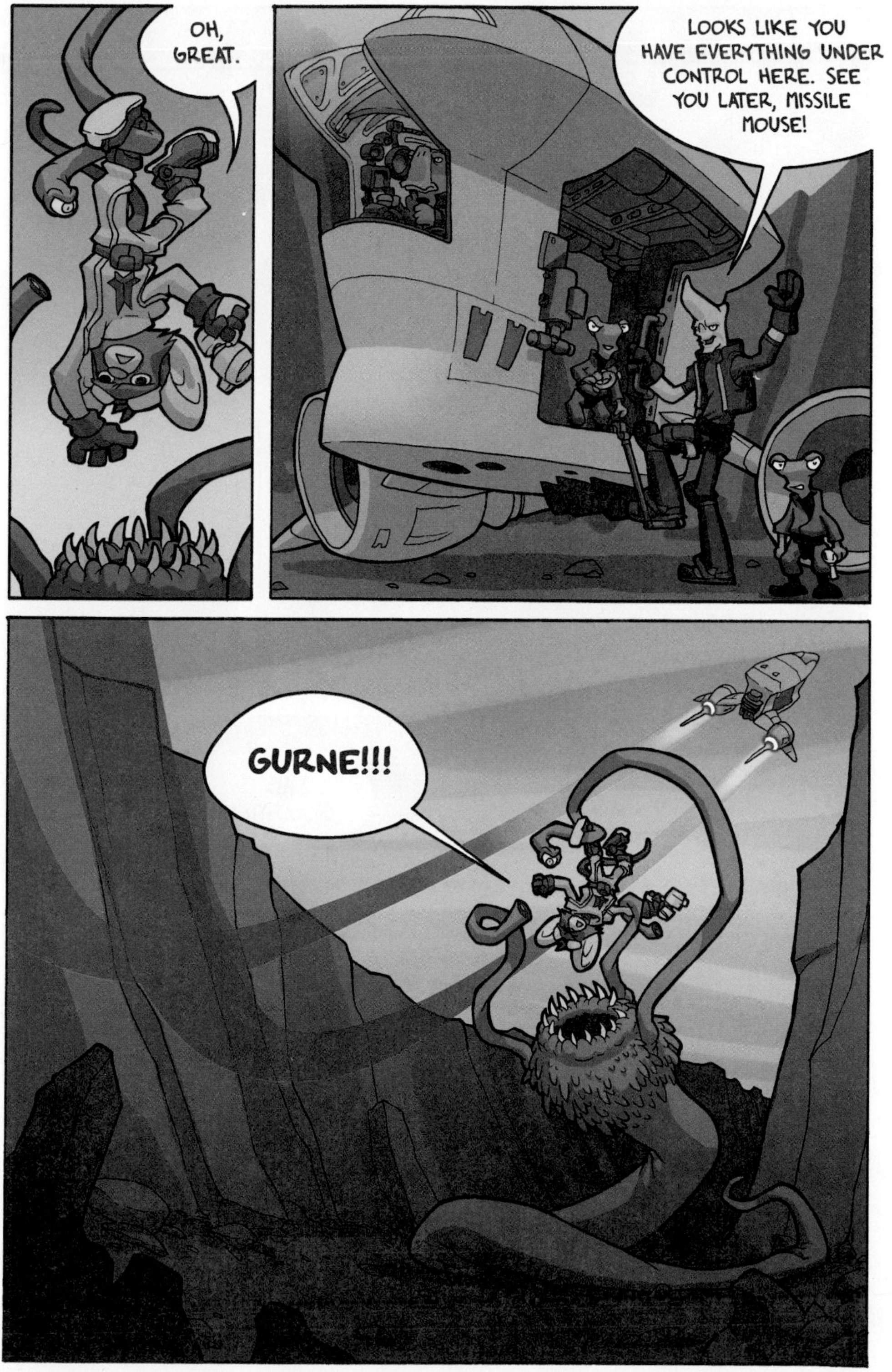
OH, GREAT.
LOOKS LIKE YOU HAVE EVERYTHING UNDER CONTROL HERE. SEE YOU LATER, MISSILE MOUSE!
GURNE!!!

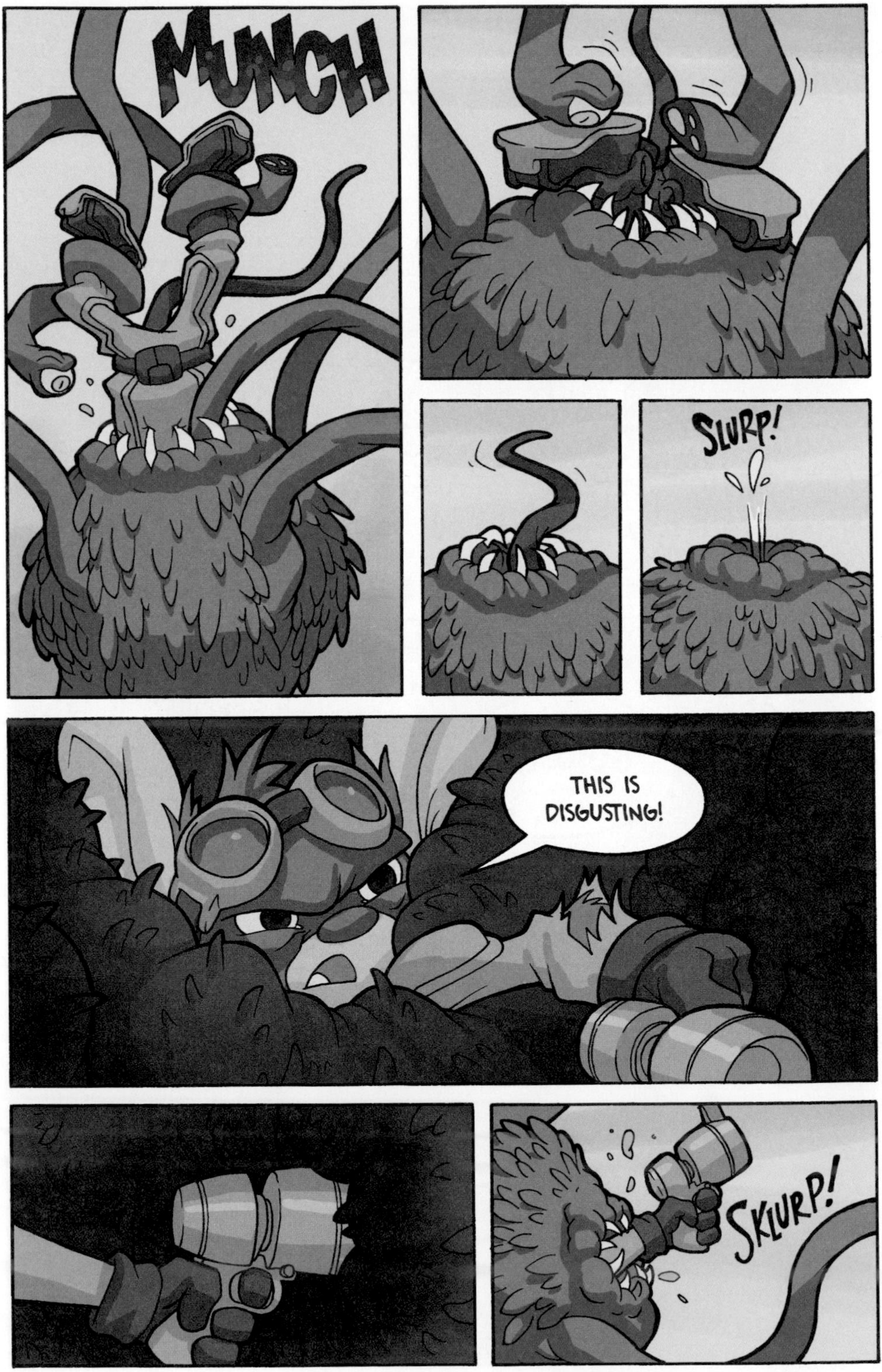
MUNCH
SLURP!
THIS IS DISGUSTING!
SKLURP!

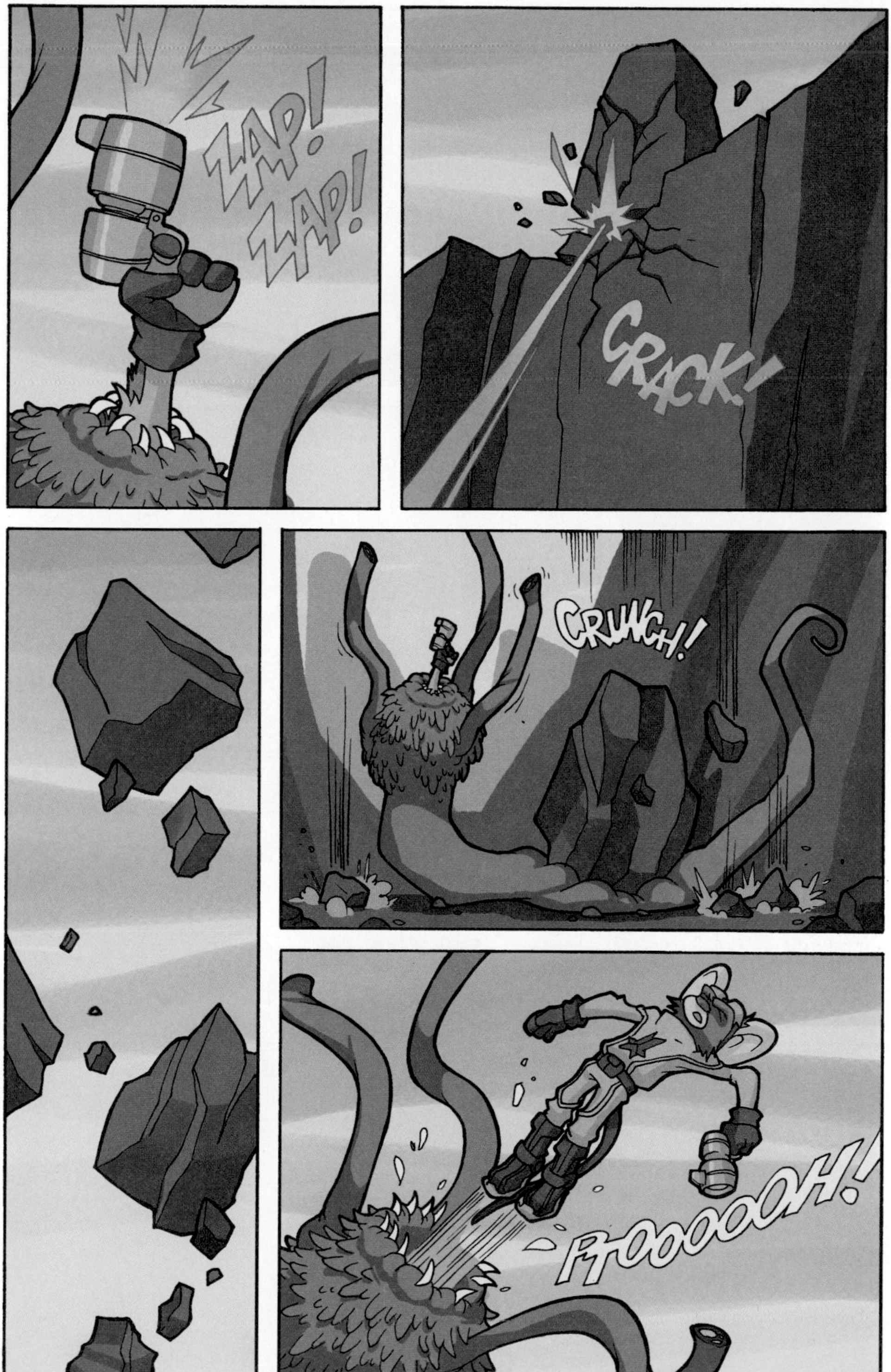
ZAP!
ZAP!
CRACK!
CRUNCH!
FTOOOOOOH!

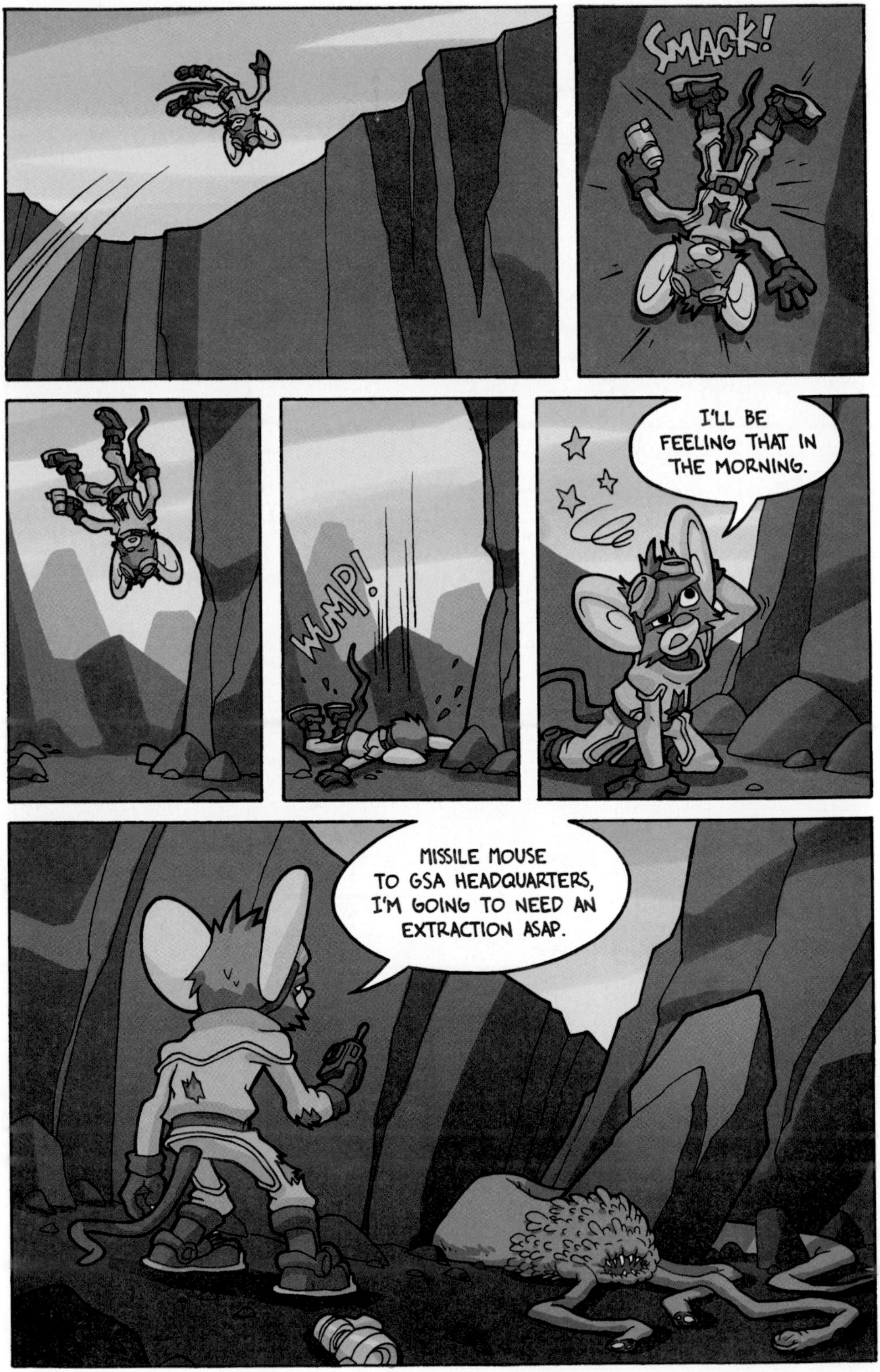
SMACK!
WUMP!
I'LL BE FEELING THAT IN THE MORNING.
MISSILE MOUSE TO GSA HEADQUARTERS, I'M GOING TO NEED AN EXTRACTION ASAP.

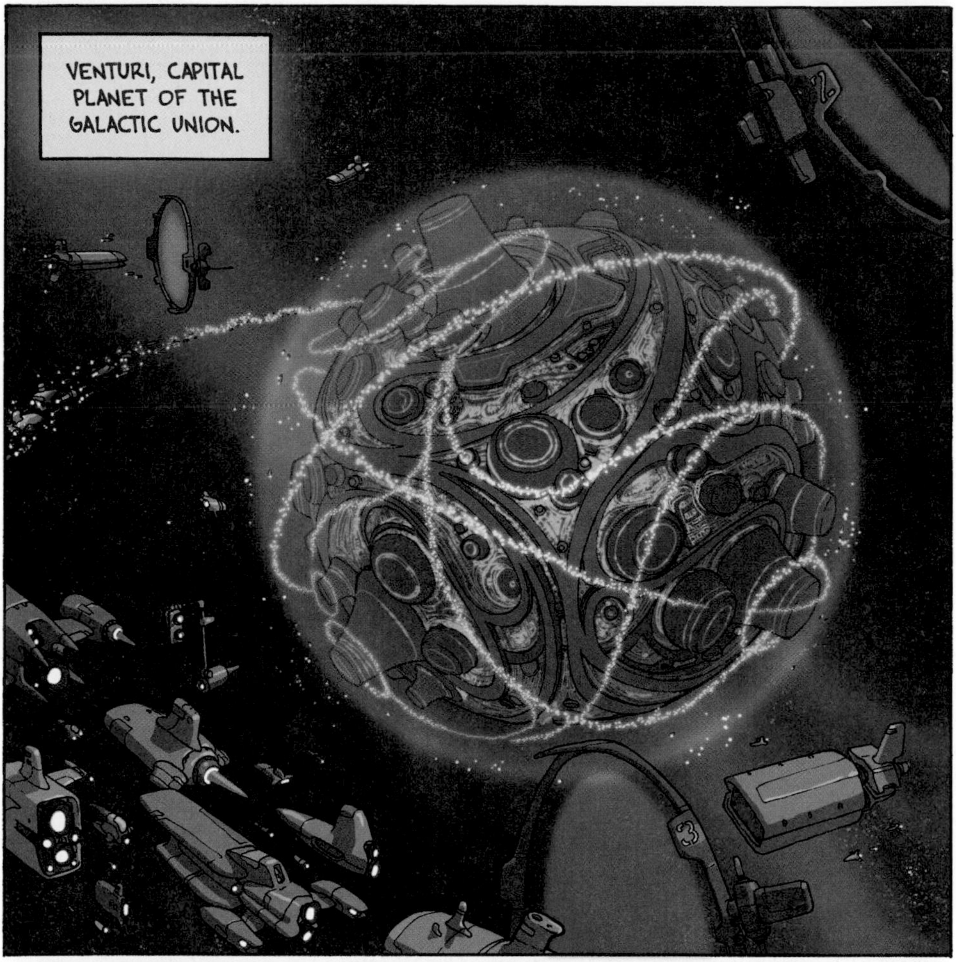
VENTURI, CAPITAL PLANET OF THE GALACTIC UNION.

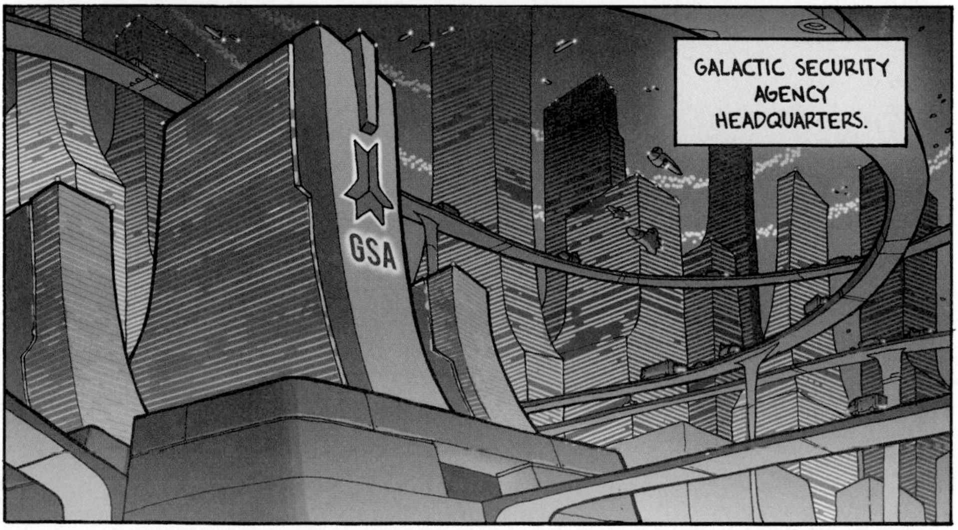
GALACTIC SECURITY AGENCY HEADQUARTERS.
GSA

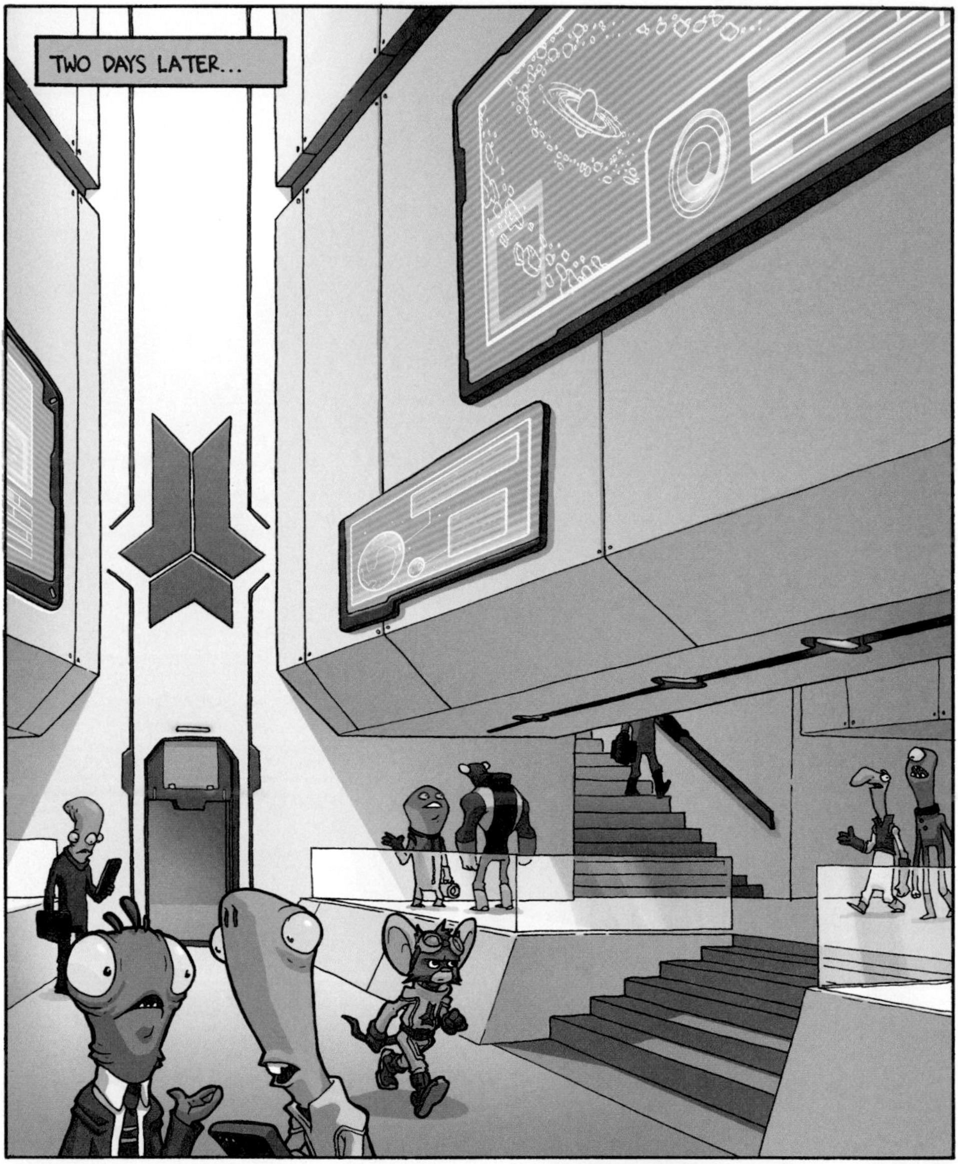
TWO DAYS LATER...

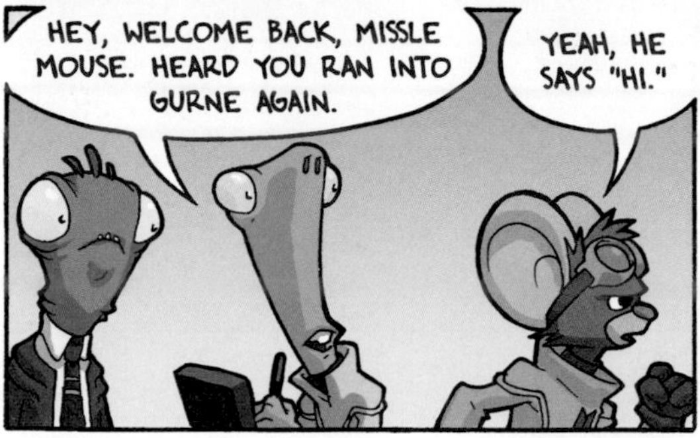
HEY, WELCOME BACK, MISSLE MOUSE. HEARD YOU RAN INTO GURNE AGAIN.
YEAH, HE SAYS "HI."

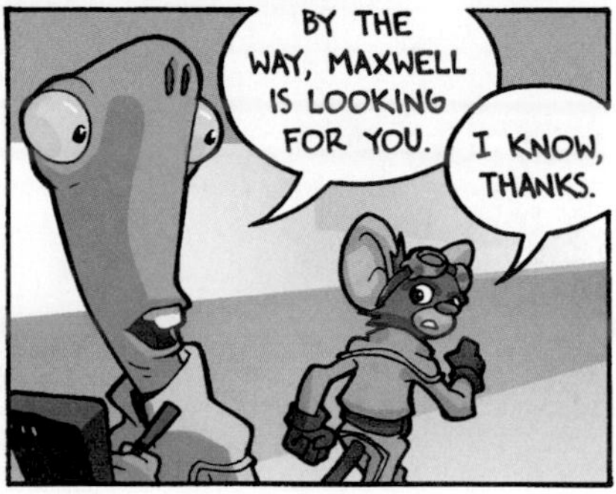
BY THE WAY, MAXWELL IS LOOKING FOR YOU.
I KNOW, THANKS.

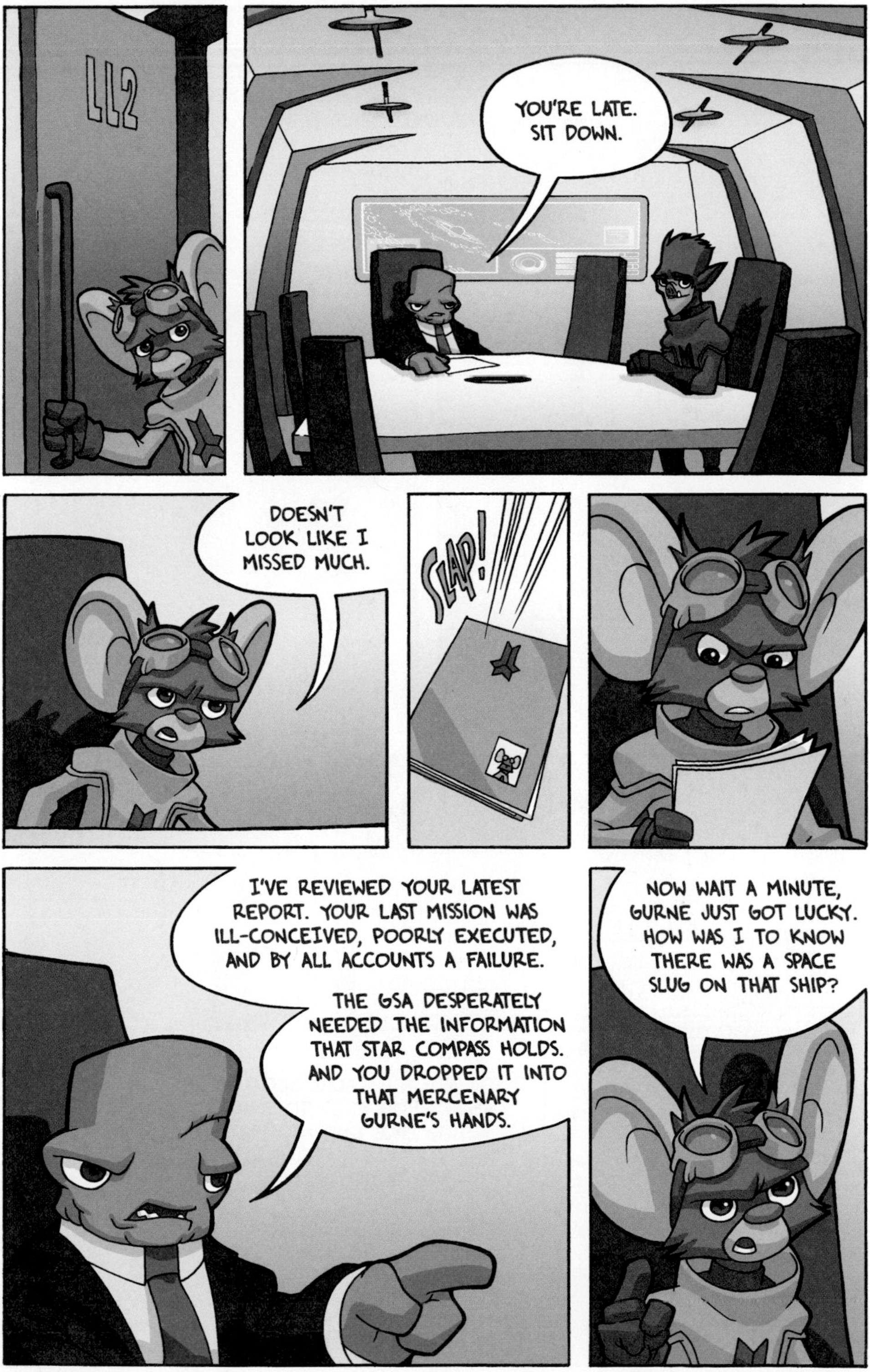
LL2
YOU'RE LATE. SIT DOWN.
DOESN'T LOOK LIKE I MISSED MUCH.
SLAP!
I'VE REVIEWED YOUR LATEST REPORT. YOUR LAST MISSION WAS ILL-CONCEIVED, POORLY EXECUTED, AND BY ALL ACCOUNTS A FAILURE.
THE GSA DESPERATELY NEEDED THE INFORMATION THAT STAR COMPASS HOLDS. AND YOU DROPPED IT INTO THAT MERCENARY GURNE'S HANDS.
NOW WAIT A MINUTE, GURNE JUST GOT LUCKY. HOW WAS I TO KNOW THERE WAS A SPACE SLUG ON THAT SHIP?

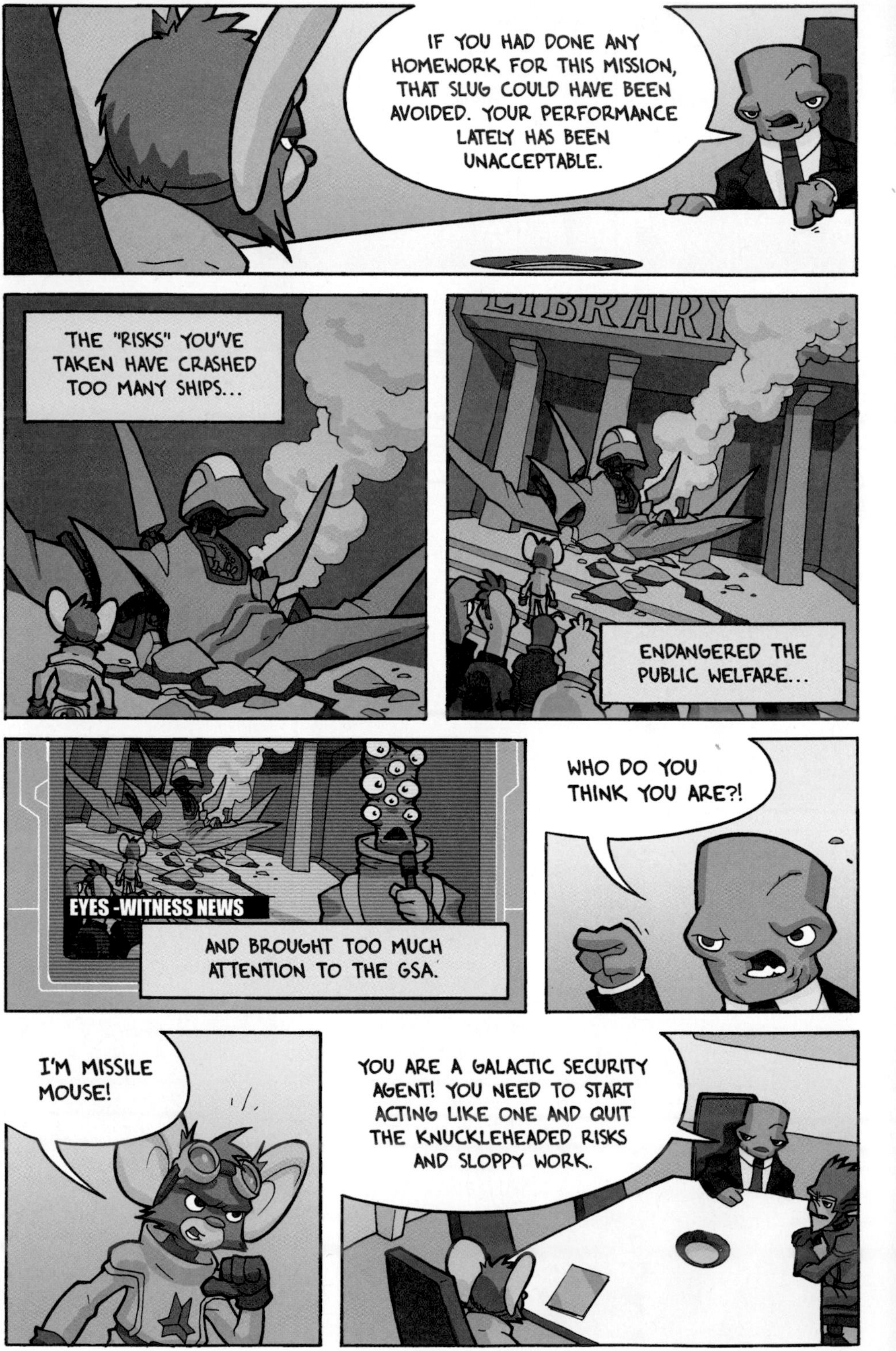
IF YOU HAD DONE ANY HOMEWORK FOR THIS MISSION, THAT SLUG COULD HAVE BEEN AVOIDED. YOUR PERFORMANCE LATELY HAS BEEN UNACCEPTABLE.
THE "RISKS" YOU'VE TAKEN HAVE CRASHED TOO MANY SHIPS...
LIBRARY
ENDANGERED THE PUBLIC WELFARE...
EYES -WITNESS NEWS
AND BROUGHT TOO MUCH ATTENTION TO THE GSA.
WHO DO YOU THINK YOU ARE?!
I'M MISSILE MOUSE!
YOU ARE A GALACTIC SECURITY AGENT! YOU NEED TO START ACTING LIKE ONE AND QUIT THE KNUCKLEHEADED RISKS AND SLOPPY WORK.

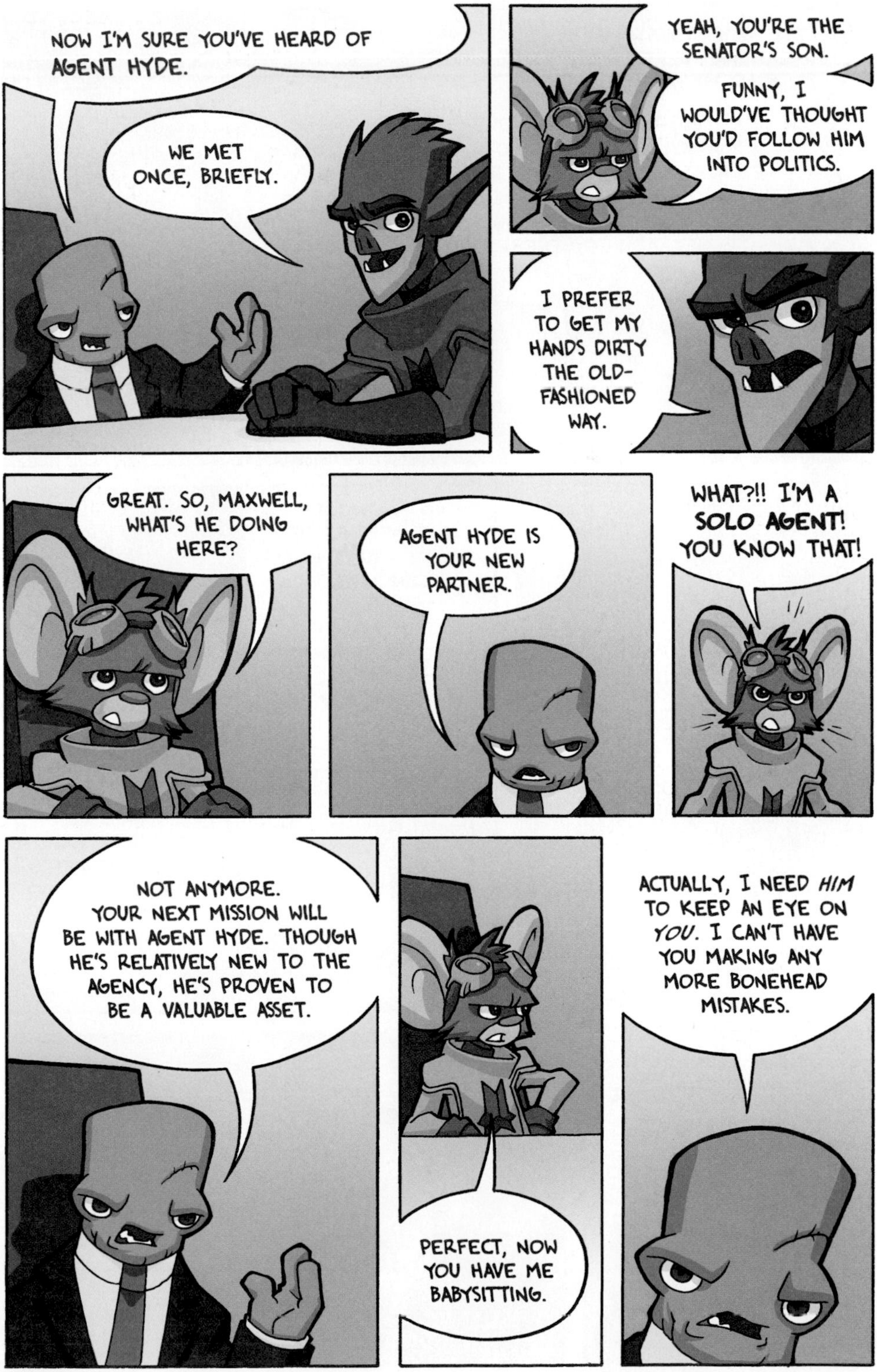
NOW I'M SURE YOU'VE HEARD OF AGENT HYDE.
WE MET ONCE, BRIEFLY.
YEAH, YOU'RE THE SENATOR'S SON.
FUNNY, I WOULD'VE THOUGHT YOU'D FOLLOW HIM INTO POLITICS.
I PREFER TO GET MY HANDS DIRTY THE OLD-FASHIONED WAY.
GREAT. SO, MAXWELL, WHAT'S HE DOING HERE?
AGENT HYDE IS YOUR NEW PARTNER.
WHAT?!! I'M A SOLO AGENT! YOU KNOW THAT!
NOT ANYMORE. YOUR NEXT MISSION WILL BE WITH AGENT HYDE. THOUGH HE'S RELATIVELY NEW TO THE AGENCY, HE'S PROVEN TO BE A VALUABLE ASSET.
PERFECT, NOW YOU HAVE ME BABYSITTING.
ACTUALLY, I NEED *HIM* TO KEEP AN EYE ON *YOU*. I CAN'T HAVE YOU MAKING ANY MORE BONEHEAD MISTAKES.

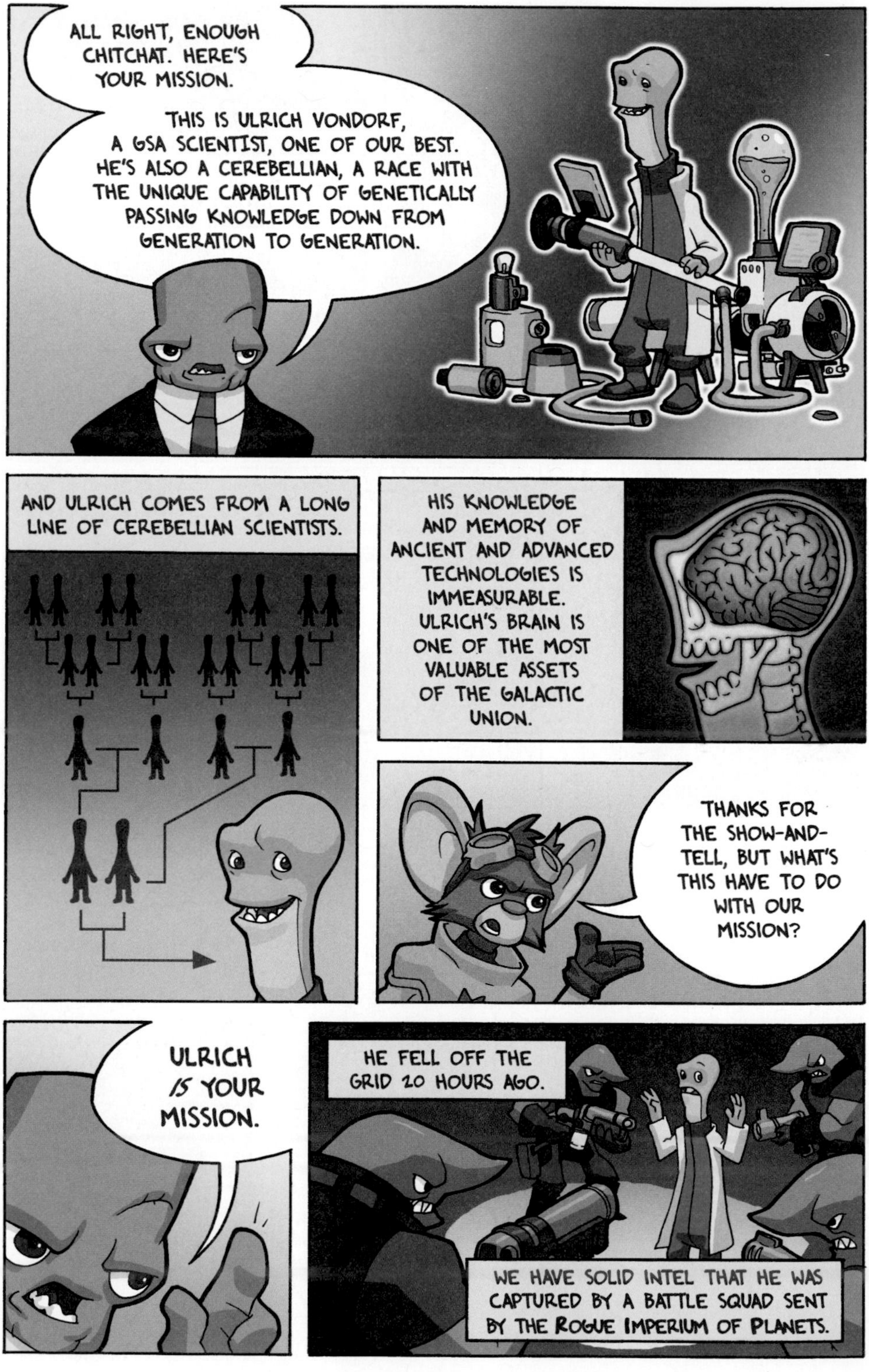
ALL RIGHT, ENOUGH CHITCHAT. HERE'S YOUR MISSION.
THIS IS ULRICH VONDORF, A GSA SCIENTIST, ONE OF OUR BEST. HE'S ALSO A CEREBELLIAN, A RACE WITH THE UNIQUE CAPABILITY OF GENETICALLY PASSING KNOWLEDGE DOWN FROM GENERATION TO GENERATION.
AND ULRICH COMES FROM A LONG LINE OF CEREBELLIAN SCIENTISTS.
HIS KNOWLEDGE AND MEMORY OF ANCIENT AND ADVANCED TECHNOLOGIES IS IMMEASURABLE. ULRICH'S BRAIN IS ONE OF THE MOST VALUABLE ASSETS OF THE GALACTIC UNION.
THANKS FOR THE SHOW-AND-TELL, BUT WHAT'S THIS HAVE TO DO WITH OUR MISSION?
ULRICH *IS* YOUR MISSION.
HE FELL OFF THE GRID 20 HOURS AGO.
WE HAVE SOLID INTEL THAT HE WAS CAPTURED BY A BATTLE SQUAD SENT BY THE ROGUE IMPERIUM OF PLANETS.

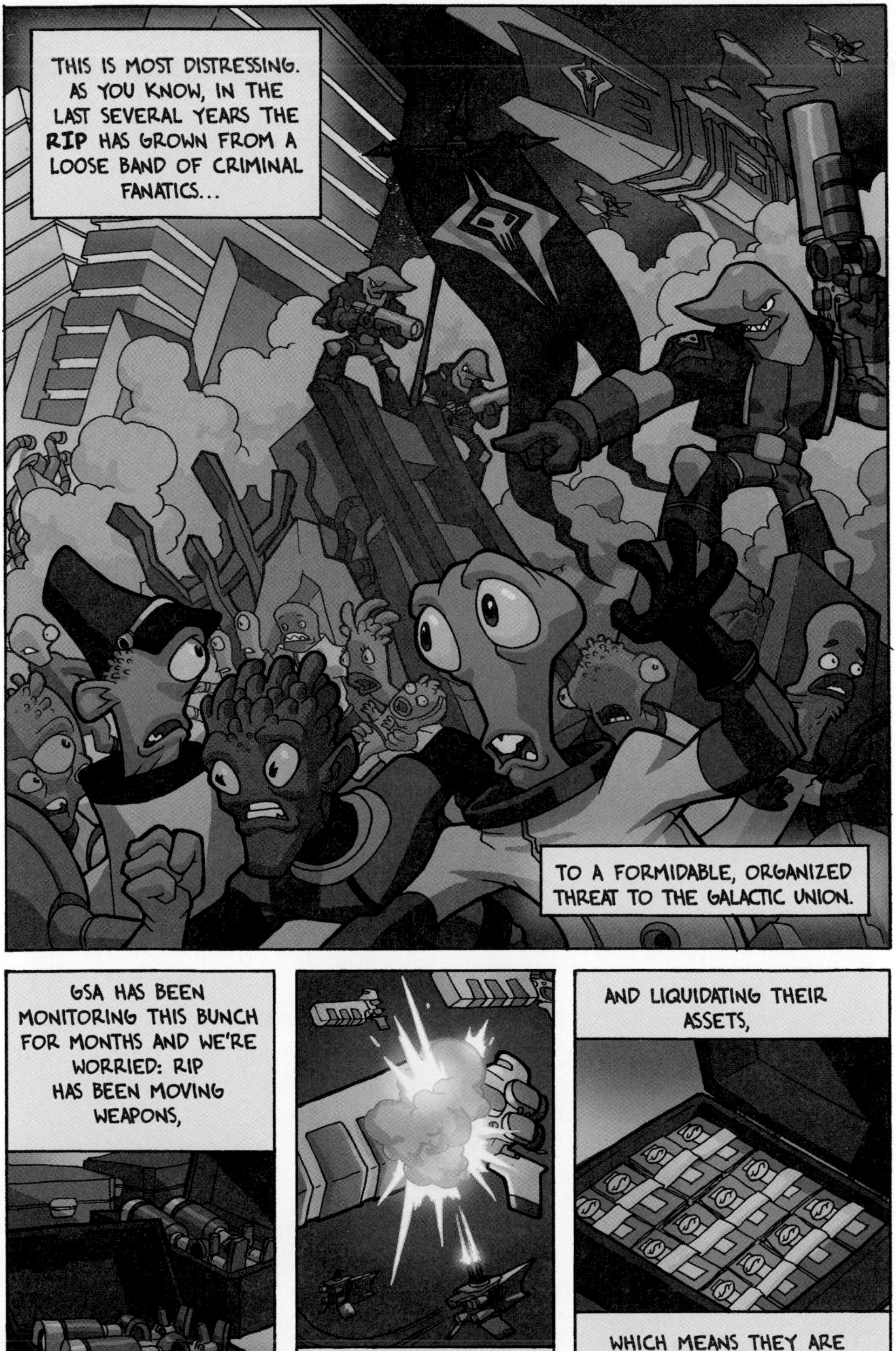
THIS IS MOST DISTRESSING. AS YOU KNOW, IN THE LAST SEVERAL YEARS THE RIP HAS GROWN FROM A LOOSE BAND OF CRIMINAL FANATICS...
TO A FORMIDABLE, ORGANIZED THREAT TO THE GALACTIC UNION.
GSA HAS BEEN MONITORING THIS BUNCH FOR MONTHS AND WE'RE WORRIED: RIP HAS BEEN MOVING WEAPONS,
ATTACKING SUPPLY SHIPS,
AND LIQUIDATING THEIR ASSETS,
WHICH MEANS THEY ARE UP TO SOMETHING BIG.

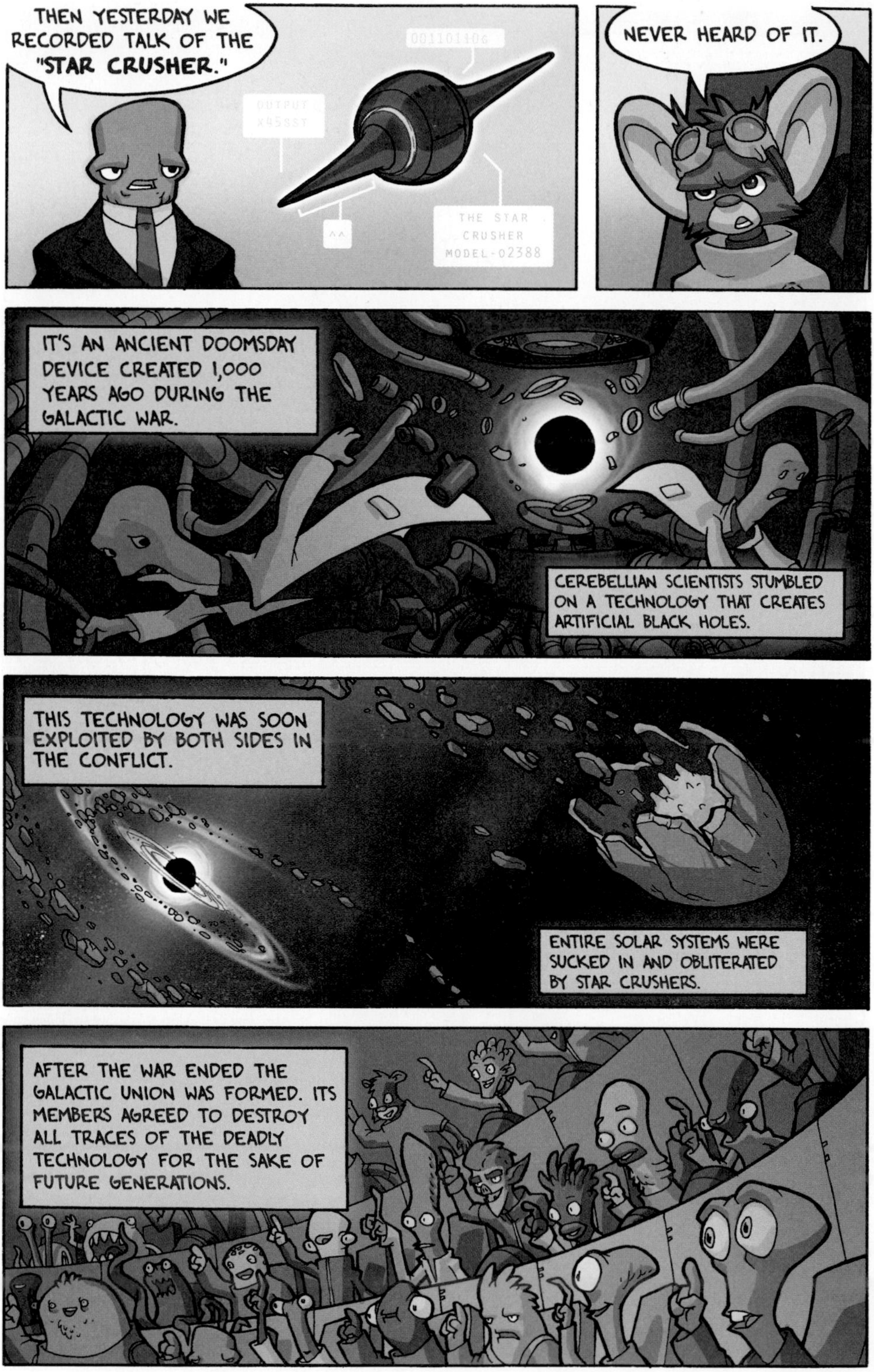
THEN YESTERDAY WE RECORDED TALK OF THE "STAR CRUSHER."
OUTPUT X45SST
^^
THE STAR CRUSHER MODEL-02388
NEVER HEARD OF IT.
IT'S AN ANCIENT DOOMSDAY DEVICE CREATED 1,000 YEARS AGO DURING THE GALACTIC WAR.
CEREBELLIAN SCIENTISTS STUMBLED ON A TECHNOLOGY THAT CREATES ARTIFICIAL BLACK HOLES.
THIS TECHNOLOGY WAS SOON EXPLOITED BY BOTH SIDES IN THE CONFLICT.
ENTIRE SOLAR SYSTEMS WERE SUCKED IN AND OBLITERATED BY STAR CRUSHERS.
AFTER THE WAR ENDED THE GALACTIC UNION WAS FORMED. ITS MEMBERS AGREED TO DESTROY ALL TRACES OF THE DEADLY TECHNOLOGY FOR THE SAKE OF FUTURE GENERATIONS.

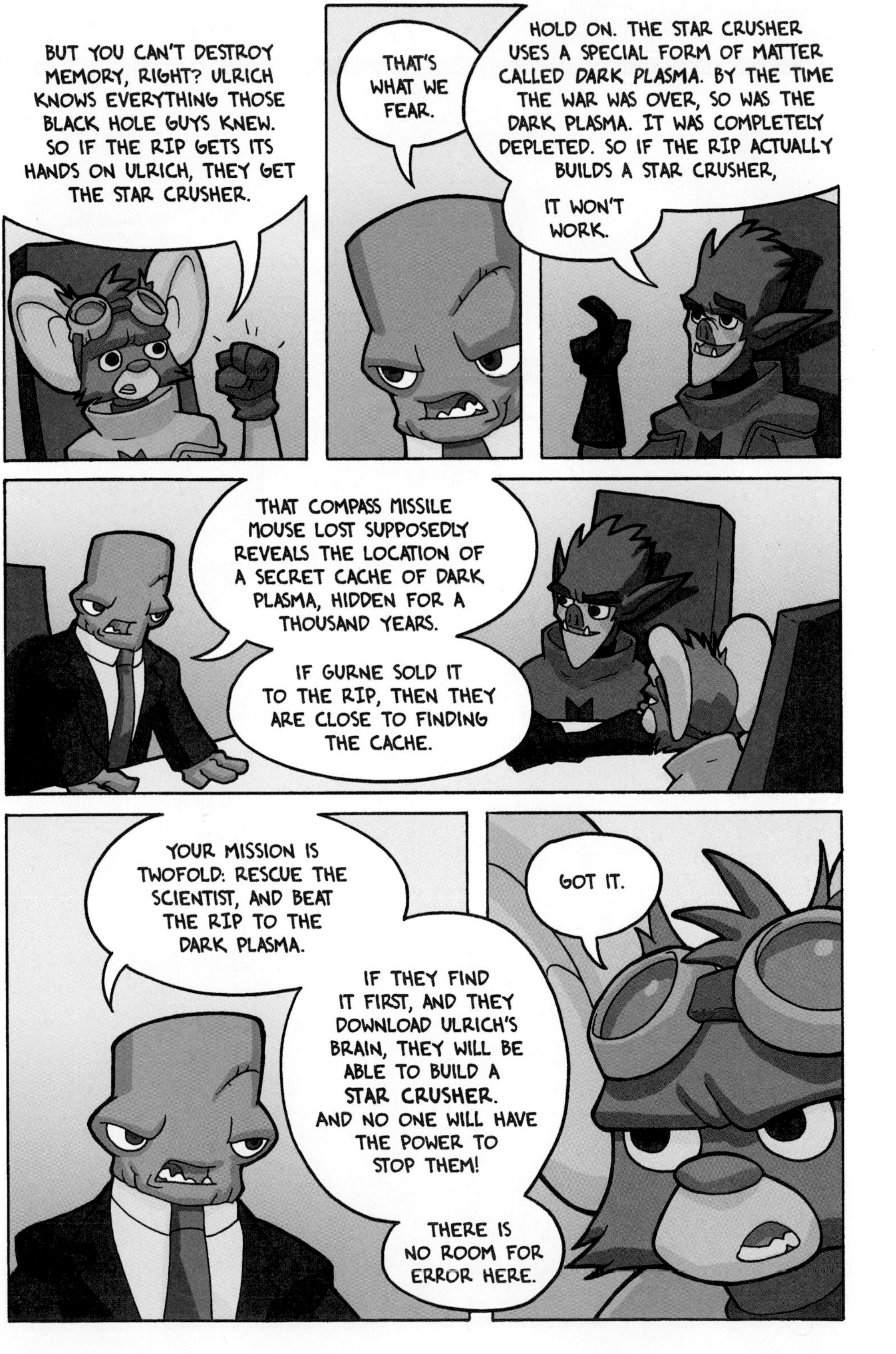
BUT YOU CAN'T DESTROY MEMORY, RIGHT? ULRICH KNOWS EVERYTHING THOSE BLACK HOLE GUYS KNEW. SO IF THE RIP GETS ITS HANDS ON ULRICH, THEY GET THE STAR CRUSHER.
THAT'S WHAT WE FEAR.
HOLD ON. THE STAR CRUSHER USES A SPECIAL FORM OF MATTER CALLED *DARK PLASMA*. BY THE TIME THE WAR WAS OVER, SO WAS THE DARK PLASMA. IT WAS COMPLETELY DEPLETED. SO IF THE RIP ACTUALLY BUILDS A STAR CRUSHER,
IT WON'T WORK.
THAT COMPASS MISSILE MOUSE LOST SUPPOSEDLY REVEALS THE LOCATION OF A SECRET CACHE OF DARK PLASMA, HIDDEN FOR A THOUSAND YEARS.
IF GURNE SOLD IT TO THE RIP, THEN THEY ARE CLOSE TO FINDING THE CACHE.
YOUR MISSION IS TWOFOLD: RESCUE THE SCIENTIST, AND BEAT THE RIP TO THE DARK PLASMA.
IF THEY FIND IT FIRST, AND THEY DOWNLOAD ULRICH'S BRAIN, THEY WILL BE ABLE TO BUILD A **STAR CRUSHER**. AND NO ONE WILL HAVE THE POWER TO STOP THEM!
THERE IS NO ROOM FOR ERROR HERE.
GOT IT.

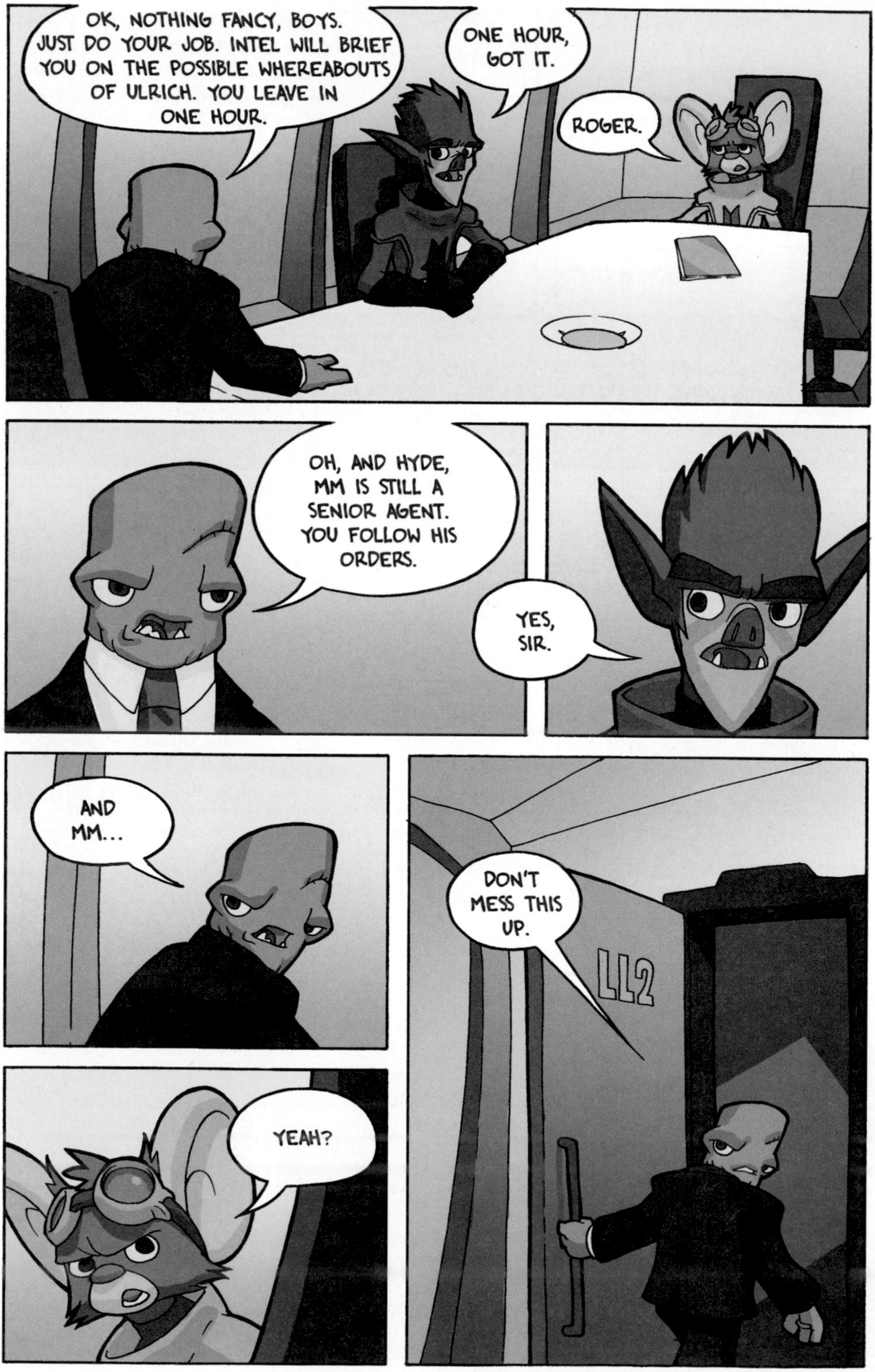
OK, NOTHING FANCY, BOYS. JUST DO YOUR JOB. INTEL WILL BRIEF YOU ON THE POSSIBLE WHEREABOUTS OF ULRICH. YOU LEAVE IN ONE HOUR.
ONE HOUR, GOT IT.
ROGER.
OH, AND HYDE, MM IS STILL A SENIOR AGENT. YOU FOLLOW HIS ORDERS.
YES, SIR.
AND MM...
YEAH?
DON'T MESS THIS UP.
LL2

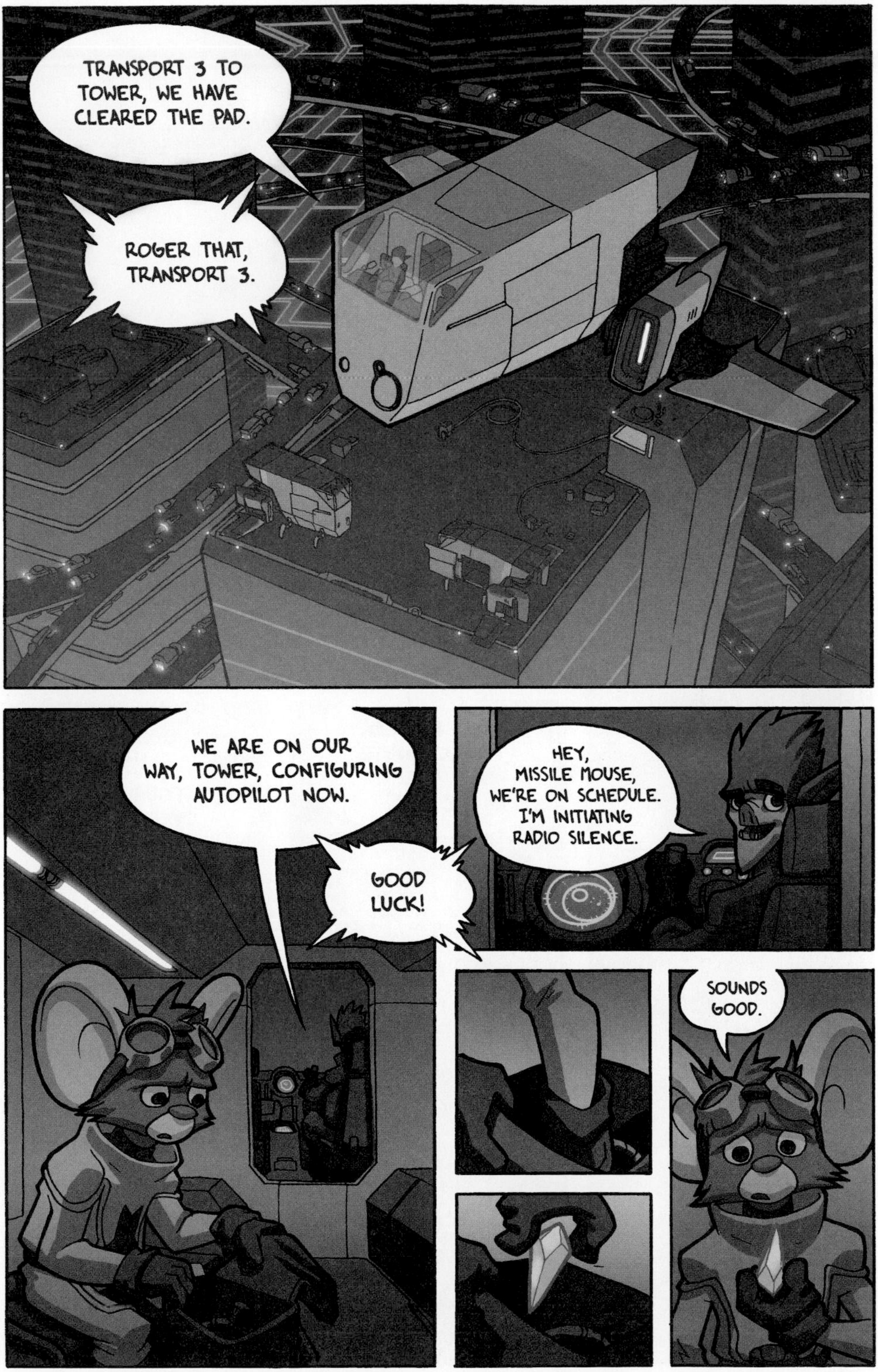
TRANSPORT 3 TO TOWER, WE HAVE CLEARED THE PAD.
ROGER THAT, TRANSPORT 3.
WE ARE ON OUR WAY, TOWER, CONFIGURING AUTOPILOT NOW.
GOOD LUCK!
HEY, MISSILE MOUSE, WE'RE ON SCHEDULE. I'M INITIATING RADIO SILENCE.
SOUNDS GOOD.

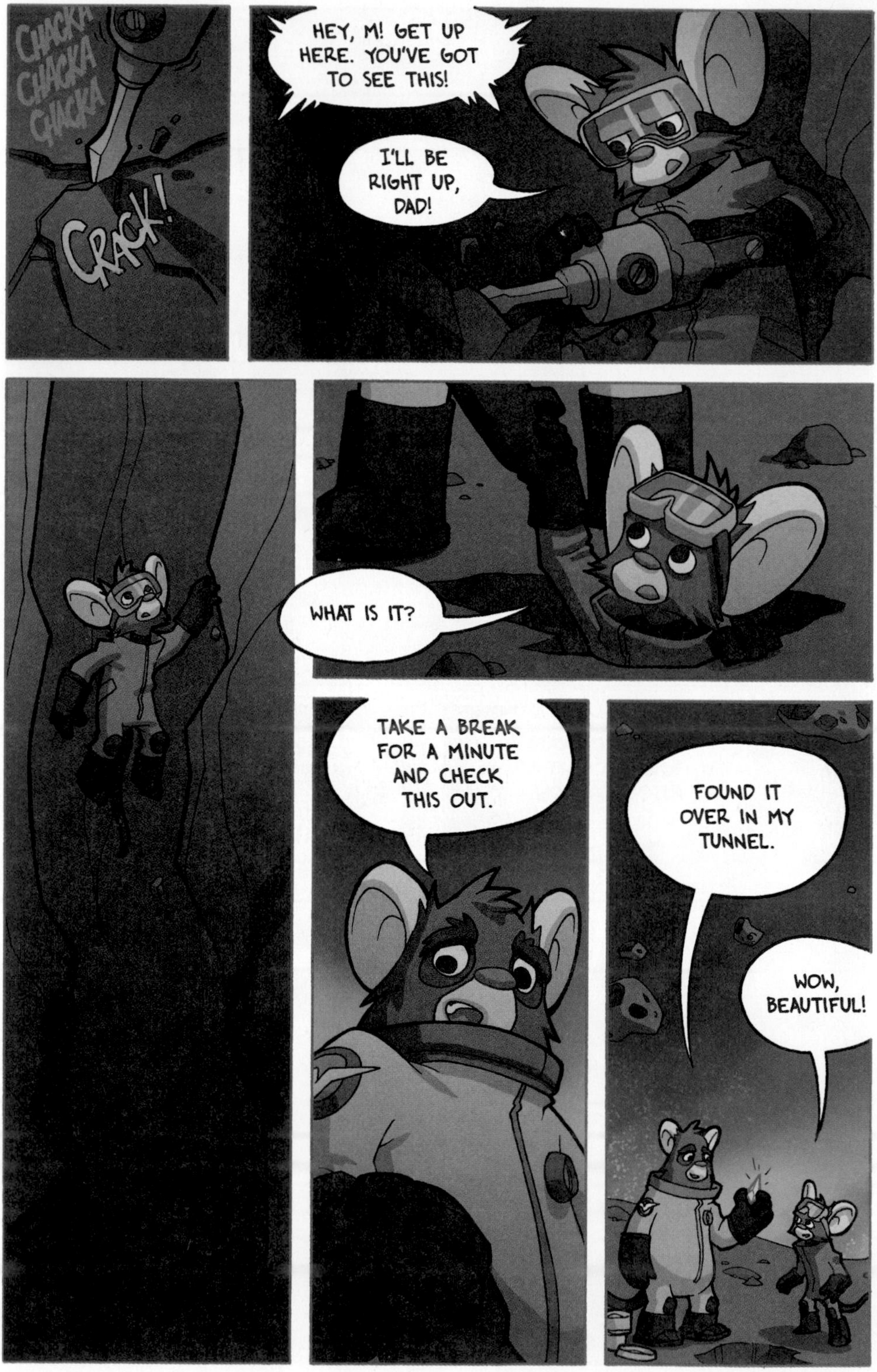
CHACKA CHACKA CHACKA
CRACK!
HEY, M! GET UP HERE. YOU'VE GOT TO SEE THIS!
I'LL BE RIGHT UP, DAD!
WHAT IS IT?
TAKE A BREAK FOR A MINUTE AND CHECK THIS OUT.
FOUND IT OVER IN MY TUNNEL.
WOW, BEAUTIFUL!

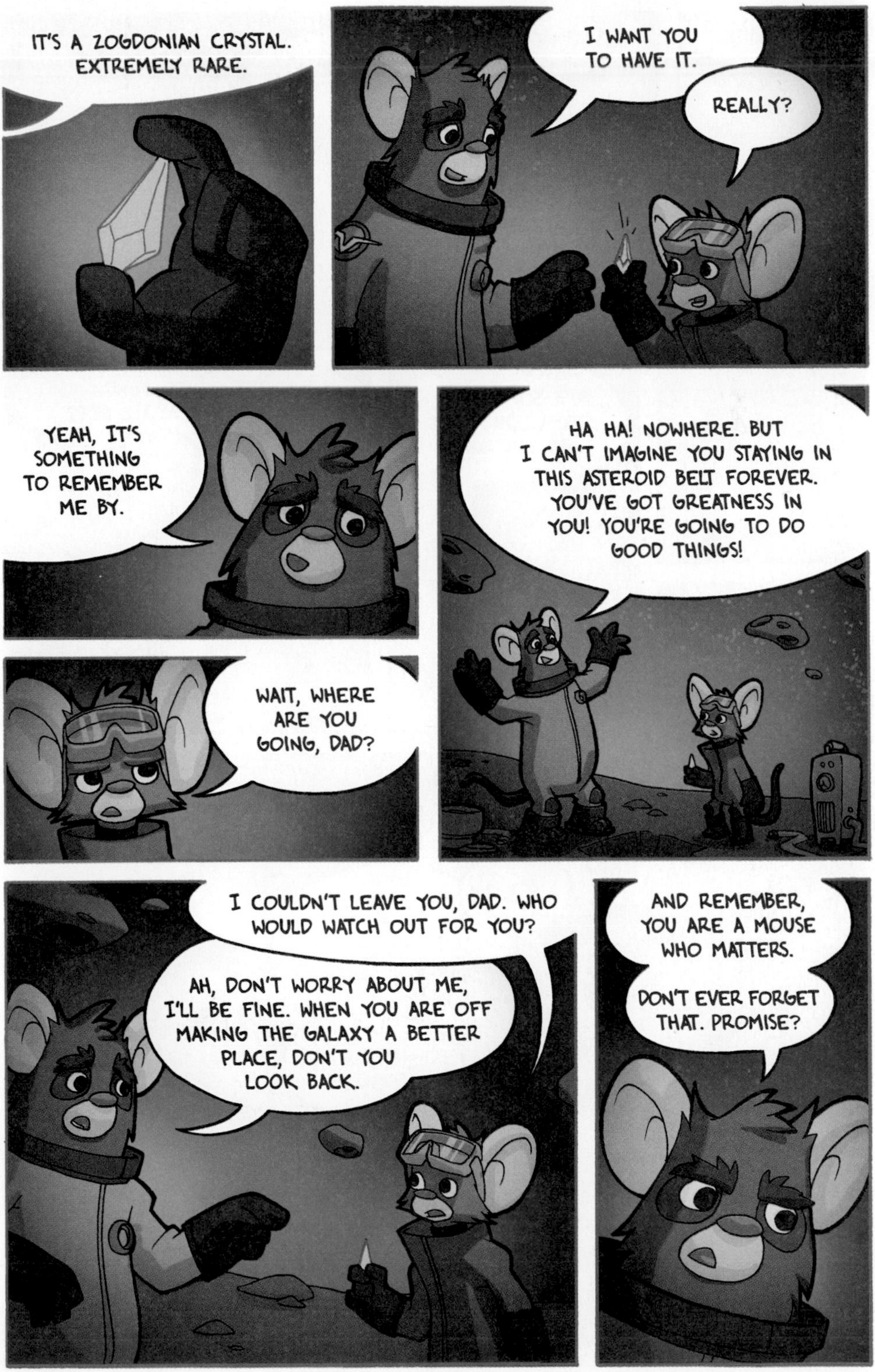
IT'S A ZOGDONIAN CRYSTAL. EXTREMELY RARE.
I WANT YOU TO HAVE IT.
REALLY?
YEAH, IT'S SOMETHING TO REMEMBER ME BY.
WAIT, WHERE ARE YOU GOING, DAD?
HA HA! NOWHERE. BUT I CAN'T IMAGINE YOU STAYING IN THIS ASTEROID BELT FOREVER. YOU'VE GOT GREATNESS IN YOU! YOU'RE GOING TO DO GOOD THINGS!
I COULDN'T LEAVE YOU, DAD. WHO WOULD WATCH OUT FOR YOU?
AH, DON'T WORRY ABOUT ME, I'LL BE FINE. WHEN YOU ARE OFF MAKING THE GALAXY A BETTER PLACE, DON'T YOU LOOK BACK.
AND REMEMBER, YOU ARE A MOUSE WHO MATTERS.
DON'T EVER FORGET THAT. PROMISE?

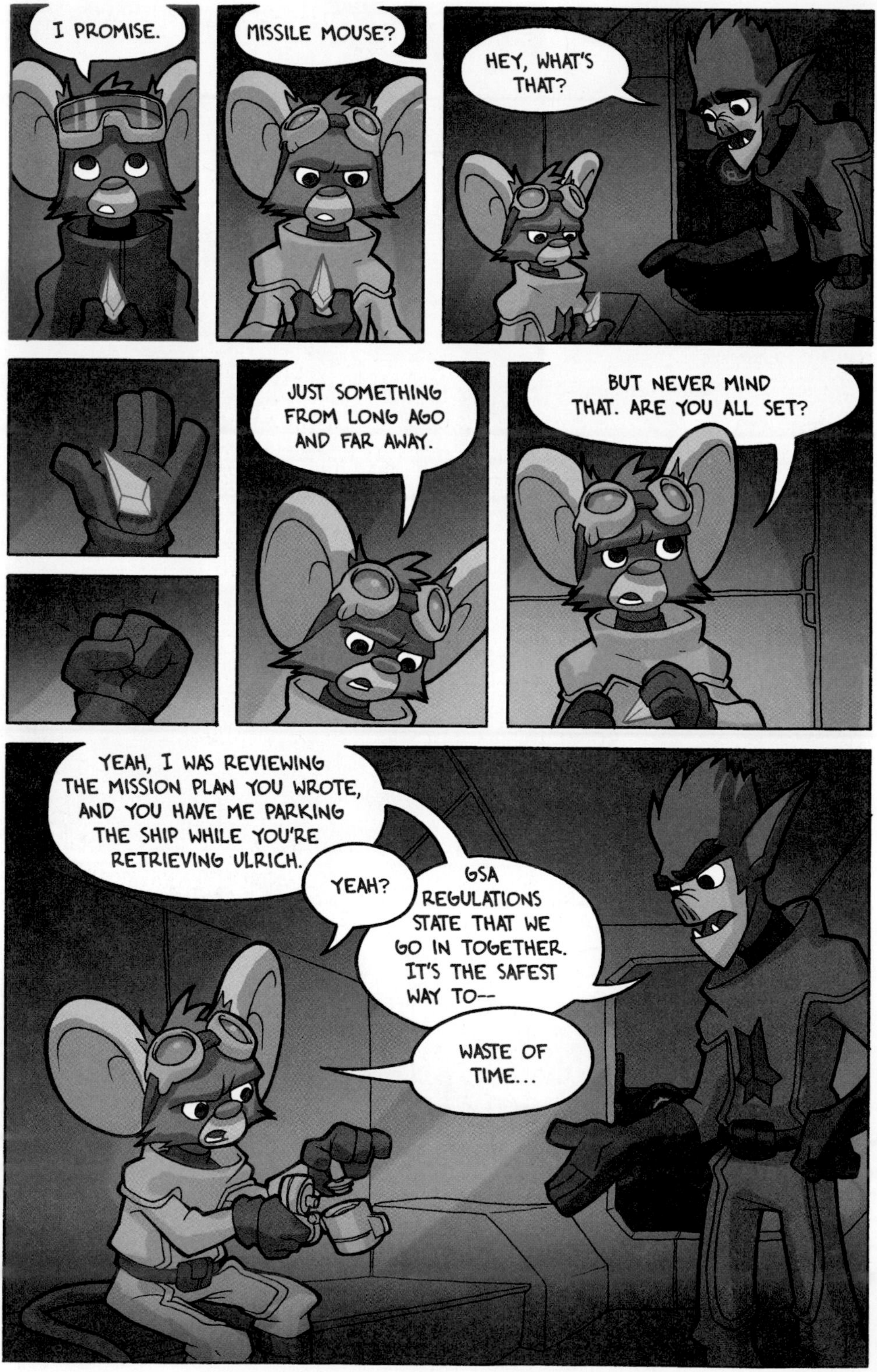
I PROMISE.
MISSILE MOUSE?
HEY, WHAT'S THAT?
JUST SOMETHING FROM LONG AGO AND FAR AWAY.
BUT NEVER MIND THAT. ARE YOU ALL SET?
YEAH, I WAS REVIEWING THE MISSION PLAN YOU WROTE, AND YOU HAVE ME PARKING THE SHIP WHILE YOU'RE RETRIEVING ULRICH.
YEAH?
GSA REGULATIONS STATE THAT WE GO IN TOGETHER. IT'S THE SAFEST WAY TO--
WASTE OF TIME...

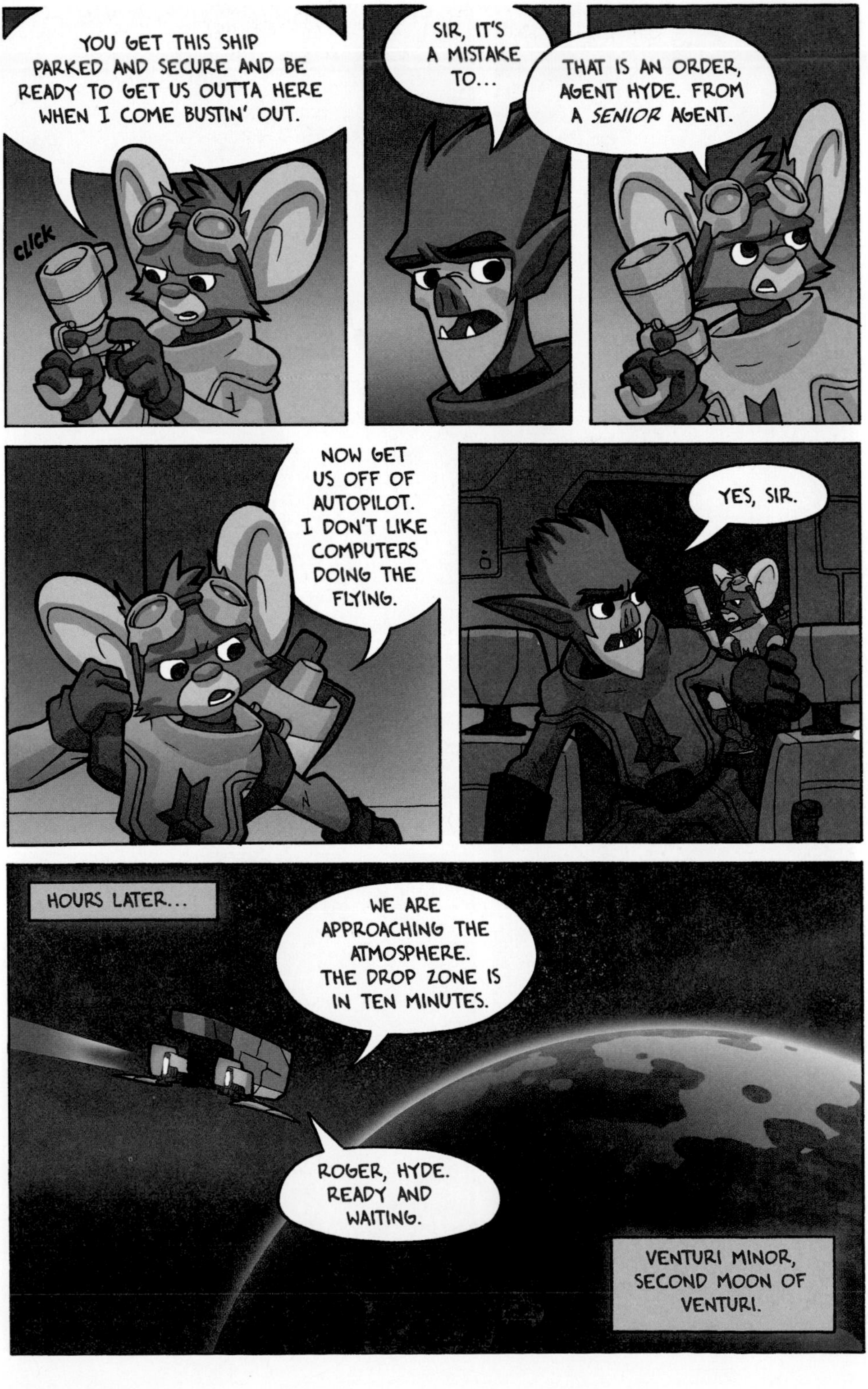
YOU GET THIS SHIP PARKED AND SECURE AND BE READY TO GET US OUTTA HERE WHEN I COME BUSTIN' OUT.
CLICK
SIR, IT'S A MISTAKE TO...
THAT IS AN ORDER, AGENT HYDE. FROM A *SENIOR* AGENT.
NOW GET US OFF OF AUTOPILOT. I DON'T LIKE COMPUTERS DOING THE FLYING.
YES, SIR.
HOURS LATER...
WE ARE APPROACHING THE ATMOSPHERE. THE DROP ZONE IS IN TEN MINUTES.
ROGER, HYDE. READY AND WAITING.
VENTURI MINOR, SECOND MOON OF VENTURI.

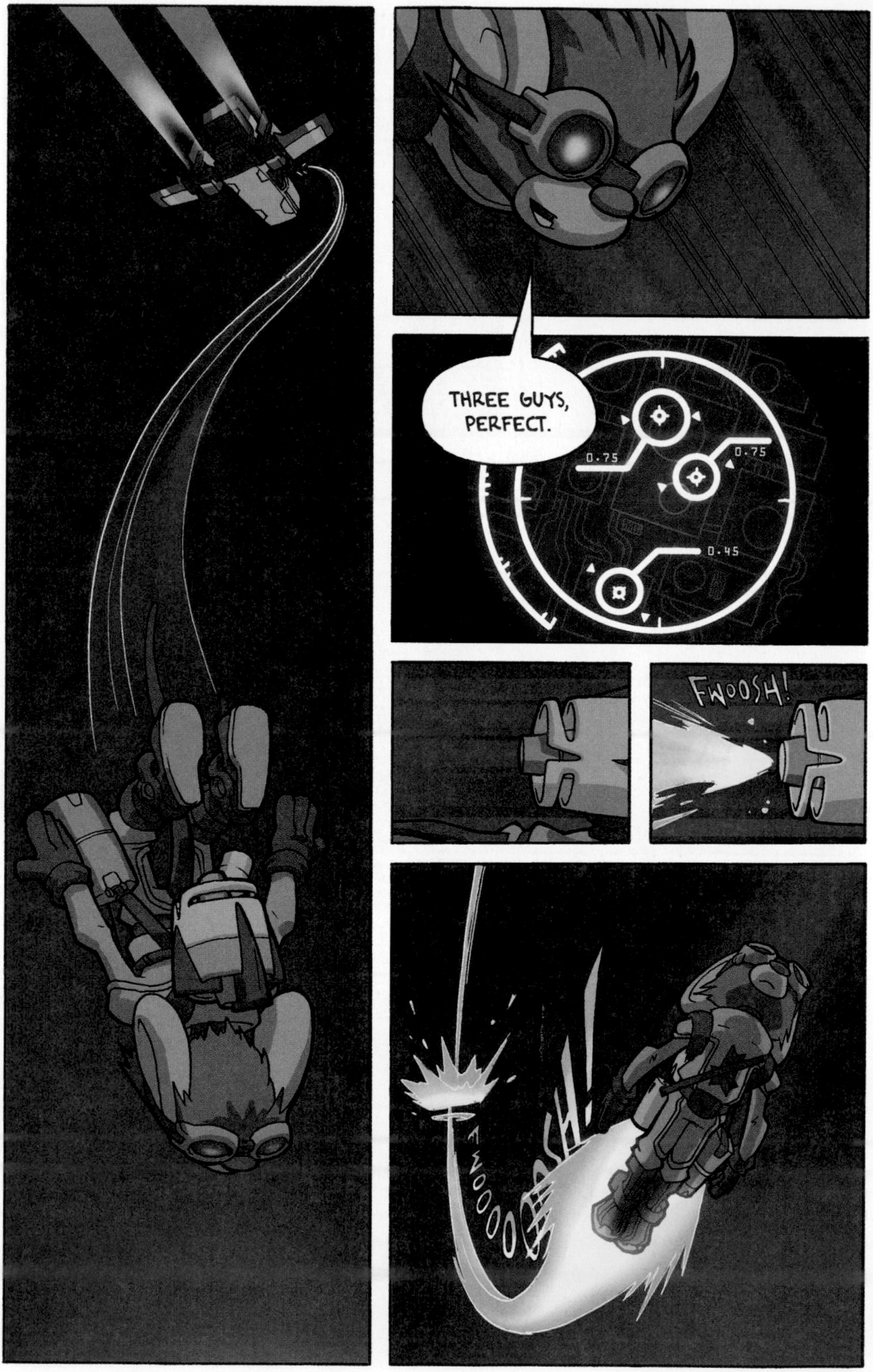
THREE GUYS, PERFECT.
0.75
0.75
0.45
FWOOSH!
FWOOOOOOSH!

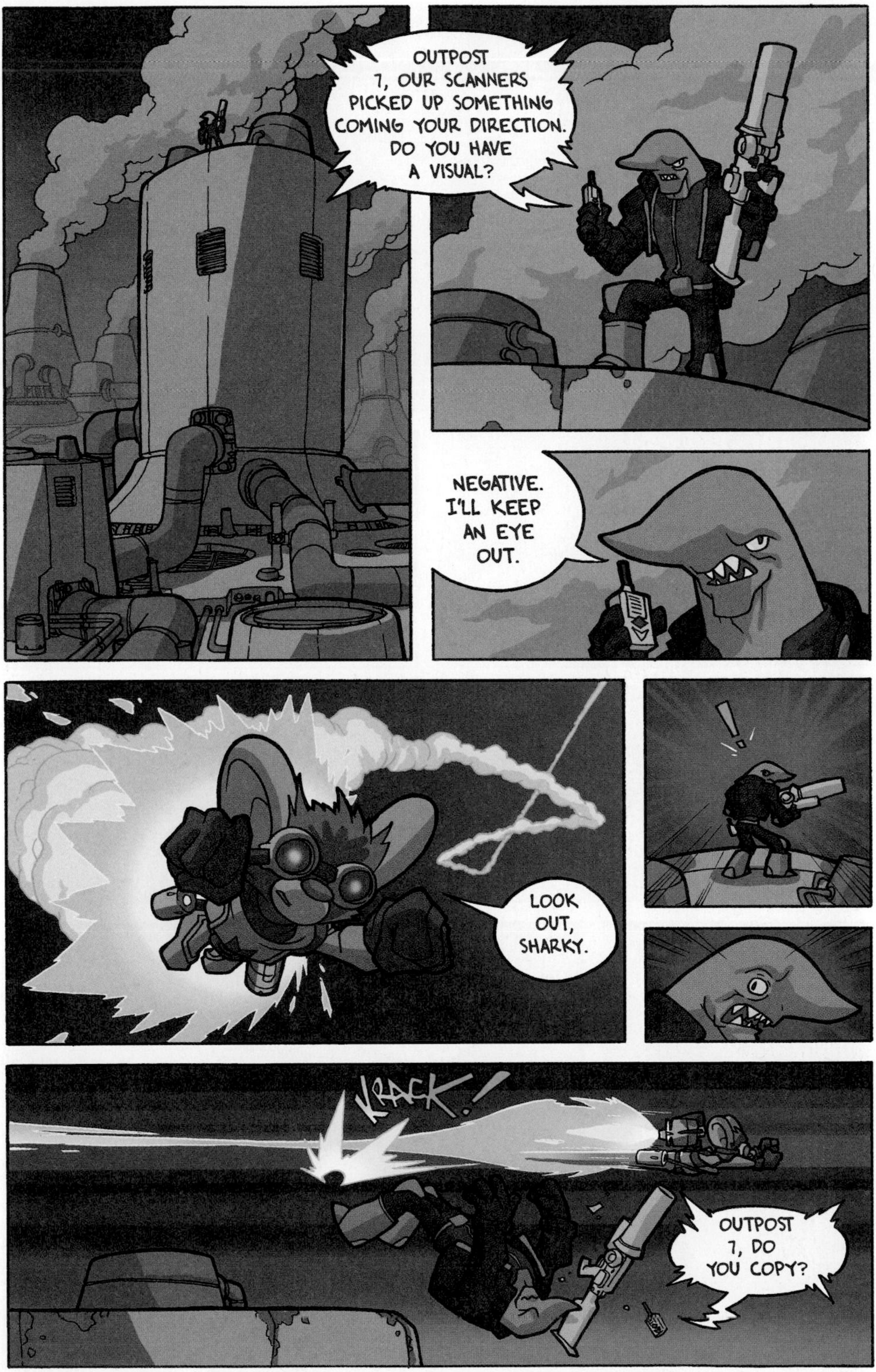
OUTPOST 7, OUR SCANNERS PICKED UP SOMETHING COMING YOUR DIRECTION. DO YOU HAVE A VISUAL?
NEGATIVE. I'LL KEEP AN EYE OUT.
LOOK OUT, SHARKY.
!
KRACK!
OUTPOST 7, DO YOU COPY?

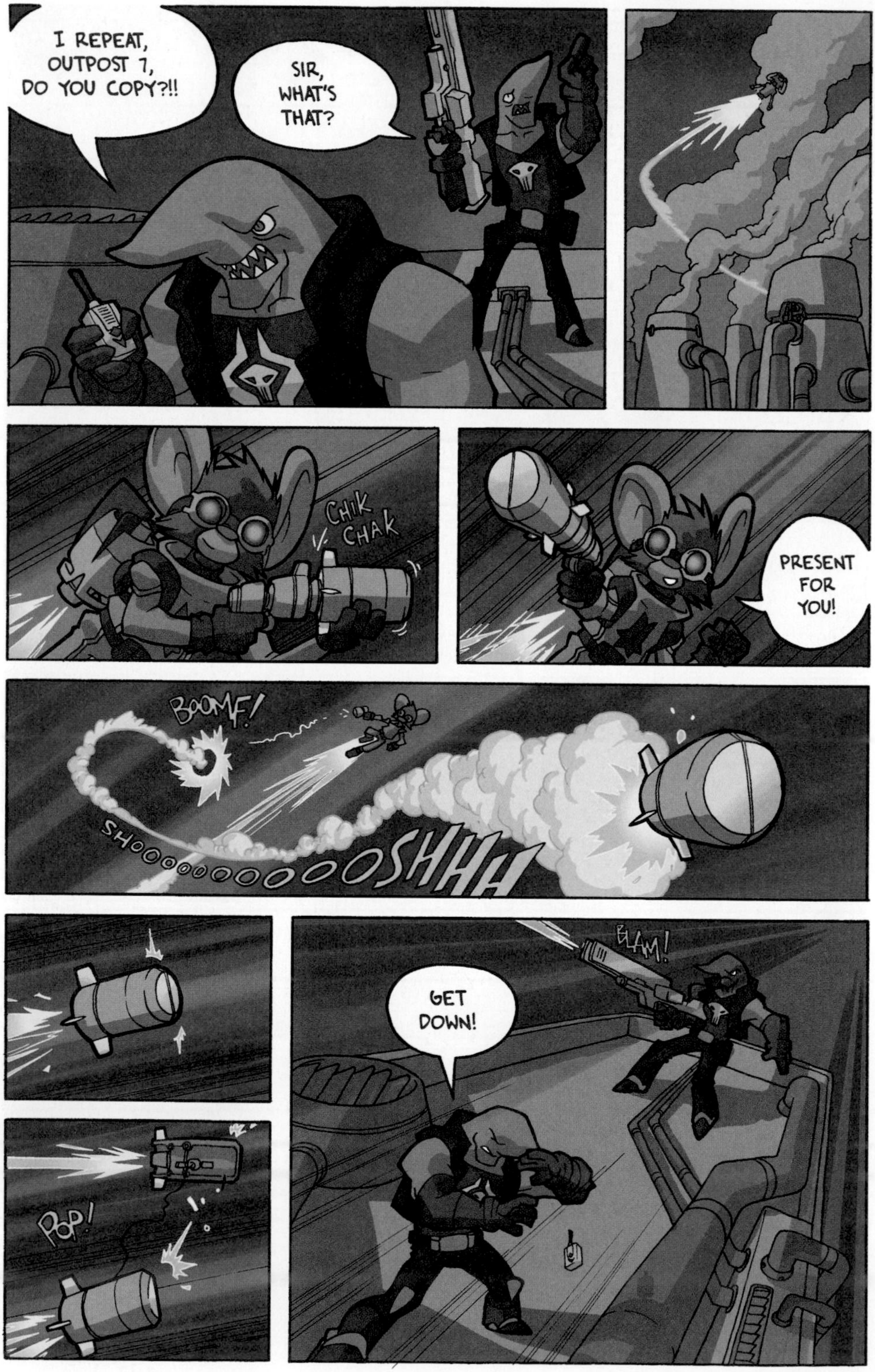
I REPEAT, OUTPOST 7, DO YOU COPY?!!
SIR, WHAT'S THAT?
CHIK CHAK
PRESENT FOR YOU!
BOOMF!
SHOOOOOOOOOOOOOOSHHH
POP!
BLAM!
GET DOWN!

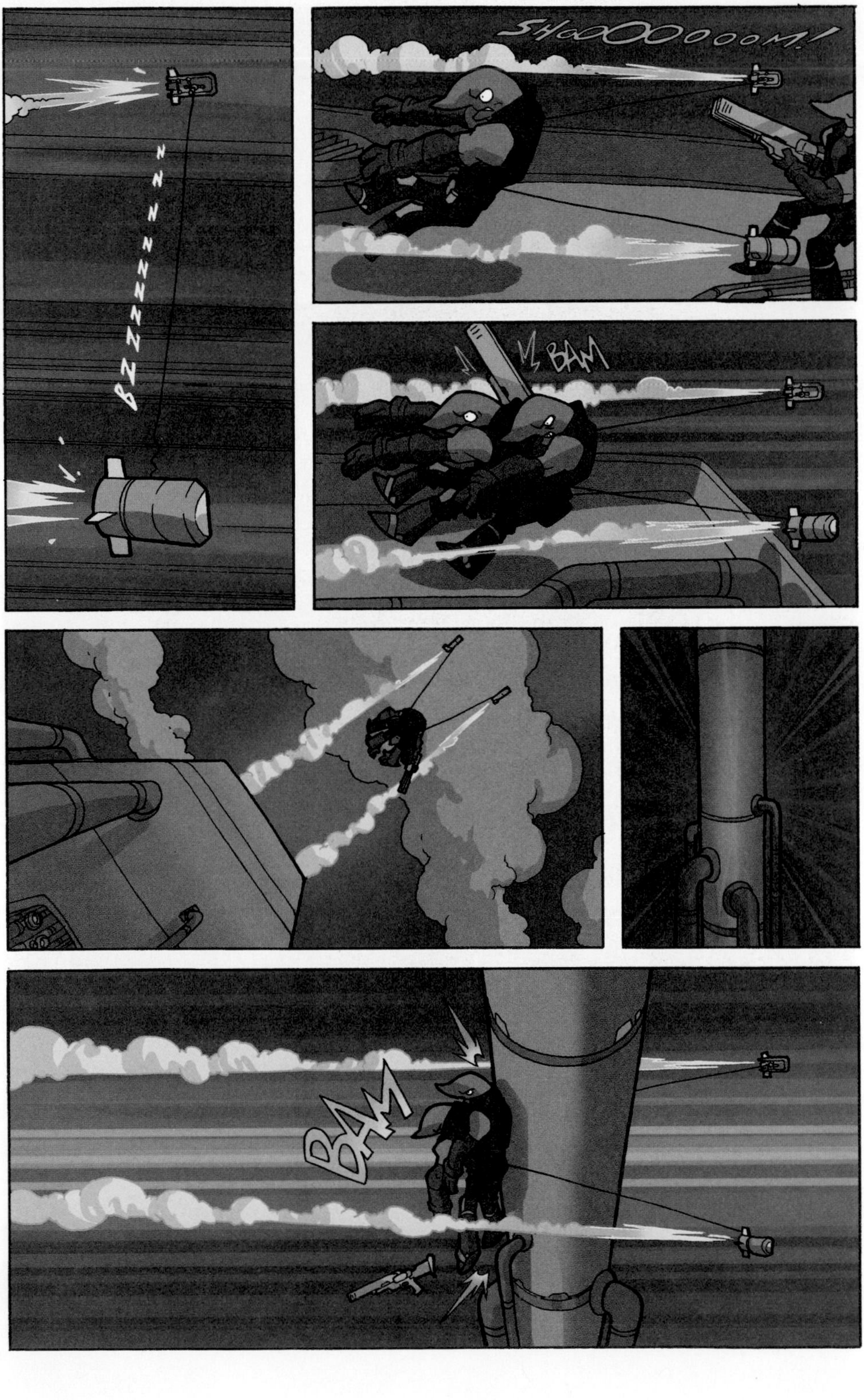
BZZZZZZZZZZZZ
SHOOOOOOOOM!
BAM
BAM

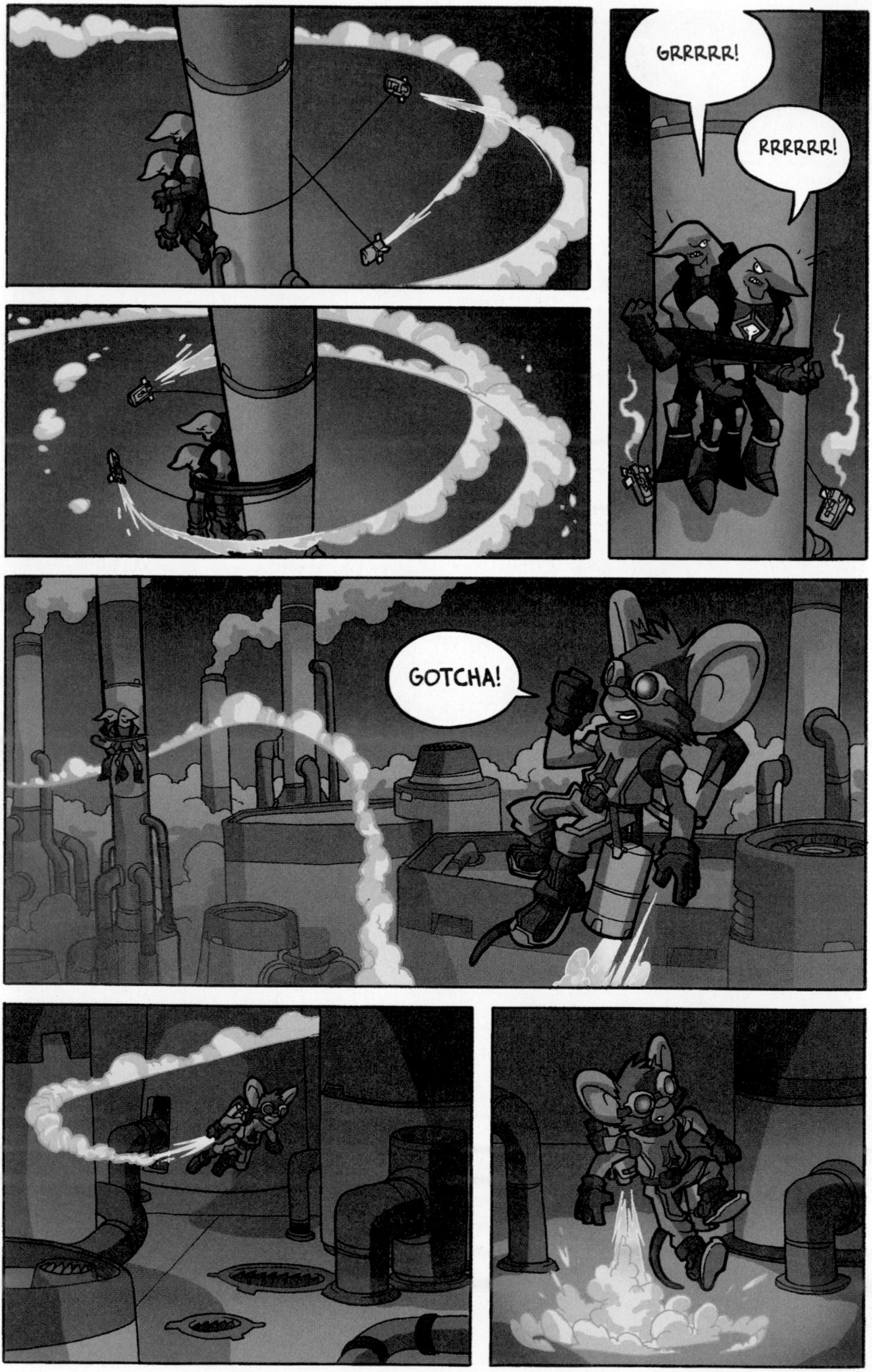
GRRRRR!
RRRRRR!
GOTCHA!

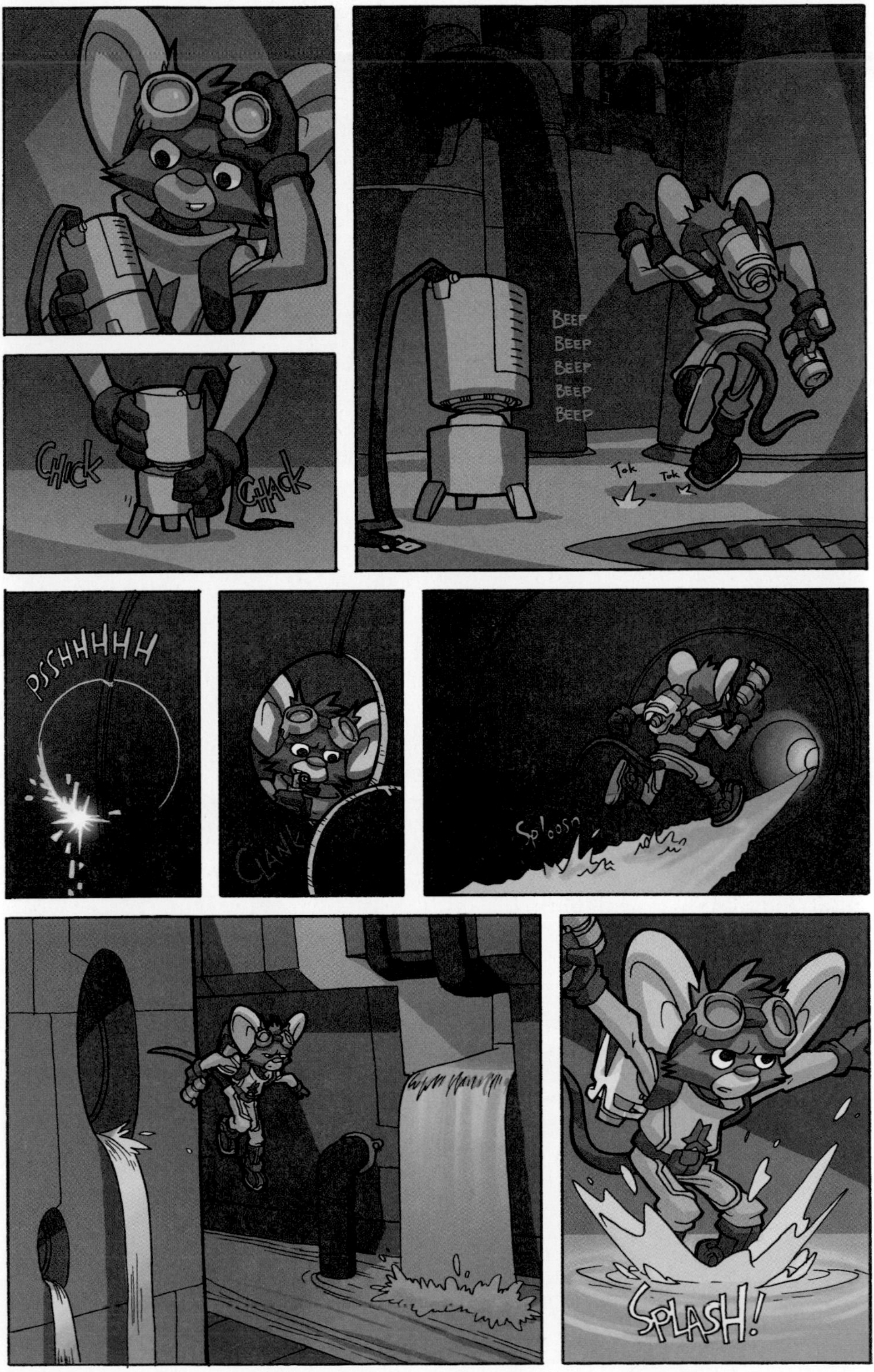

CHICK
CHACK
BEEP
BEEP
BEEP
BEEP
BEEP
Tok
Tok
PSSHHHHH
CLANK
Sploosh
SPLASH!

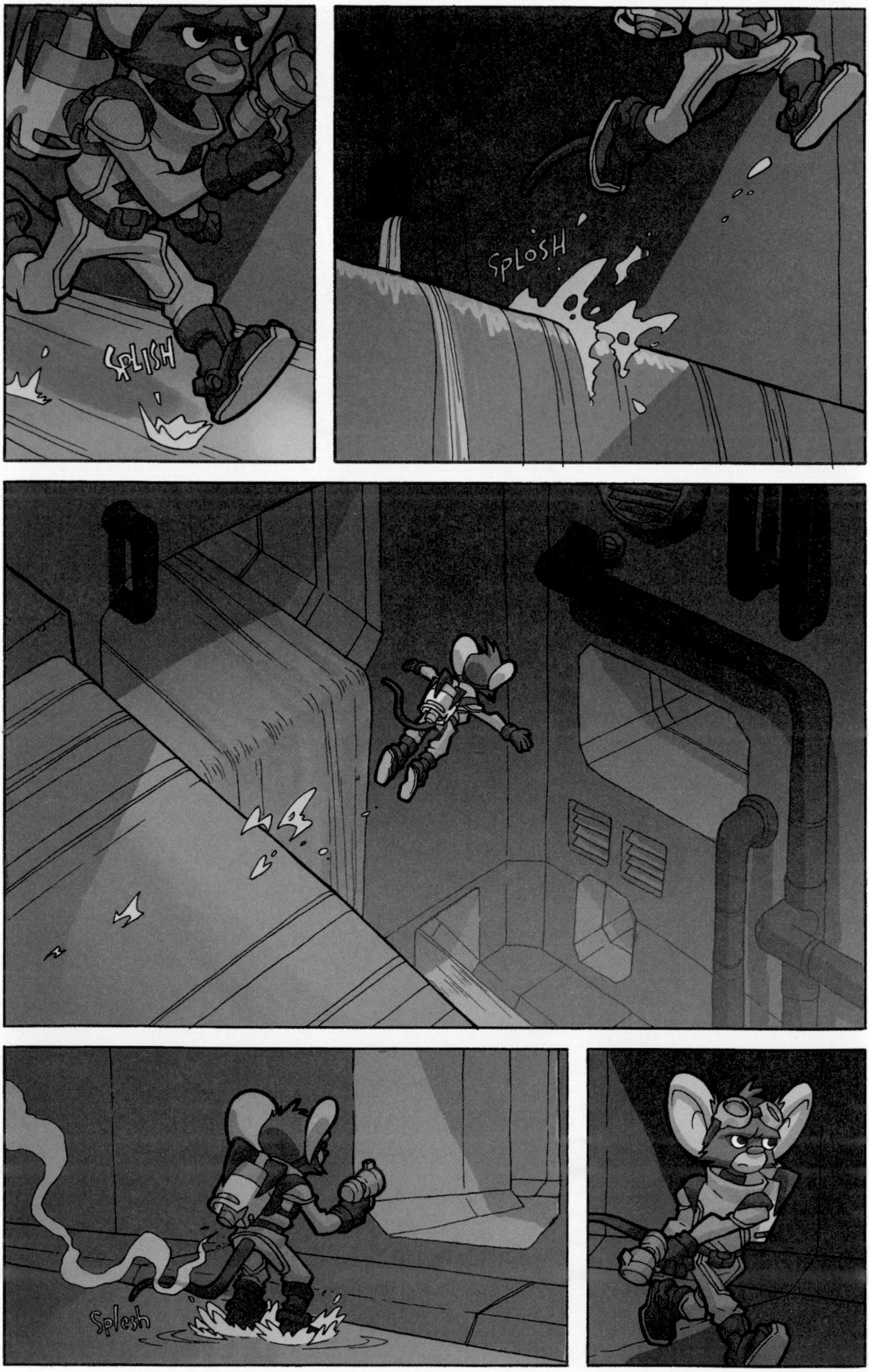
SPLISH
SPLOSH
Splesh

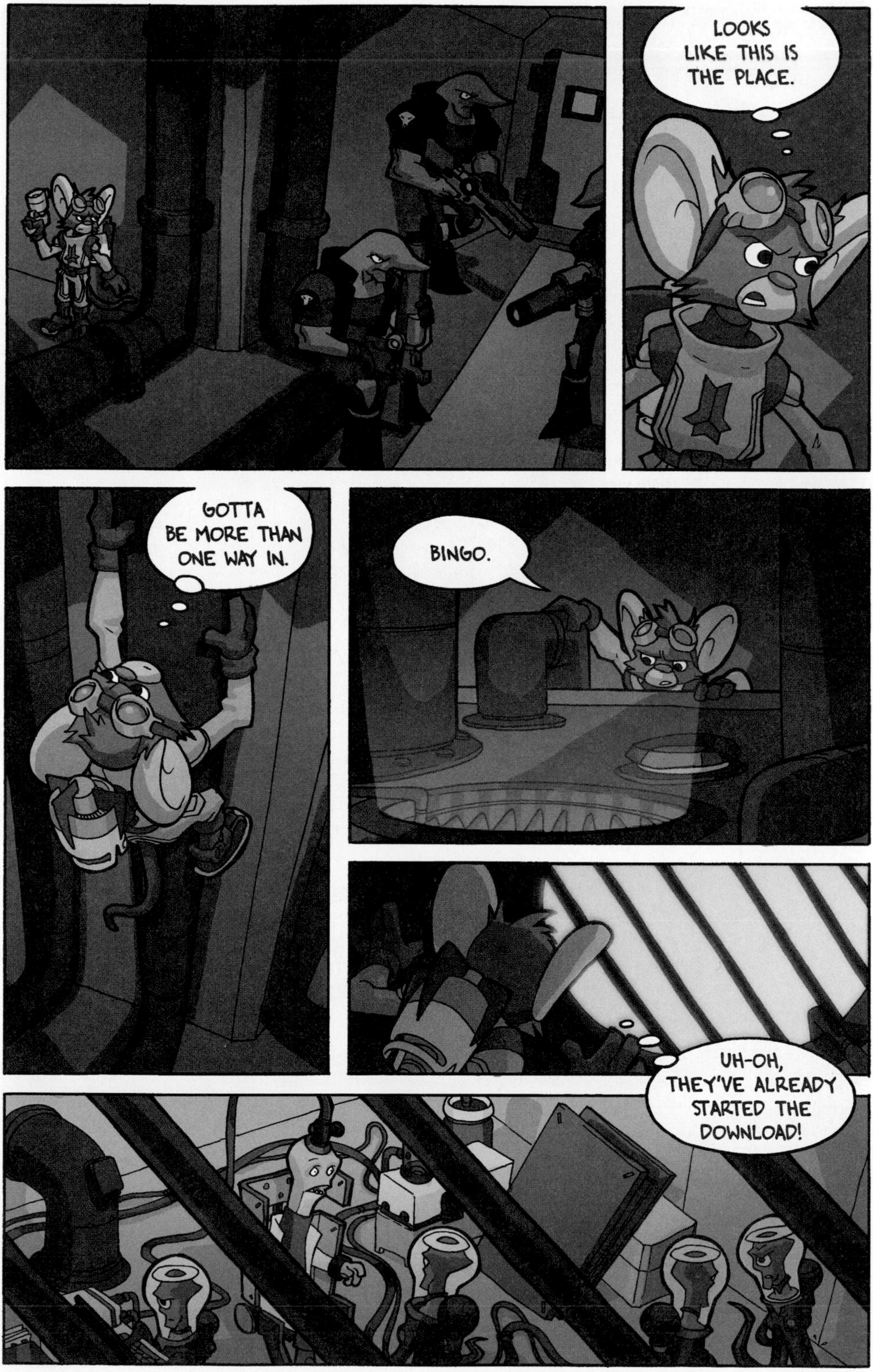
LOOKS LIKE THIS IS THE PLACE.
GOTTA BE MORE THAN ONE WAY IN.
BINGO.
UH-OH, THEY'VE ALREADY STARTED THE DOWNLOAD!

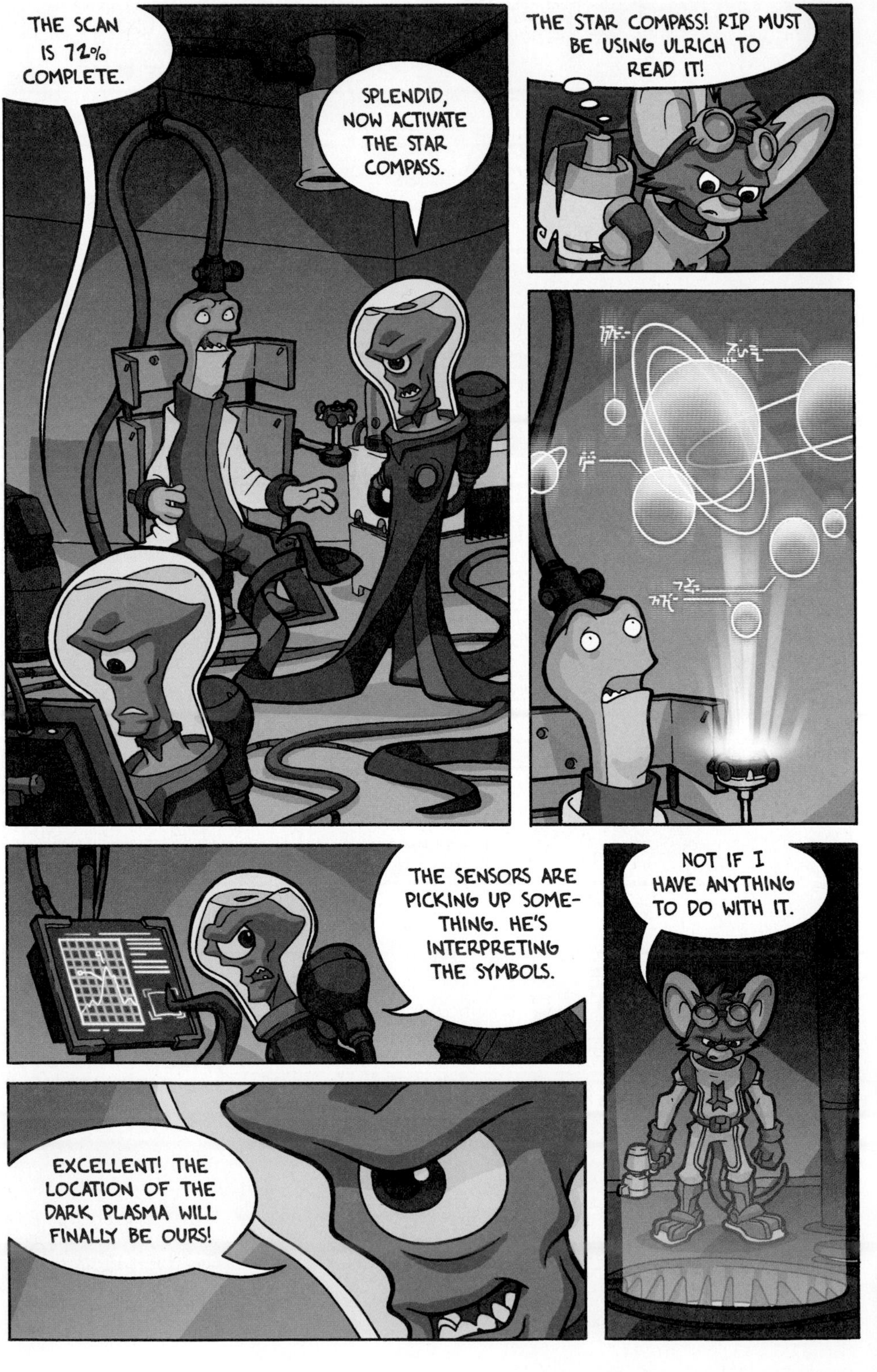
THE SCAN IS 72% COMPLETE.
SPLENDID, NOW ACTIVATE THE STAR COMPASS.
THE STAR COMPASS! RIP MUST BE USING ULRICH TO READ IT!
THE SENSORS ARE PICKING UP SOMETHING. HE'S INTERPRETING THE SYMBOLS.
EXCELLENT! THE LOCATION OF THE DARK PLASMA WILL FINALLY BE OURS!
NOT IF I HAVE ANYTHING TO DO WITH IT.

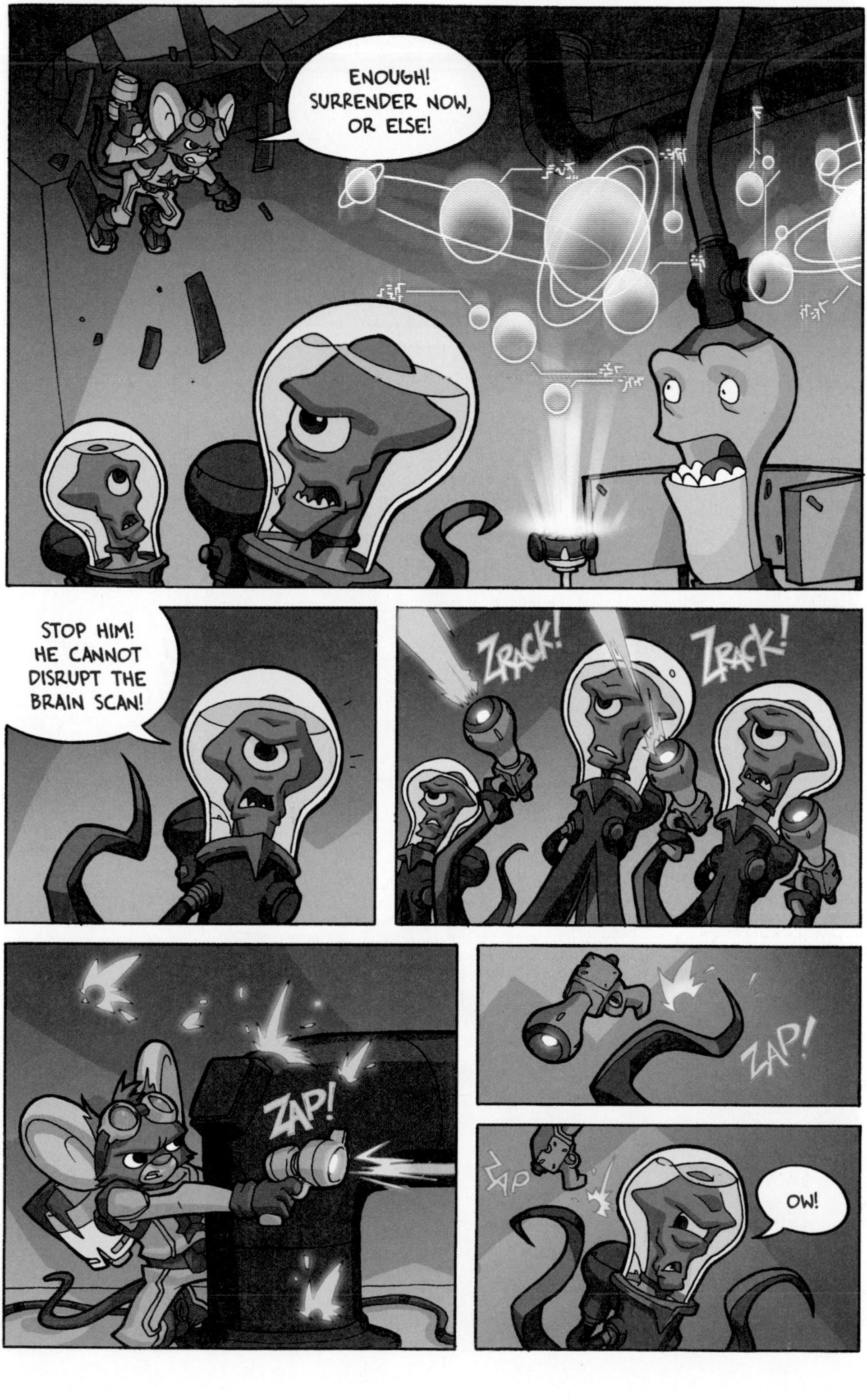
ENOUGH! SURRENDER NOW, OR ELSE!
STOP HIM! HE CANNOT DISRUPT THE BRAIN SCAN!
ZRACK!
ZRACK!
ZAP!
ZAP!
ZAP
OW!

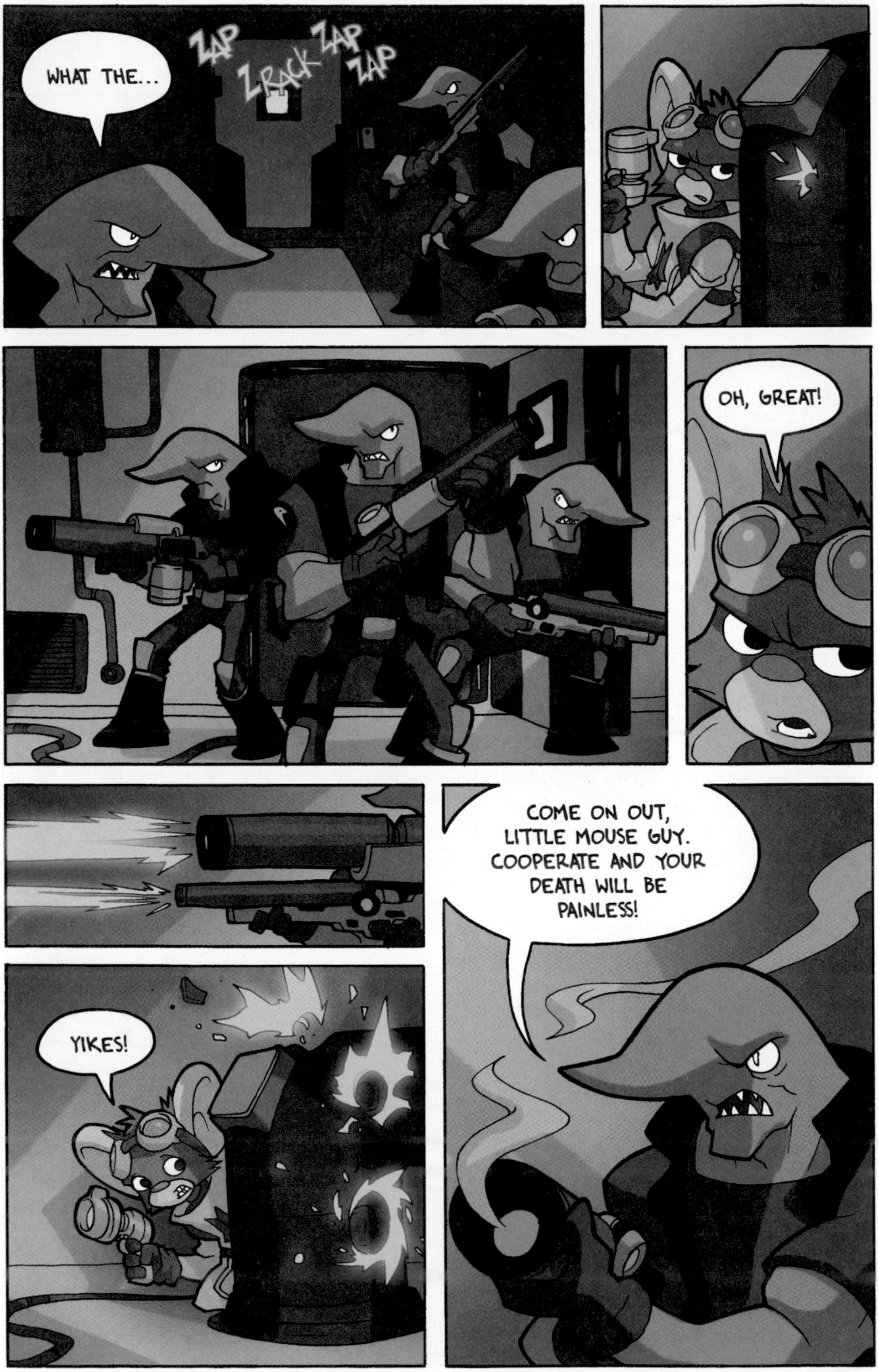
WHAT THE...
ZAP
ZRACK
ZAP
ZAP
OH, GREAT!
COME ON OUT, LITTLE MOUSE GUY. COOPERATE AND YOUR DEATH WILL BE PAINLESS!
YIKES!

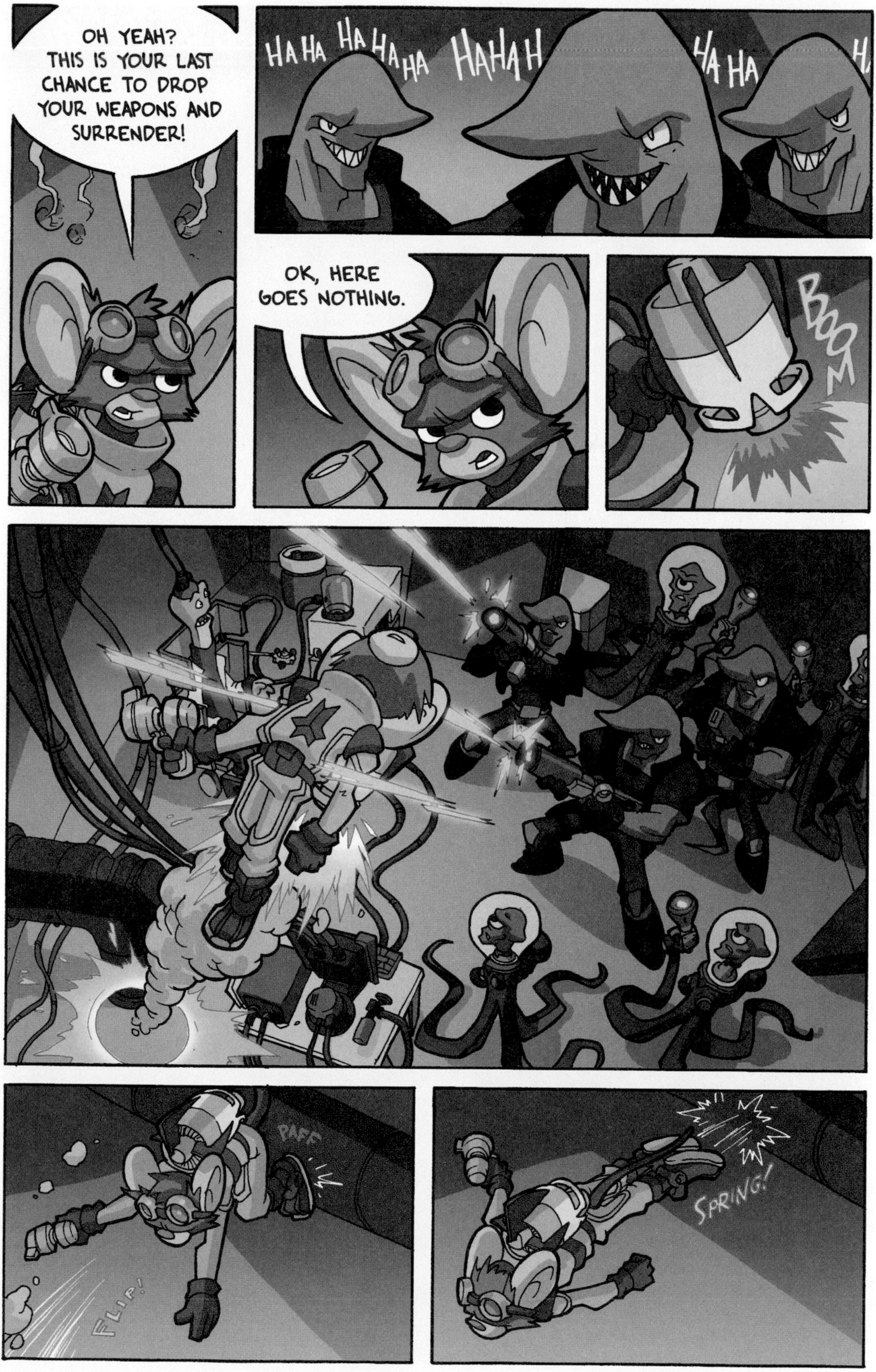
OH YEAH? THIS IS YOUR LAST CHANCE TO DROP YOUR WEAPONS AND SURRENDER!
HA HA HA HA HA HAHAH HA HA
OK, HERE GOES NOTHING.
BOOM
PAFF
FLIP!
SPRING!

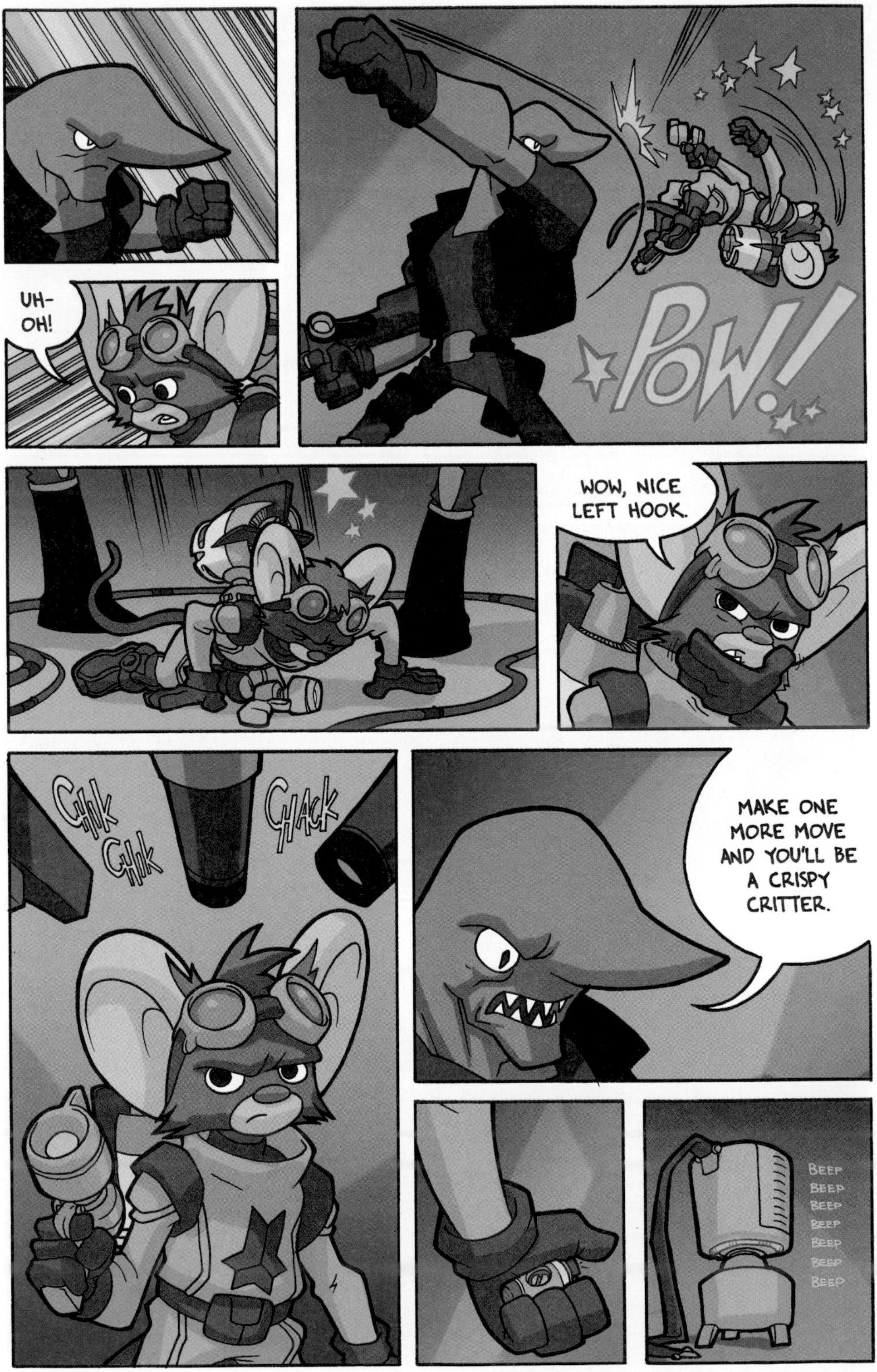
UH-OH!
POW!
WOW, NICE LEFT HOOK.
CHIK CHIK
CHACK
MAKE ONE MORE MOVE AND YOU'LL BE A CRISPY CRITTER.
BEEP BEEP BEEP BEEP BEEP BEEP BEEP

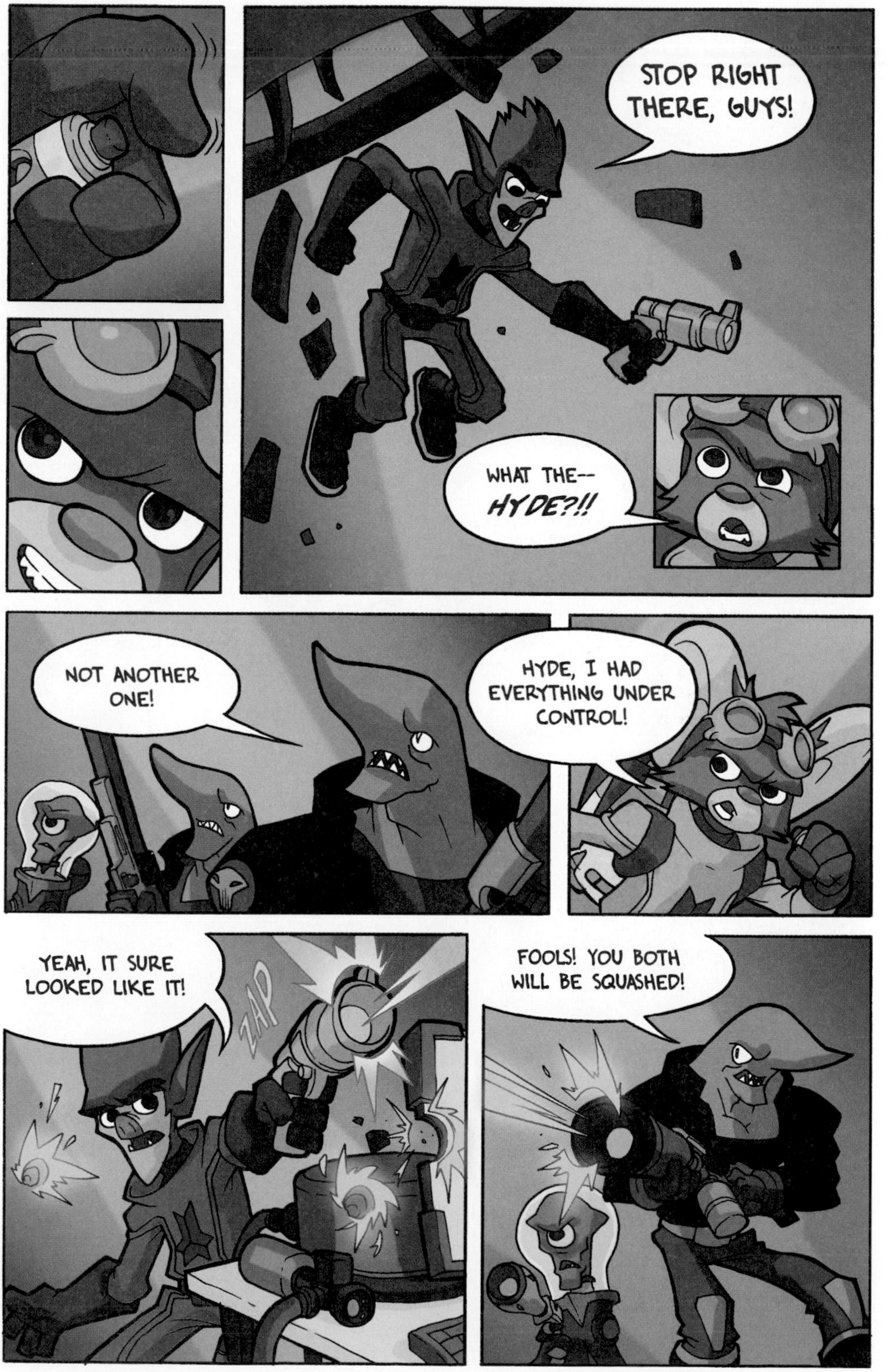
STOP RIGHT THERE, GUYS!
WHAT THE-- HYDE?!!
NOT ANOTHER ONE!
HYDE, I HAD EVERYTHING UNDER CONTROL!
YEAH, IT SURE LOOKED LIKE IT!
ZAP
FOOLS! YOU BOTH WILL BE SQUASHED!

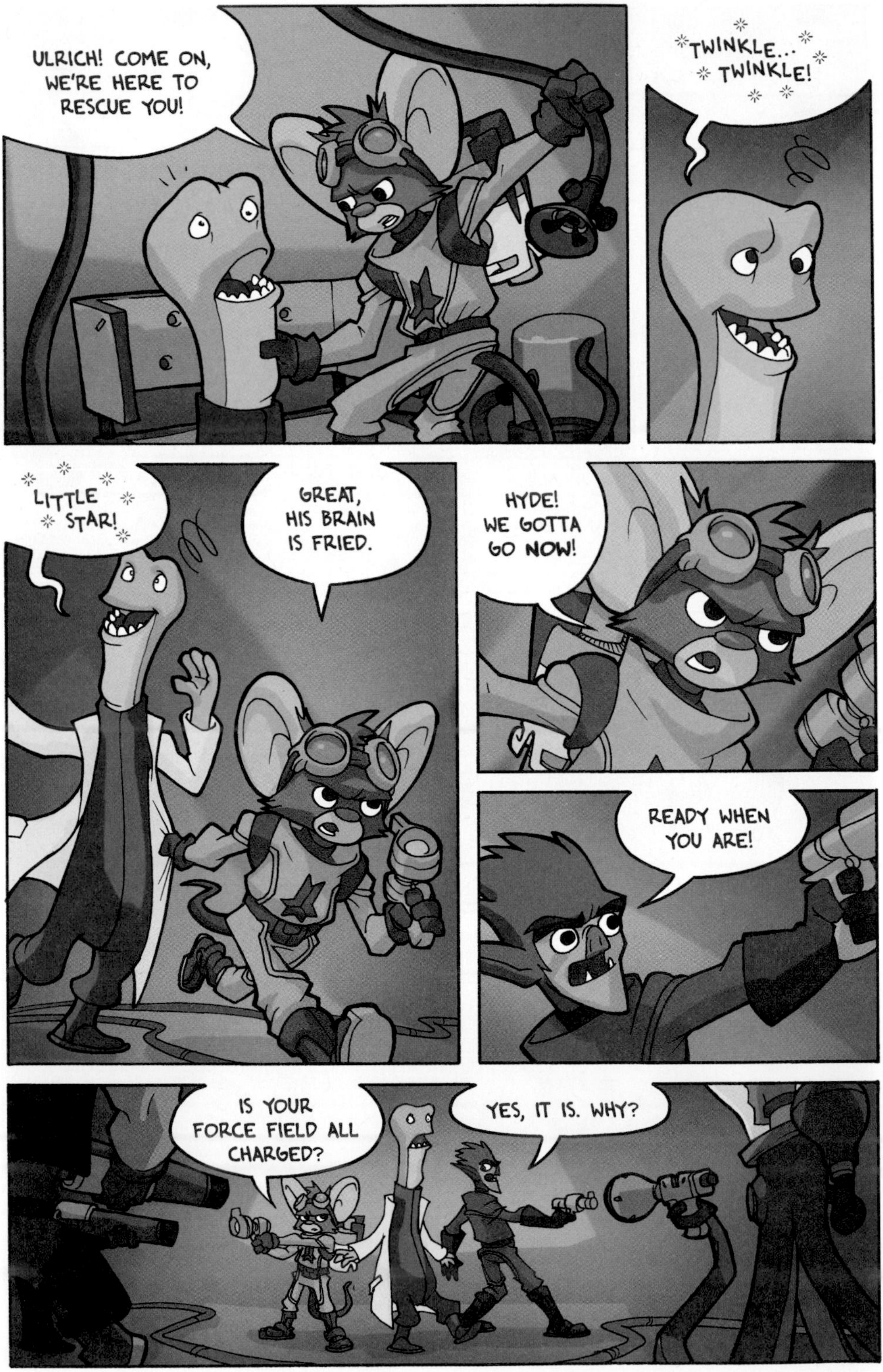
ULRICH! COME ON, WE'RE HERE TO RESCUE YOU!
TWINKLE... TWINKLE!
LITTLE STAR!
GREAT, HIS BRAIN IS FRIED.
HYDE! WE GOTTA GO NOW!
READY WHEN YOU ARE!
IS YOUR FORCE FIELD ALL CHARGED?
YES, IT IS. WHY?

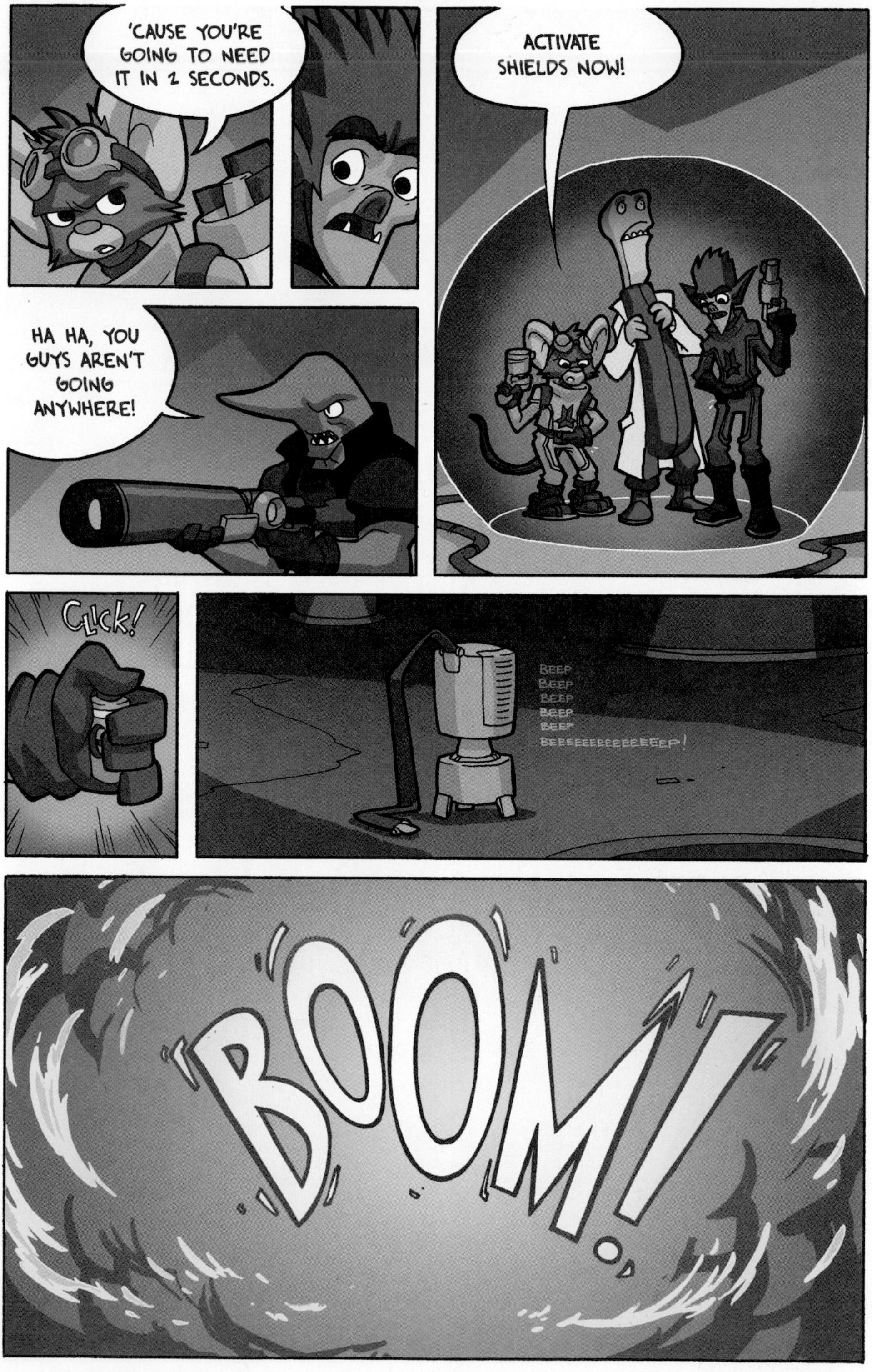
'CAUSE YOU'RE GOING TO NEED IT IN 2 SECONDS.
ACTIVATE SHIELDS NOW!
HA HA, YOU GUYS AREN'T GOING ANYWHERE!
CLICK!
BEEP
BEEP
BEEP
BEEP
BEEP
BEEEEEEEEEEEEEEP!
BOOM!

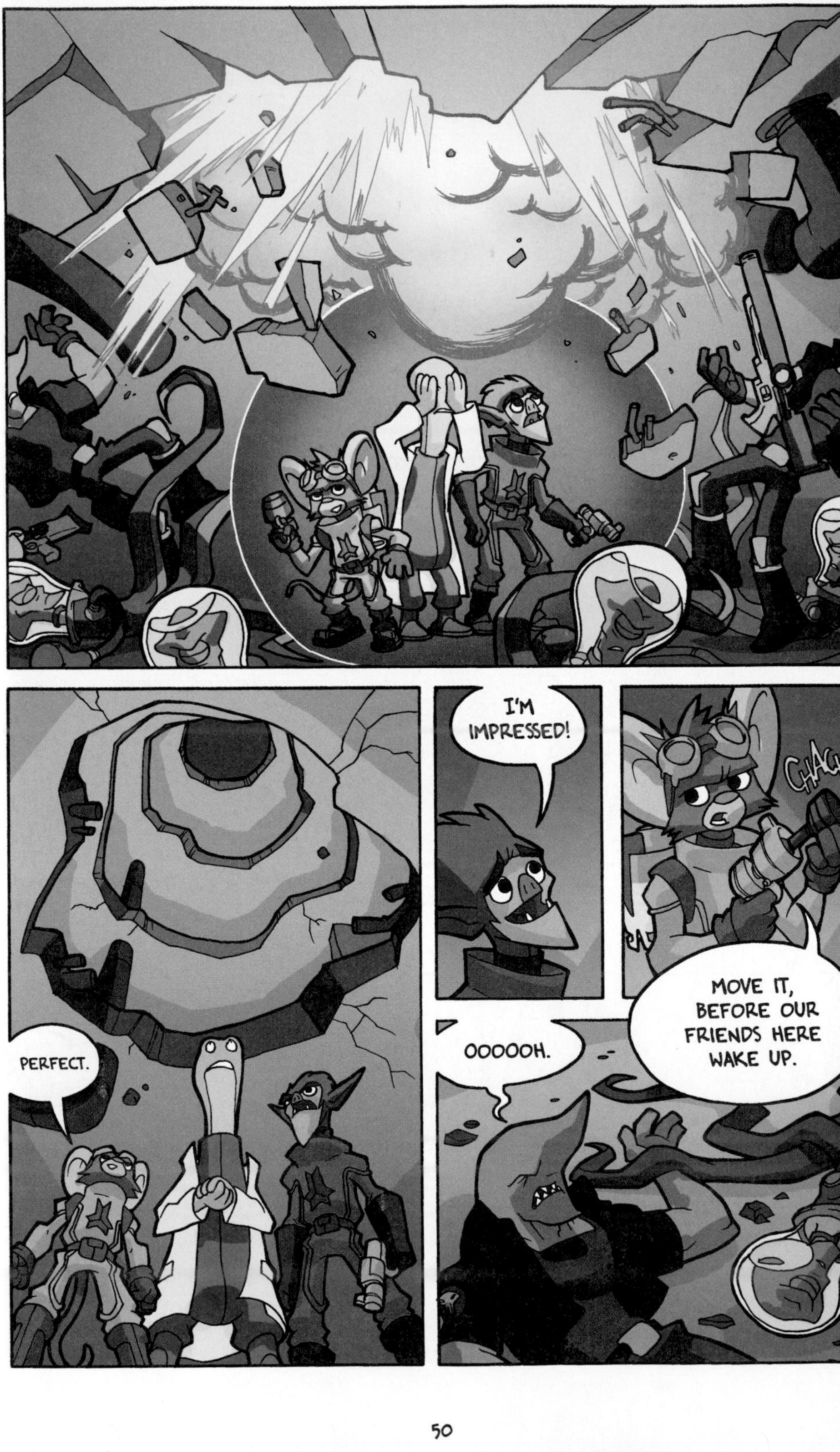
PERFECT.
I'M IMPRESSED!
CHACK
MOVE IT, BEFORE OUR FRIENDS HERE WAKE UP.
OOOOOH.

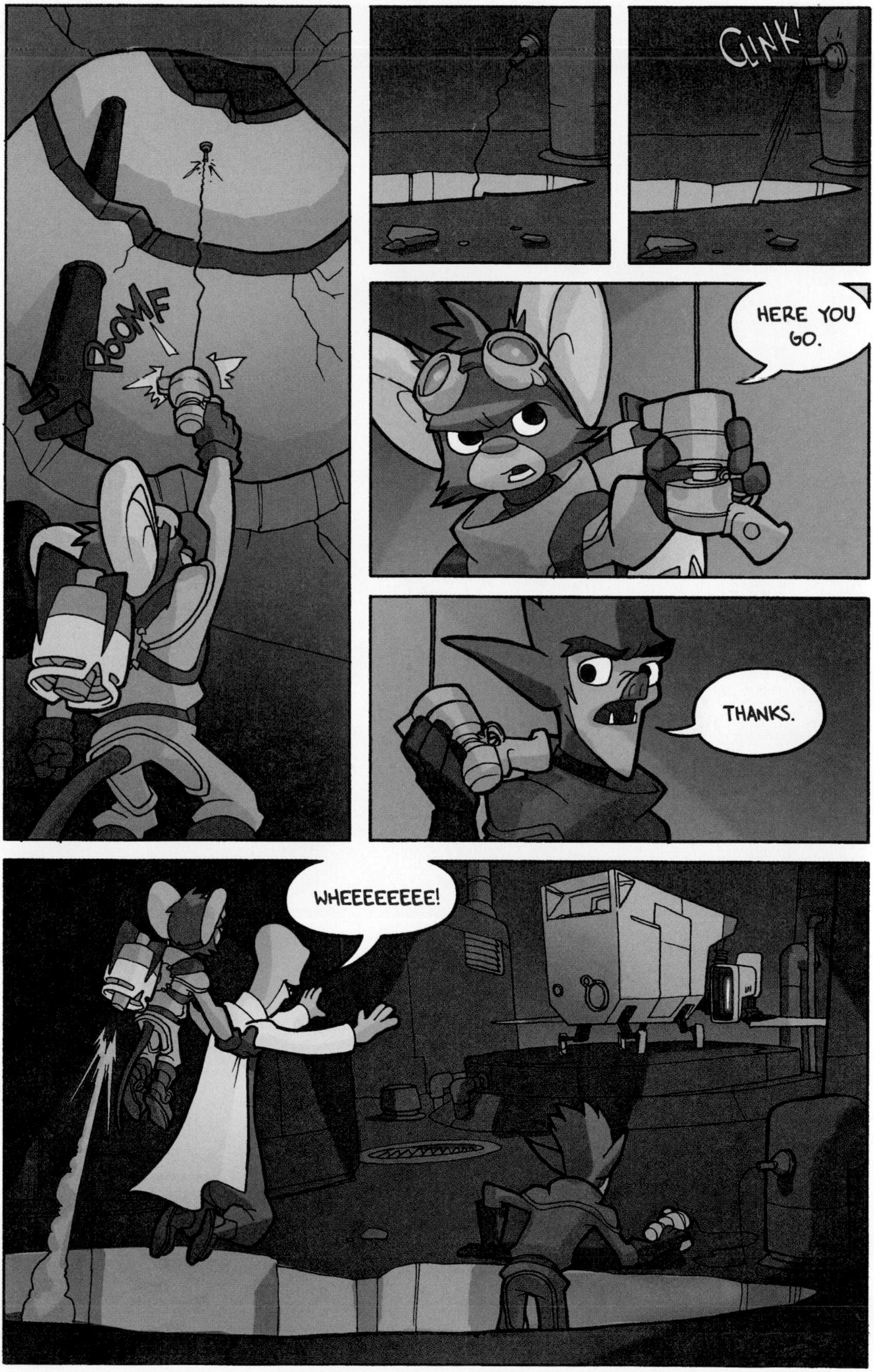
ROOMF
CLINK!
HERE YOU GO.
THANKS.
WHEEEEEEEE!

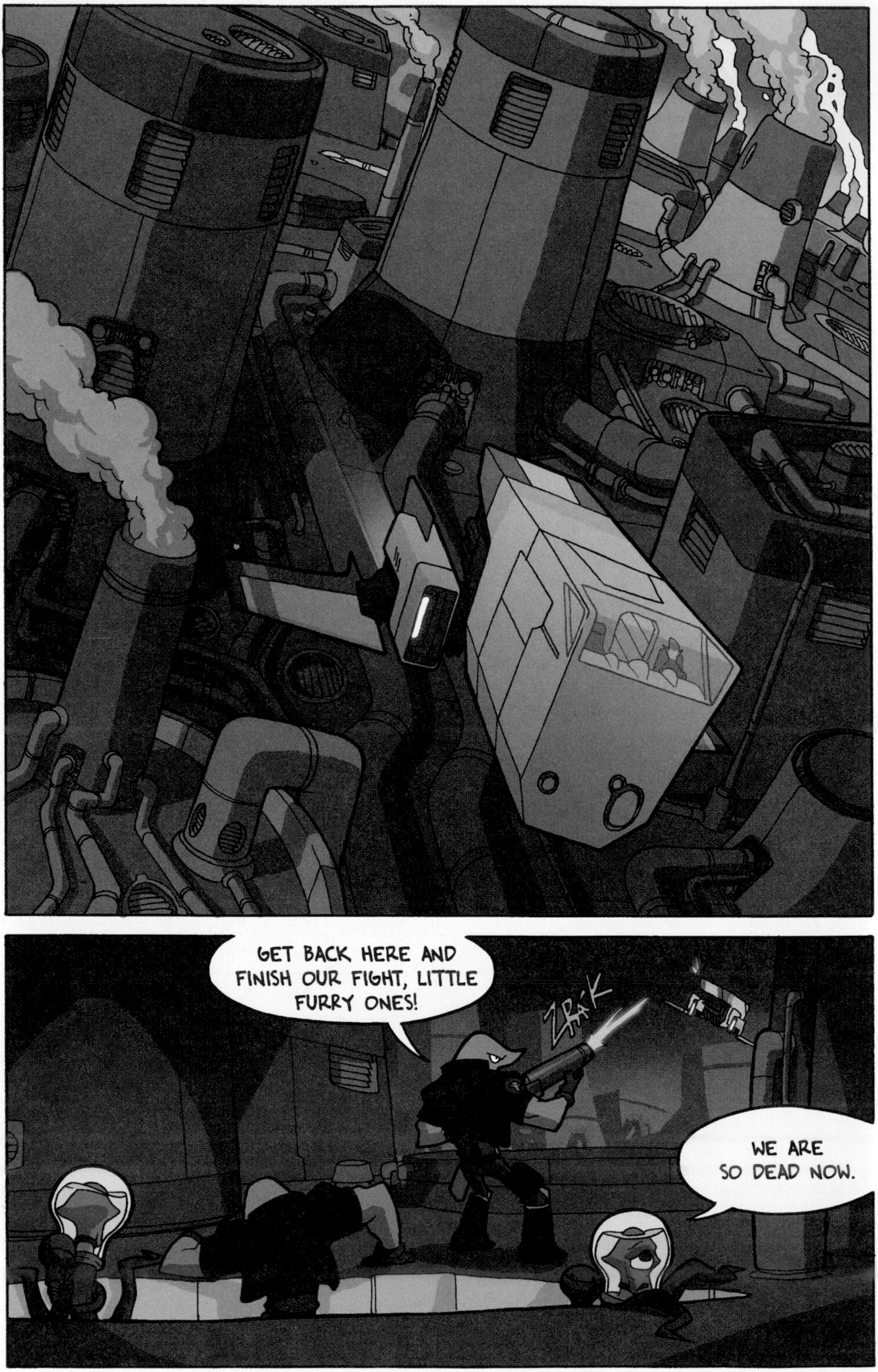
GET BACK HERE AND FINISH OUR FIGHT, LITTLE FURRY ONES!
ZRAK
WE ARE SO DEAD NOW.

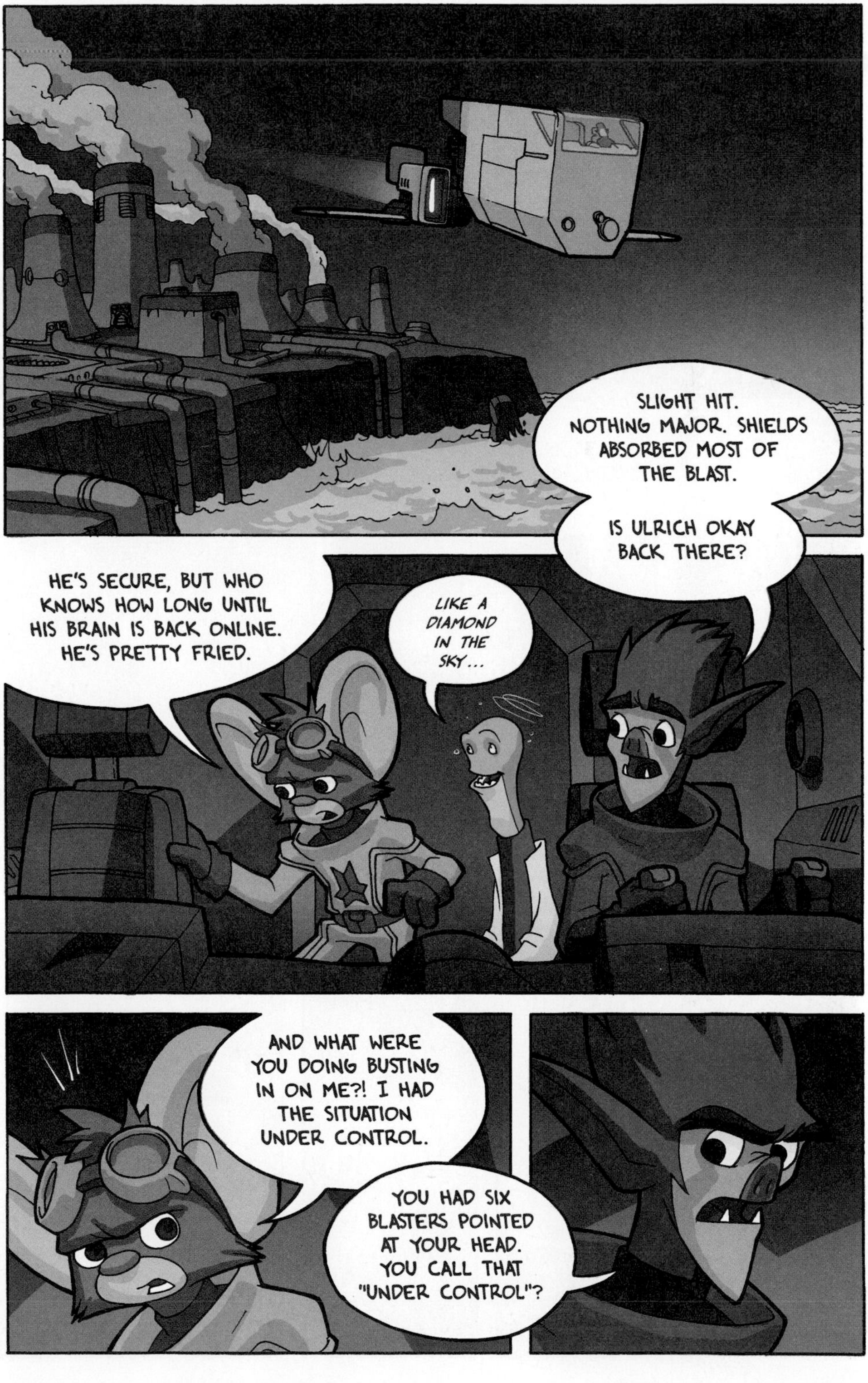
SLIGHT HIT. NOTHING MAJOR. SHIELDS ABSORBED MOST OF THE BLAST.
IS ULRICH OKAY BACK THERE?
HE'S SECURE, BUT WHO KNOWS HOW LONG UNTIL HIS BRAIN IS BACK ONLINE. HE'S PRETTY FRIED.
LIKE A DIAMOND IN THE SKY...
AND WHAT WERE YOU DOING BUSTING IN ON ME?! I HAD THE SITUATION UNDER CONTROL.
YOU HAD SIX BLASTERS POINTED AT YOUR HEAD. YOU CALL THAT "UNDER CONTROL"?

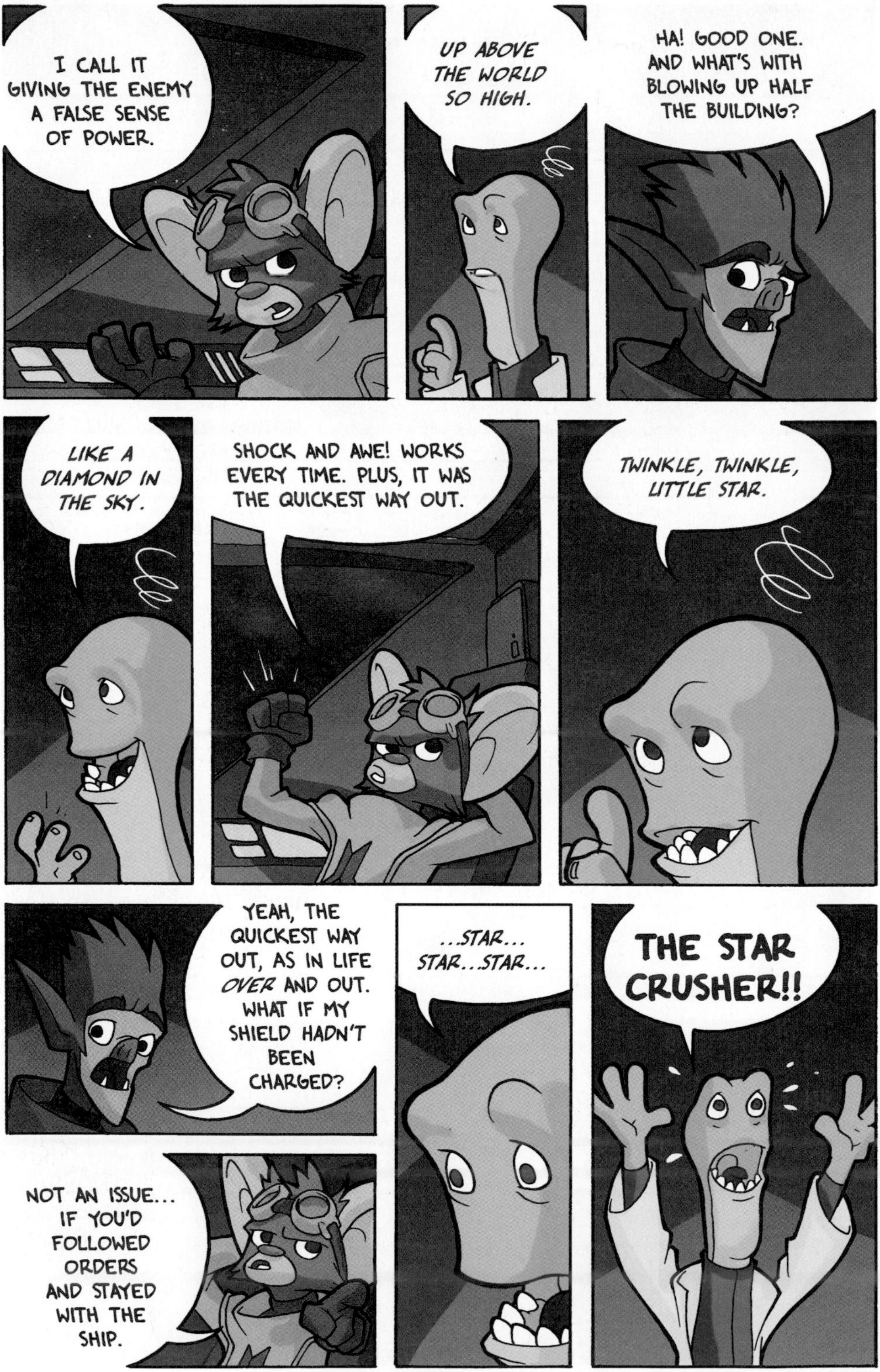
I CALL IT GIVING THE ENEMY A FALSE SENSE OF POWER.
UP ABOVE THE WORLD SO HIGH.
HA! GOOD ONE. AND WHAT'S WITH BLOWING UP HALF THE BUILDING?
LIKE A DIAMOND IN THE SKY.
SHOCK AND AWE! WORKS EVERY TIME. PLUS, IT WAS THE QUICKEST WAY OUT.
TWINKLE, TWINKLE, LITTLE STAR.
YEAH, THE QUICKEST WAY OUT, AS IN LIFE OVER AND OUT. WHAT IF MY SHIELD HADN'T BEEN CHARGED?
NOT AN ISSUE... IF YOU'D FOLLOWED ORDERS AND STAYED WITH THE SHIP.
...STAR... STAR...STAR...
THE STAR CRUSHER!!

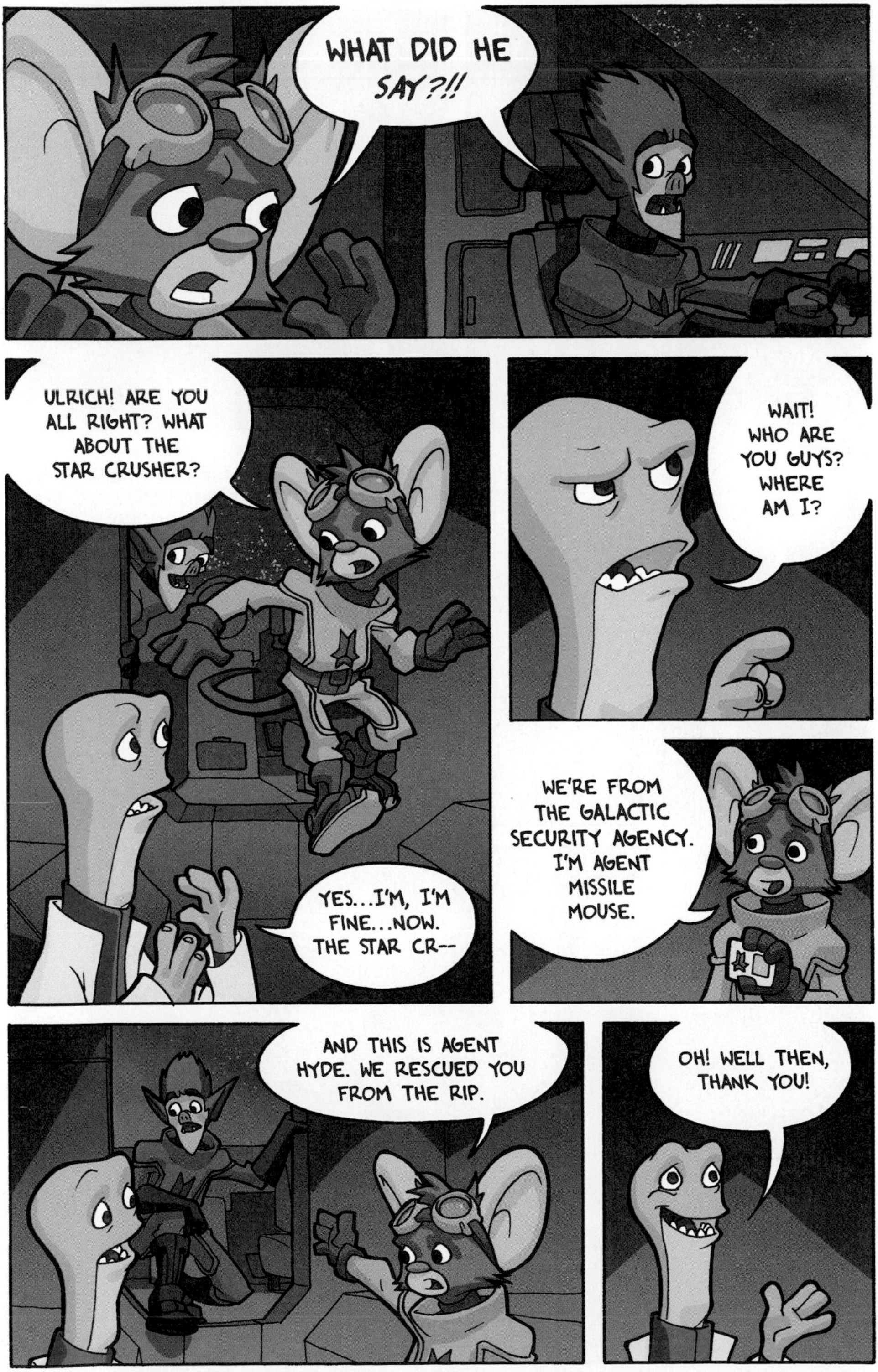

WHAT DID HE SAY?!!
ULRICH! ARE YOU ALL RIGHT? WHAT ABOUT THE STAR CRUSHER?
YES...I'M, I'M FINE...NOW. THE STAR CR--
WAIT! WHO ARE YOU GUYS? WHERE AM I?
WE'RE FROM THE GALACTIC SECURITY AGENCY. I'M AGENT MISSILE MOUSE.
AND THIS IS AGENT HYDE. WE RESCUED YOU FROM THE RIP.
OH! WELL THEN, THANK YOU!

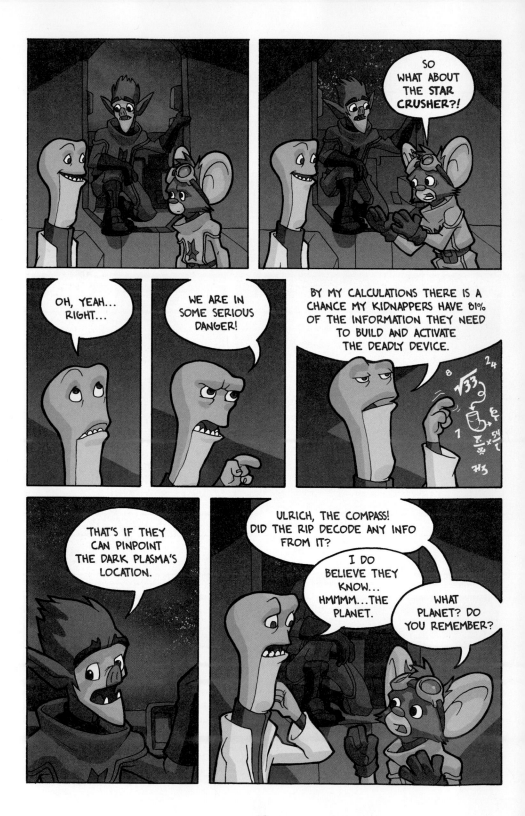

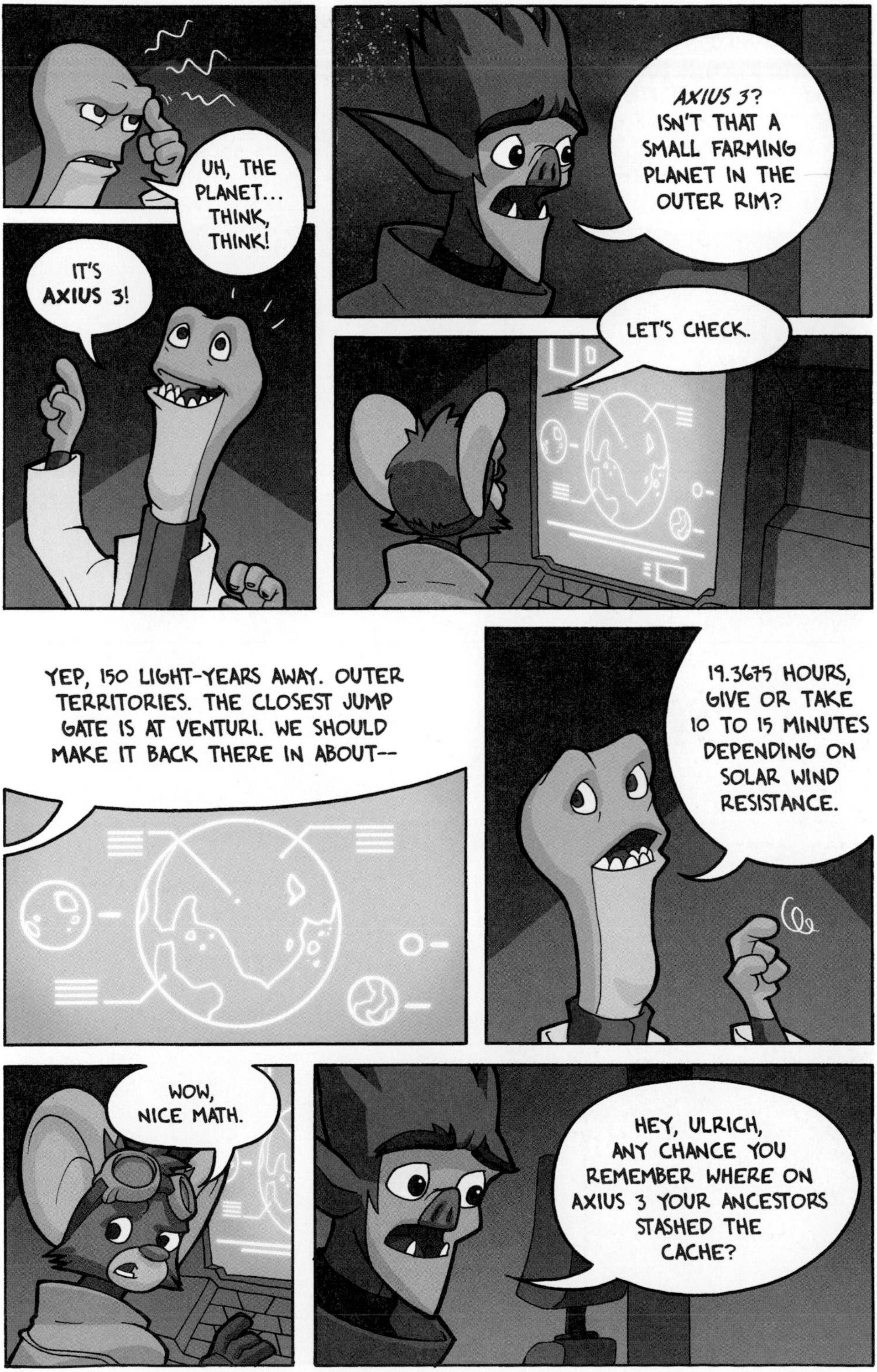
UH, THE PLANET... THINK, THINK!
AXIUS 3? ISN'T THAT A SMALL FARMING PLANET IN THE OUTER RIM?
IT'S AXIUS 3!
LET'S CHECK.
YEP, 150 LIGHT-YEARS AWAY. OUTER TERRITORIES. THE CLOSEST JUMP GATE IS AT VENTURI. WE SHOULD MAKE IT BACK THERE IN ABOUT--
19.3675 HOURS, GIVE OR TAKE 10 TO 15 MINUTES DEPENDING ON SOLAR WIND RESISTANCE.
WOW, NICE MATH.
HEY, ULRICH, ANY CHANCE YOU REMEMBER WHERE ON AXIUS 3 YOUR ANCESTORS STASHED THE CACHE?

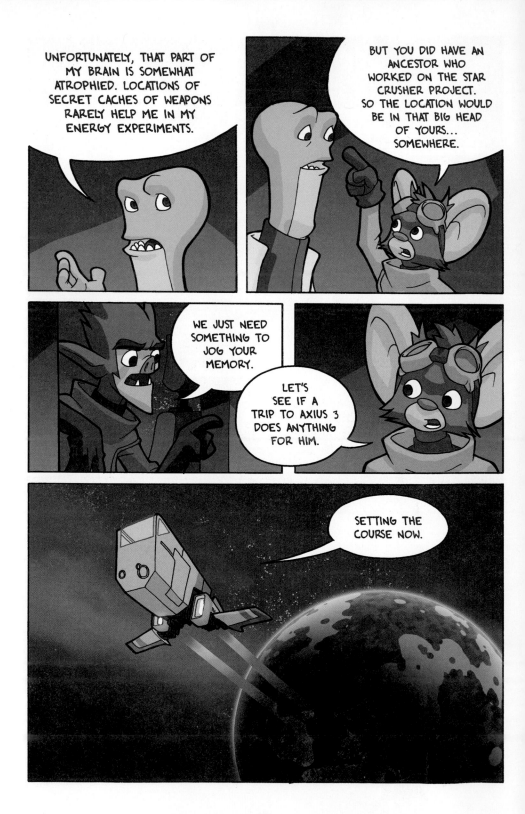

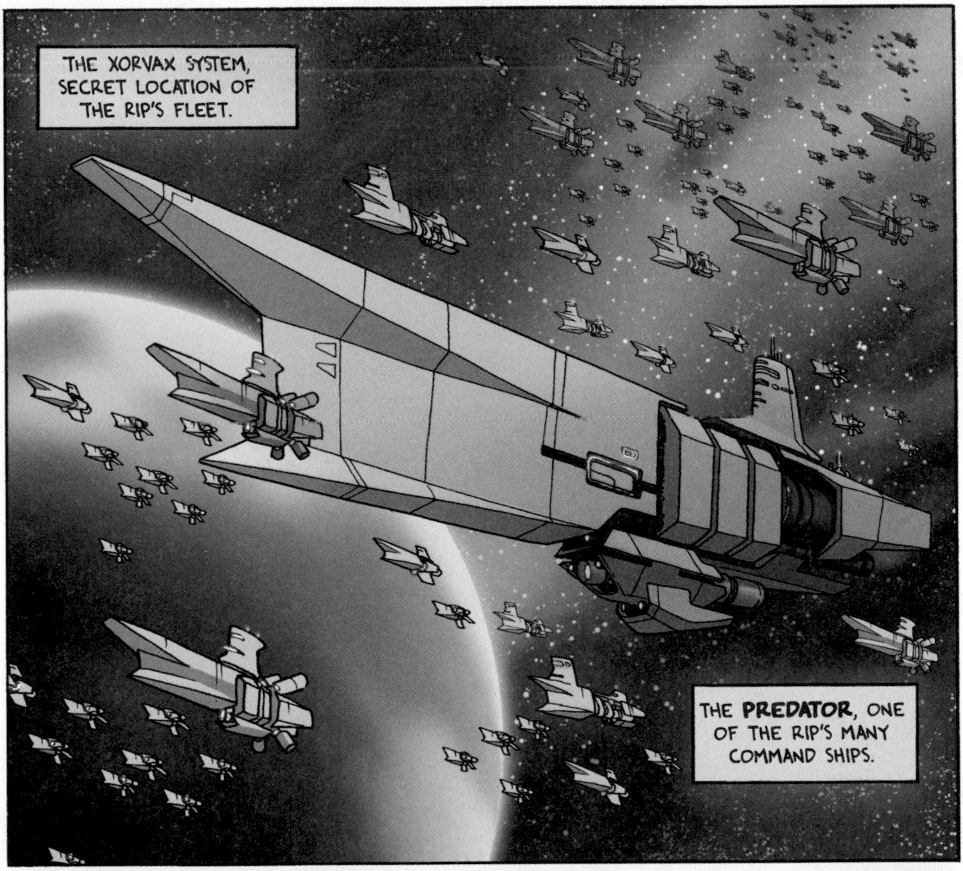
THE XORVAX SYSTEM, SECRET LOCATION OF THE RIP'S FLEET.
THE **PREDATOR**, ONE OF THE RIP'S MANY COMMAND SHIPS.

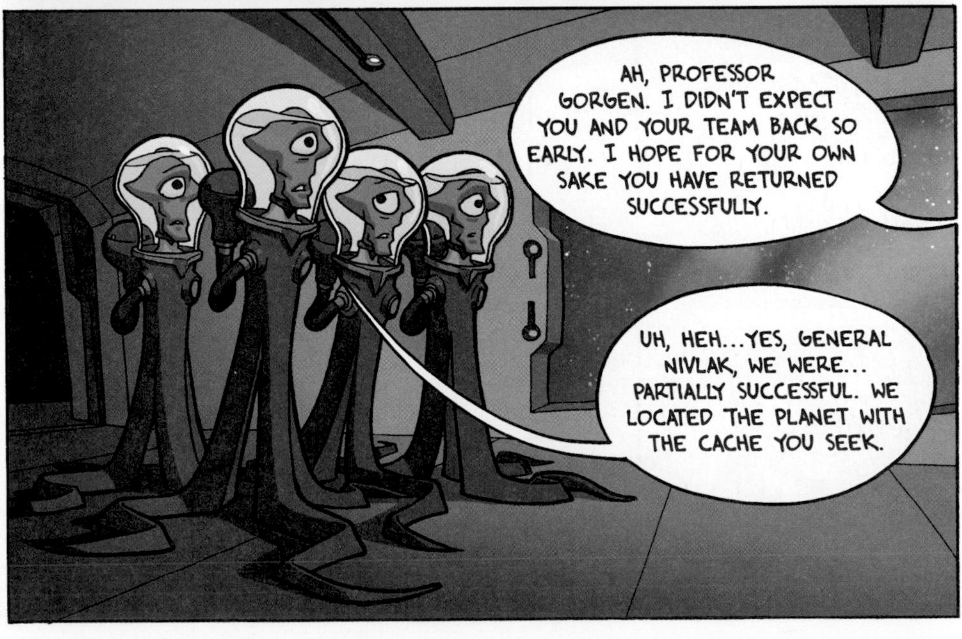
AH, PROFESSOR GORGEN. I DIDN'T EXPECT YOU AND YOUR TEAM BACK SO EARLY. I HOPE FOR YOUR OWN SAKE YOU HAVE RETURNED SUCCESSFULLY.
UH, HEH...YES, GENERAL NIVLAK, WE WERE... PARTIALLY SUCCESSFUL. WE LOCATED THE PLANET WITH THE CACHE YOU SEEK.

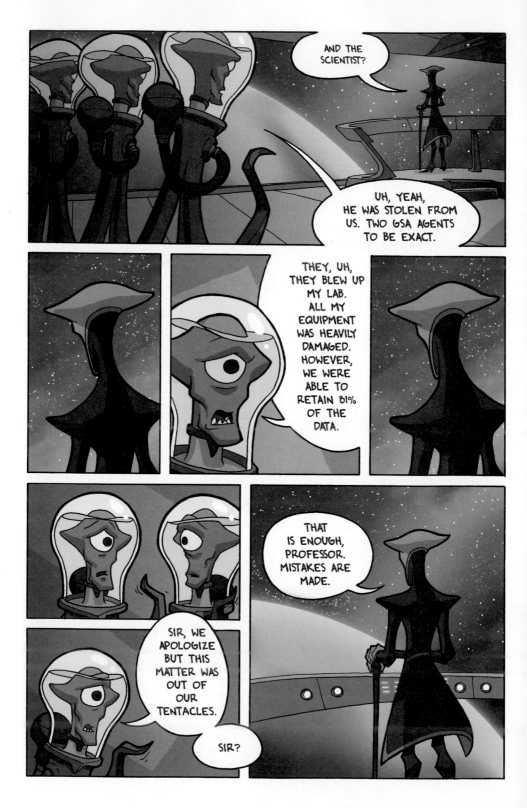

60

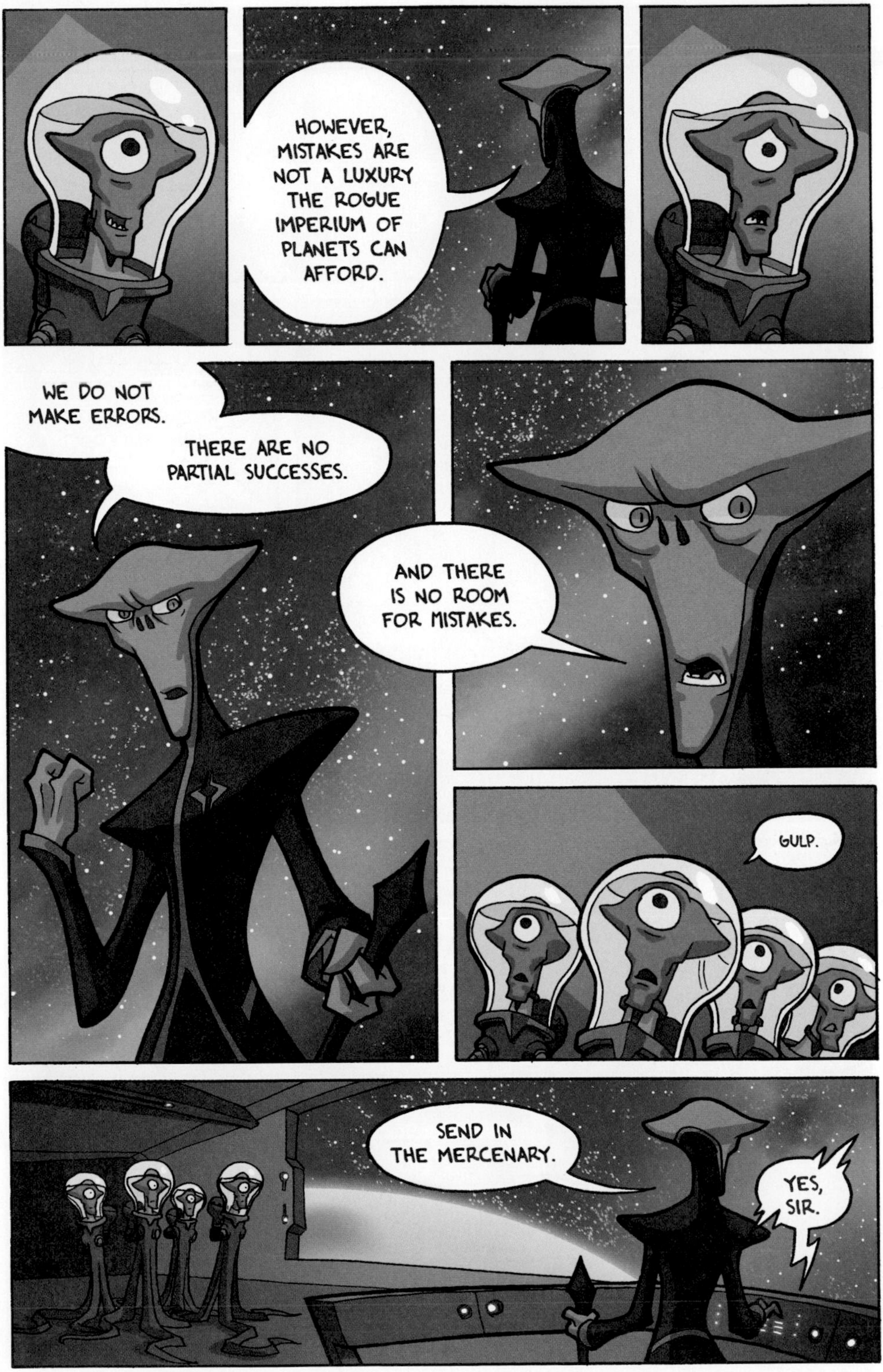
HOWEVER, MISTAKES ARE NOT A LUXURY THE ROGUE IMPERIUM OF PLANETS CAN AFFORD.
WE DO NOT MAKE ERRORS.
THERE ARE NO PARTIAL SUCCESSES.
AND THERE IS NO ROOM FOR MISTAKES.
GULP.
SEND IN THE MERCENARY.
YES, SIR.

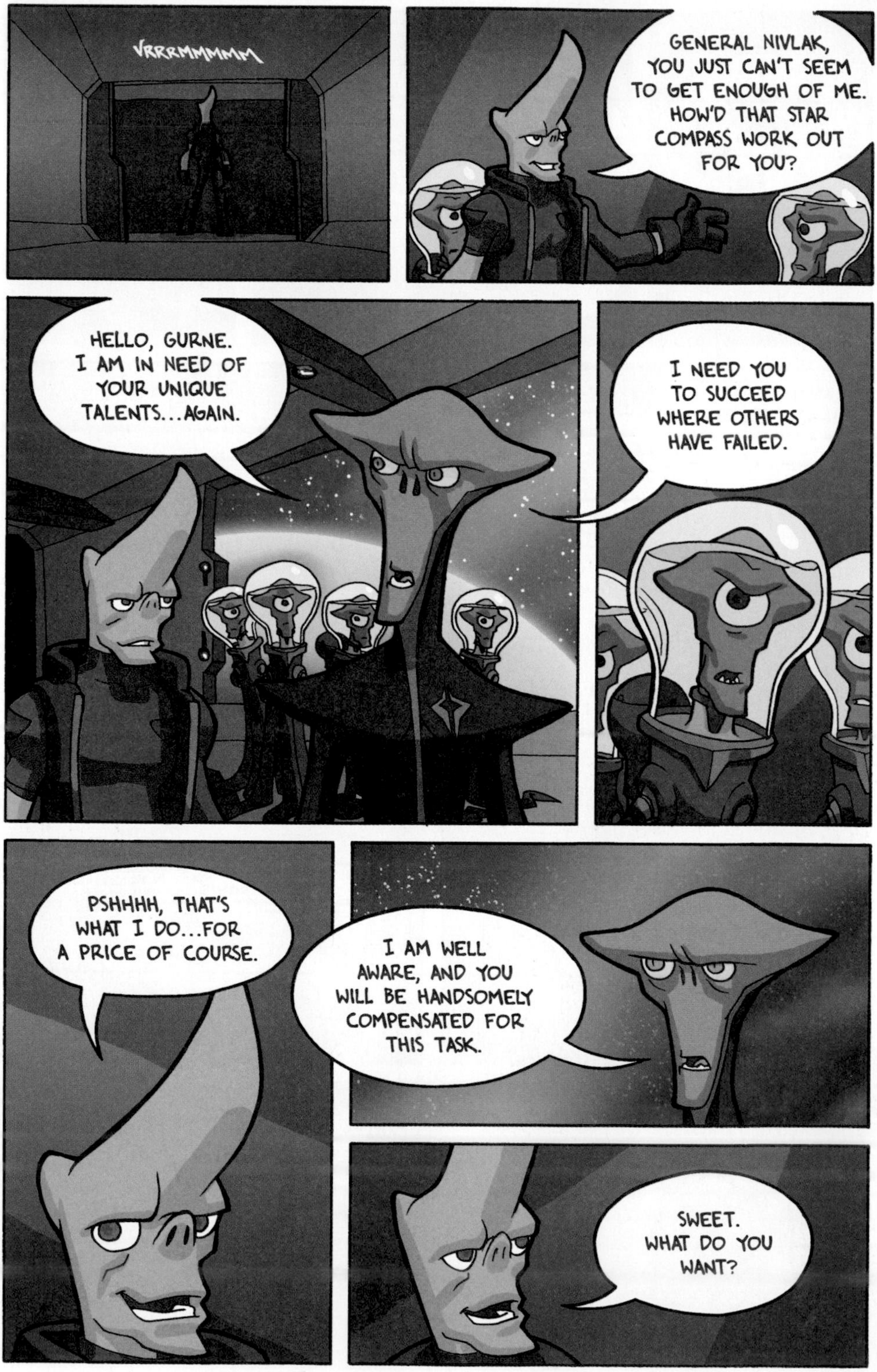
VRRRMMMMMM
GENERAL NIVLAK, YOU JUST CAN'T SEEM TO GET ENOUGH OF ME. HOW'D THAT STAR COMPASS WORK OUT FOR YOU?
HELLO, GURNE. I AM IN NEED OF YOUR UNIQUE TALENTS...AGAIN.
I NEED YOU TO SUCCEED WHERE OTHERS HAVE FAILED.
PSHHHH, THAT'S WHAT I DO...FOR A PRICE OF COURSE.
I AM WELL AWARE, AND YOU WILL BE HANDSOMELY COMPENSATED FOR THIS TASK.
SWEET. WHAT DO YOU WANT?

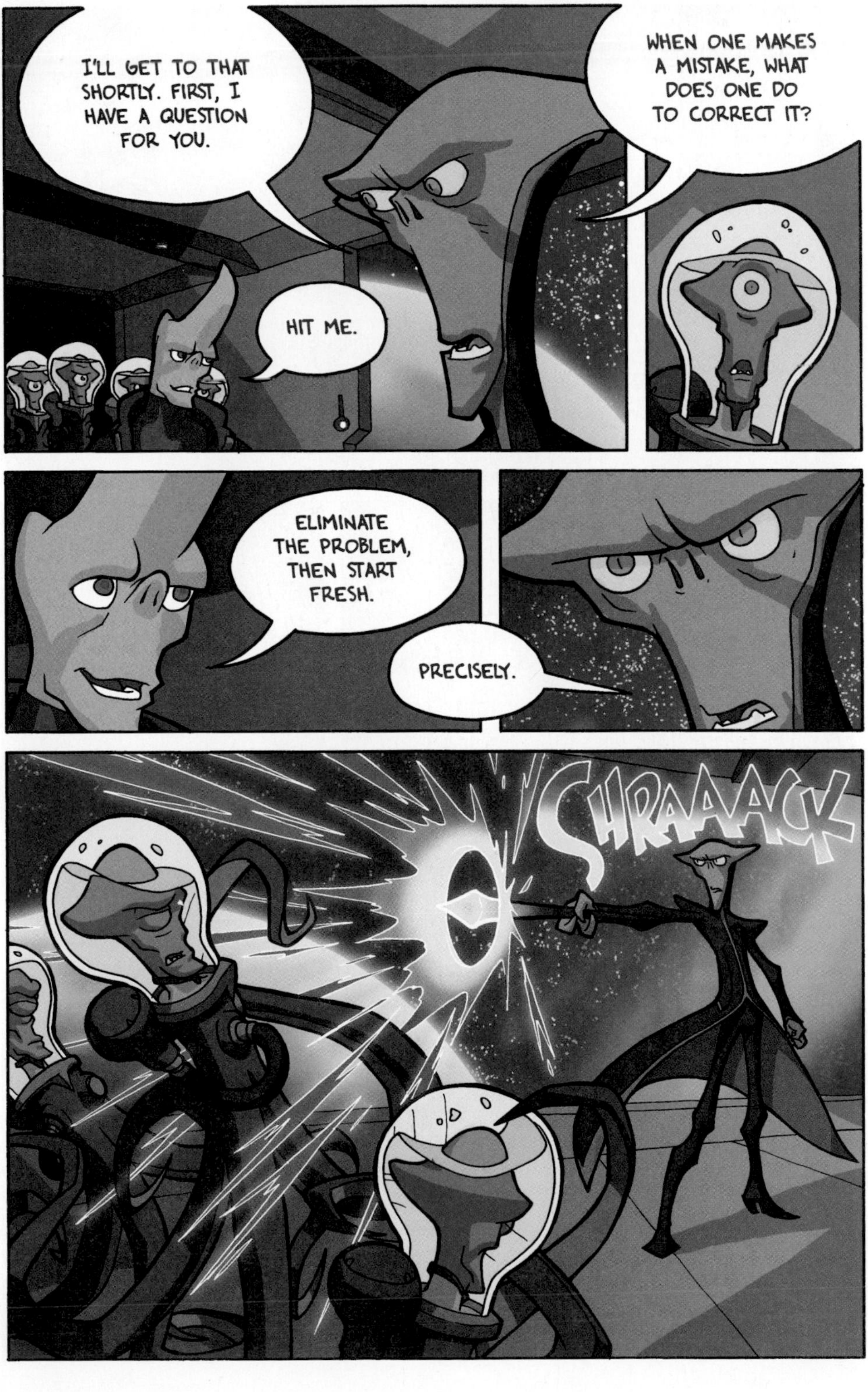
I'LL GET TO THAT SHORTLY. FIRST, I HAVE A QUESTION FOR YOU.
HIT ME.
WHEN ONE MAKES A MISTAKE, WHAT DOES ONE DO TO CORRECT IT?
ELIMINATE THE PROBLEM, THEN START FRESH.
PRECISELY.
SHRAAACK

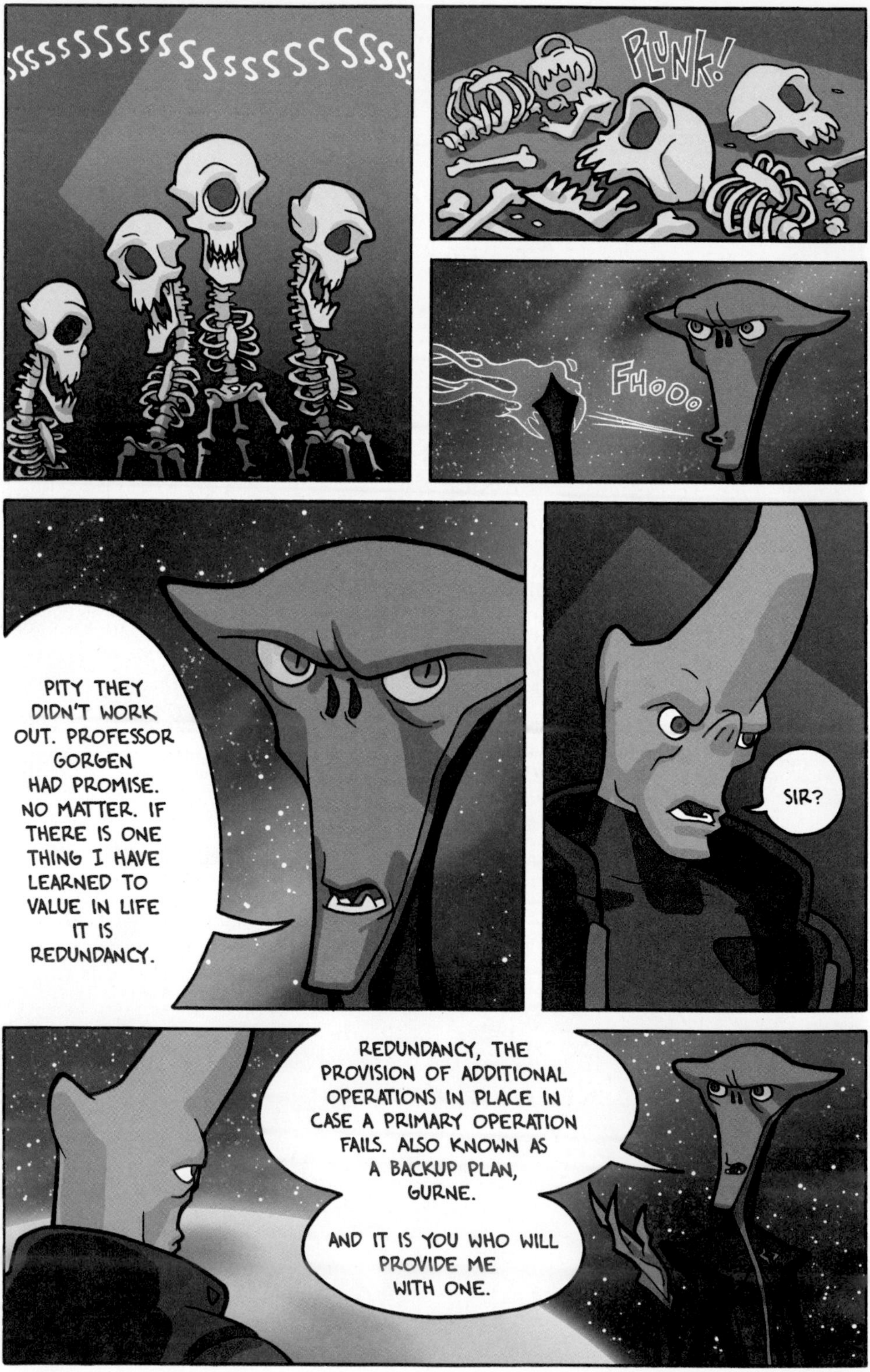
SSSSSSSSSSSSSSSSSSSSSS
PLUNK!
FHOOO
PITY THEY DIDN'T WORK OUT. PROFESSOR GORGEN HAD PROMISE. NO MATTER. IF THERE IS ONE THING I HAVE LEARNED TO VALUE IN LIFE IT IS REDUNDANCY.
SIR?
REDUNDANCY, THE PROVISION OF ADDITIONAL OPERATIONS IN PLACE IN CASE A PRIMARY OPERATION FAILS. ALSO KNOWN AS A BACKUP PLAN, GURNE.
AND IT IS YOU WHO WILL PROVIDE ME WITH ONE.

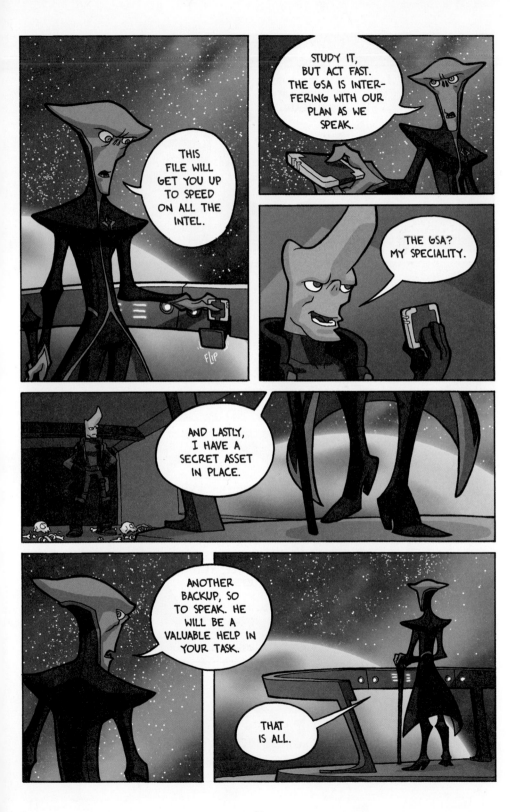

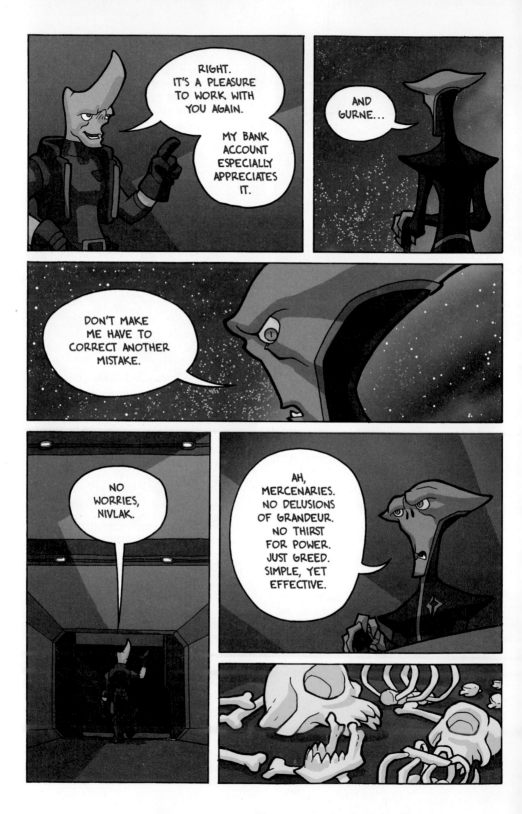

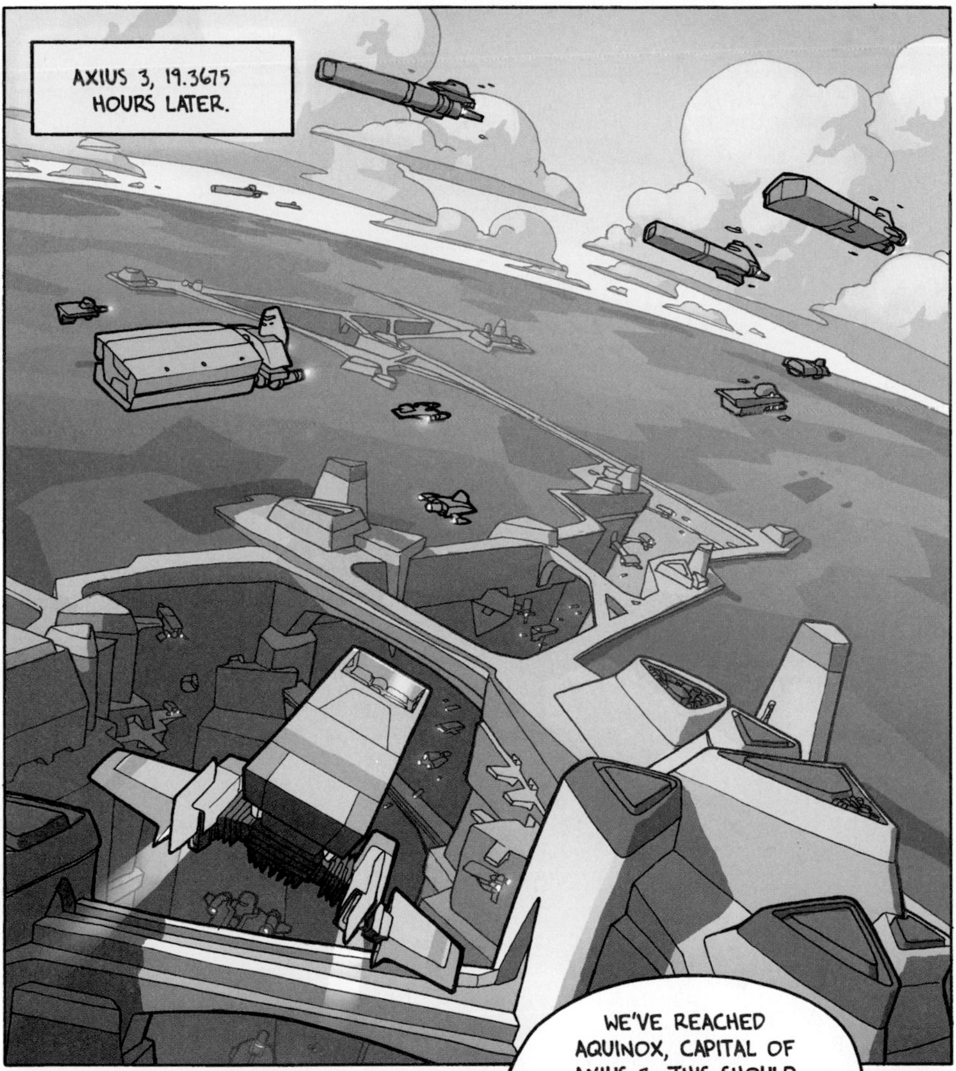
AXIUS 3, 19.3675 HOURS LATER.

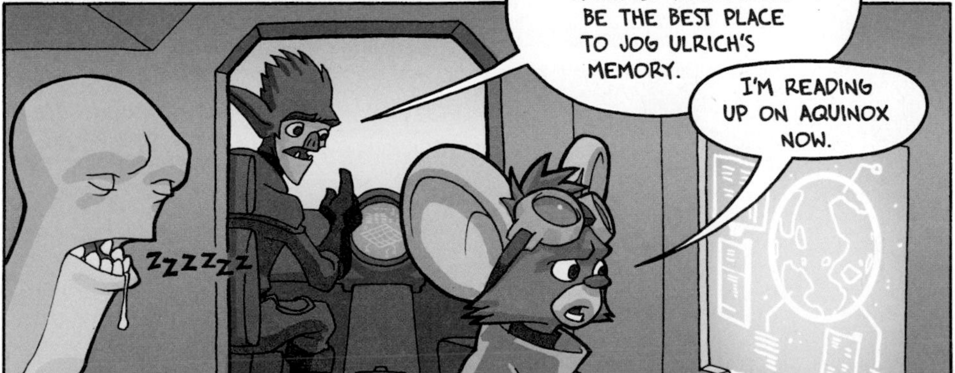
WE'VE REACHED AQUINOX, CAPITAL OF AXIUS 3. THIS SHOULD BE THE BEST PLACE TO JOG ULRICH'S MEMORY.
I'M READING UP ON AQUINOX NOW.
ZZZZZZ

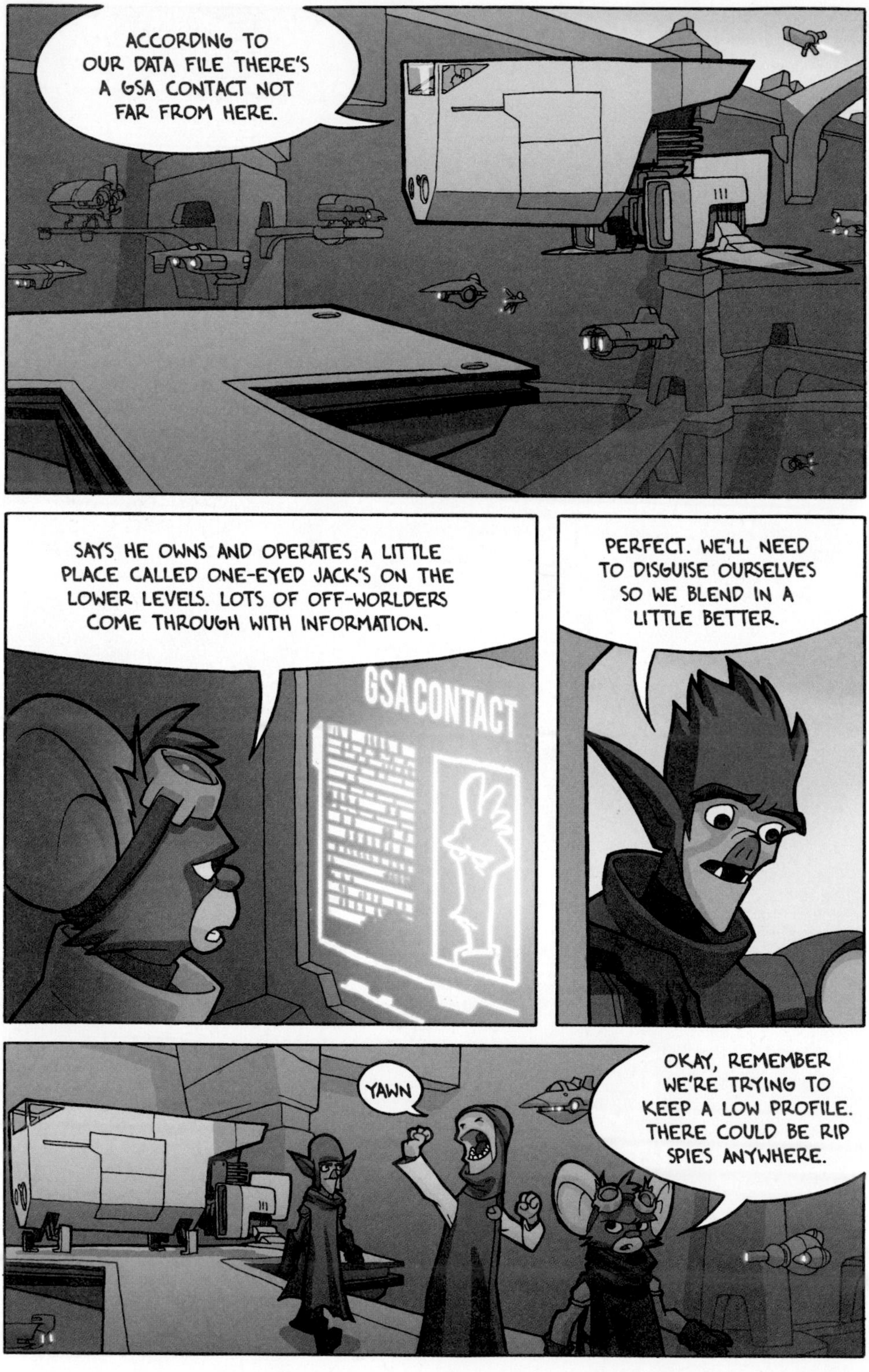
ACCORDING TO OUR DATA FILE THERE'S A GSA CONTACT NOT FAR FROM HERE.
SAYS HE OWNS AND OPERATES A LITTLE PLACE CALLED ONE-EYED JACK'S ON THE LOWER LEVELS. LOTS OF OFF-WORLDERS COME THROUGH WITH INFORMATION.
GSA CONTACT
PERFECT. WE'LL NEED TO DISGUISE OURSELVES SO WE BLEND IN A LITTLE BETTER.
YAWN
OKAY, REMEMBER WE'RE TRYING TO KEEP A LOW PROFILE. THERE COULD BE RIP SPIES ANYWHERE.

71

74

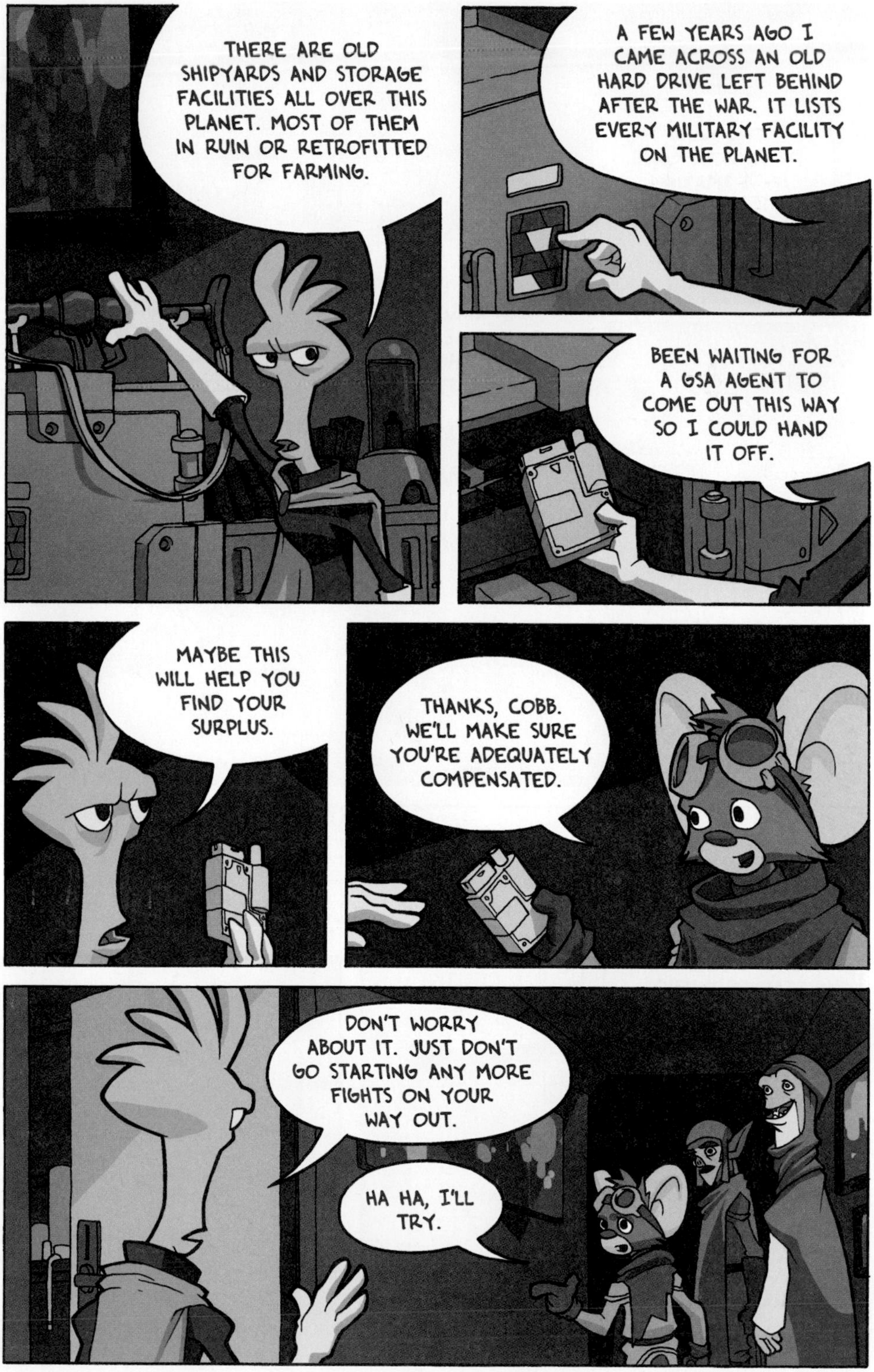
THERE ARE OLD SHIPYARDS AND STORAGE FACILITIES ALL OVER THIS PLANET. MOST OF THEM IN RUIN OR RETROFITTED FOR FARMING.
A FEW YEARS AGO I CAME ACROSS AN OLD HARD DRIVE LEFT BEHIND AFTER THE WAR. IT LISTS EVERY MILITARY FACILITY ON THE PLANET.
BEEN WAITING FOR A GSA AGENT TO COME OUT THIS WAY SO I COULD HAND IT OFF.
MAYBE THIS WILL HELP YOU FIND YOUR SURPLUS.
THANKS, COBB. WE'LL MAKE SURE YOU'RE ADEQUATELY COMPENSATED.
DON'T WORRY ABOUT IT. JUST DON'T GO STARTING ANY MORE FIGHTS ON YOUR WAY OUT.
HA HA, I'LL TRY.

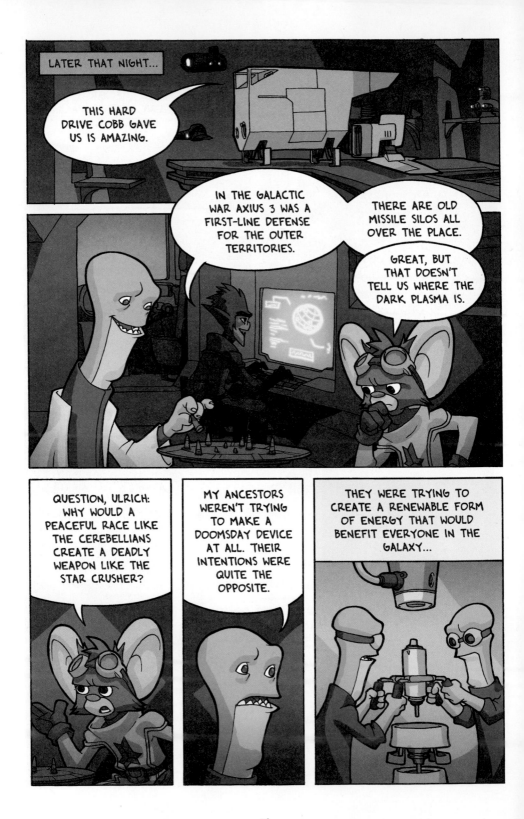

LATER THAT NIGHT...

THIS HARD DRIVE COBB GAVE US IS AMAZING.

IN THE GALACTIC WAR AXIUS 3 WAS A FIRST-LINE DEFENSE FOR THE OUTER TERRITORIES.

THERE ARE OLD MISSILE SILOS ALL OVER THE PLACE.

GREAT, BUT THAT DOESN'T TELL US WHERE THE DARK PLASMA IS.

QUESTION, ULRICH: WHY WOULD A PEACEFUL RACE LIKE THE CEREBELLIANS CREATE A DEADLY WEAPON LIKE THE STAR CRUSHER?

MY ANCESTORS WEREN'T TRYING TO MAKE A DOOMSDAY DEVICE AT ALL. THEIR INTENTIONS WERE QUITE THE OPPOSITE.

THEY WERE TRYING TO CREATE A RENEWABLE FORM OF ENERGY THAT WOULD BENEFIT EVERYONE IN THE GALAXY...

THEIR GOAL WAS TO TAKE THE FINITE BUT POWERFUL SUPPLY OF DARK PLASMA AND TURN IT INTO AN INFINITE SUPPLY OF ENERGY.

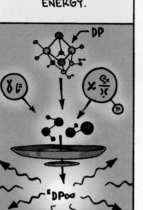

IMAGINE A DARK PLASMA-INFUSED TREE THAT GREW HIGHLY ENERGIZED FRUIT POWERFUL ENOUGH TO FUEL A FLEET OF SPACE CRUISERS.

IN THEIR EXPERIMENTS THEY DISCOVERED THAT ORGANIC MATTER, WHEN FUSED WITH DARK PLASMA, TURNED ITSELF INTO PURE ENERGY.

BUT EVERY EXPERIMENT ENDED IN FAILURE. THE PLASMA-CHARGED MATTER COULDN'T HANDLE THE PURE ENERGY. IT COLLAPSED ON ITSELF, CREATING A BLACK HOLE EVERY TIME.

THE MILITARY HEARD OF THE CEREBELLIAN EXPERIMENTS AND DEMANDED THE TECHNOLOGY BE TURNED INTO A WEAPON, THE STAR CRUSHER.

SPIES THEN TOOK THE TECH TO THE OTHER SIDE AND **BOOM**...

HALF THE GALAXY DESTROYED.

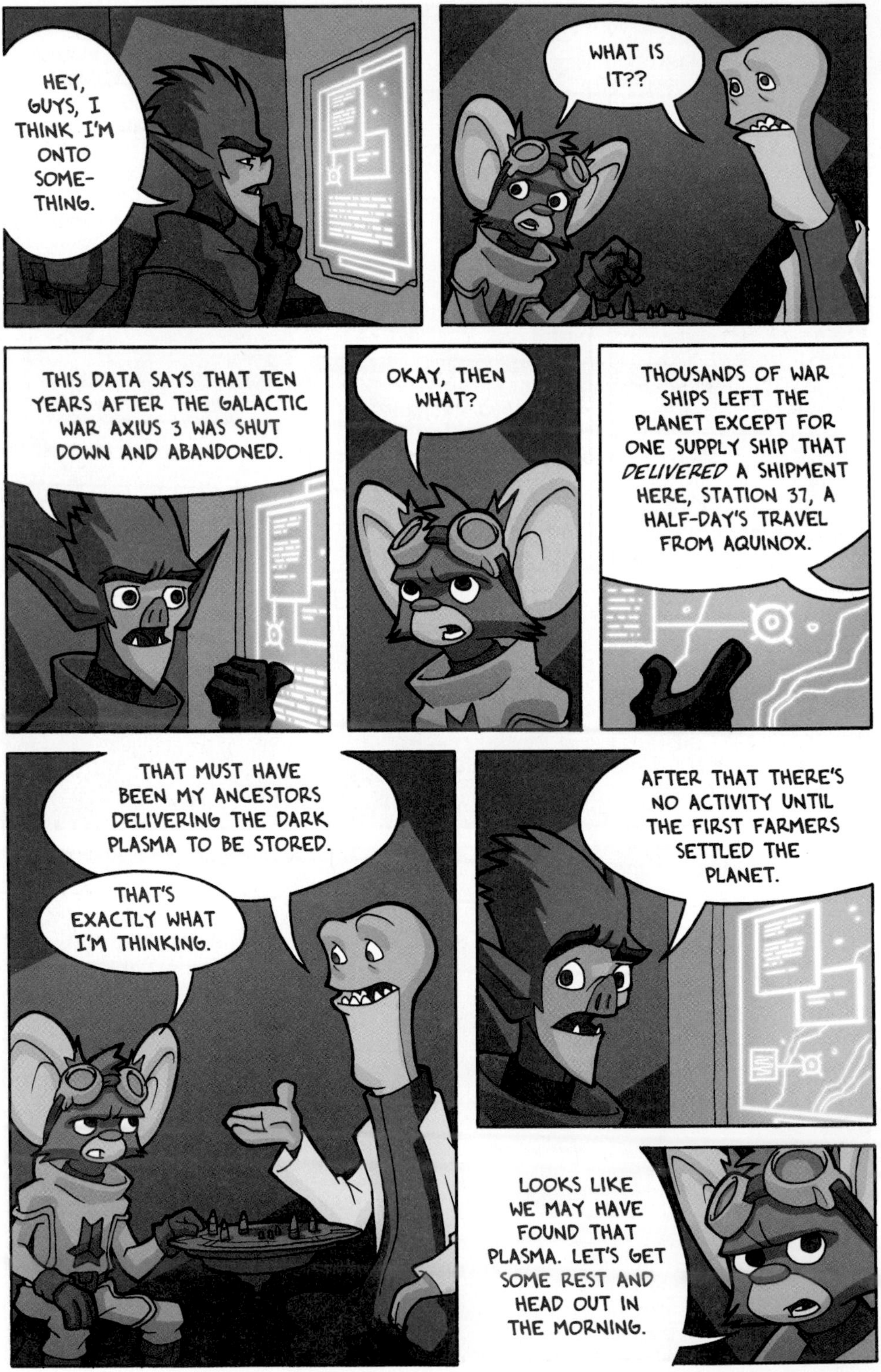
HEY, GUYS, I THINK I'M ONTO SOME-THING.
WHAT IS IT??
THIS DATA SAYS THAT TEN YEARS AFTER THE GALACTIC WAR AXIUS 3 WAS SHUT DOWN AND ABANDONED.
OKAY, THEN WHAT?
THOUSANDS OF WAR SHIPS LEFT THE PLANET EXCEPT FOR ONE SUPPLY SHIP THAT *DELIVERED* A SHIPMENT HERE, STATION 37, A HALF-DAY'S TRAVEL FROM AQUINOX.
THAT MUST HAVE BEEN MY ANCESTORS DELIVERING THE DARK PLASMA TO BE STORED.
THAT'S EXACTLY WHAT I'M THINKING.
AFTER THAT THERE'S NO ACTIVITY UNTIL THE FIRST FARMERS SETTLED THE PLANET.
LOOKS LIKE WE MAY HAVE FOUND THAT PLASMA. LET'S GET SOME REST AND HEAD OUT IN THE MORNING.

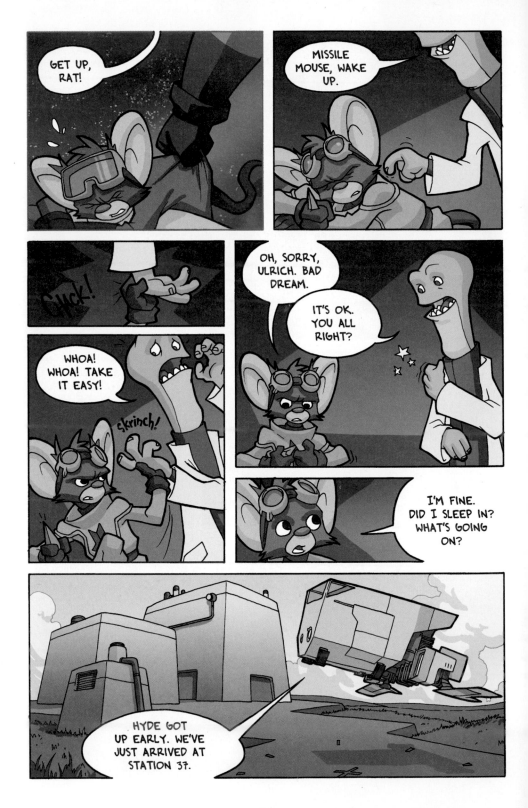

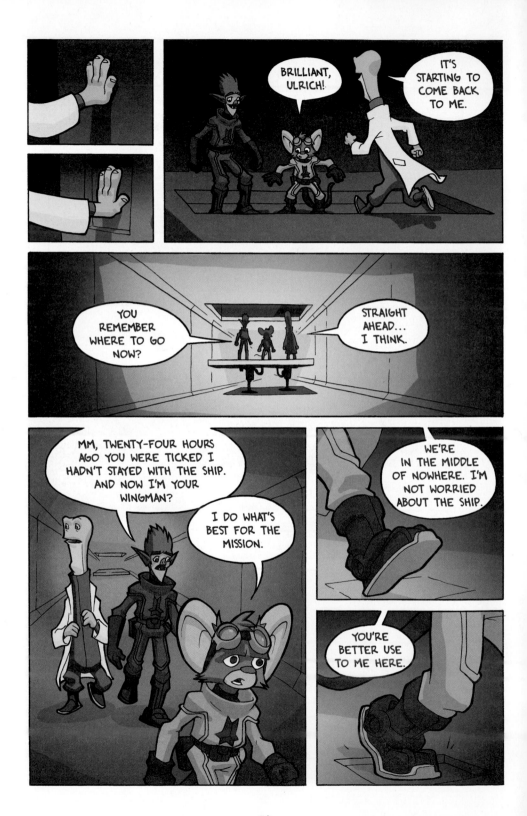

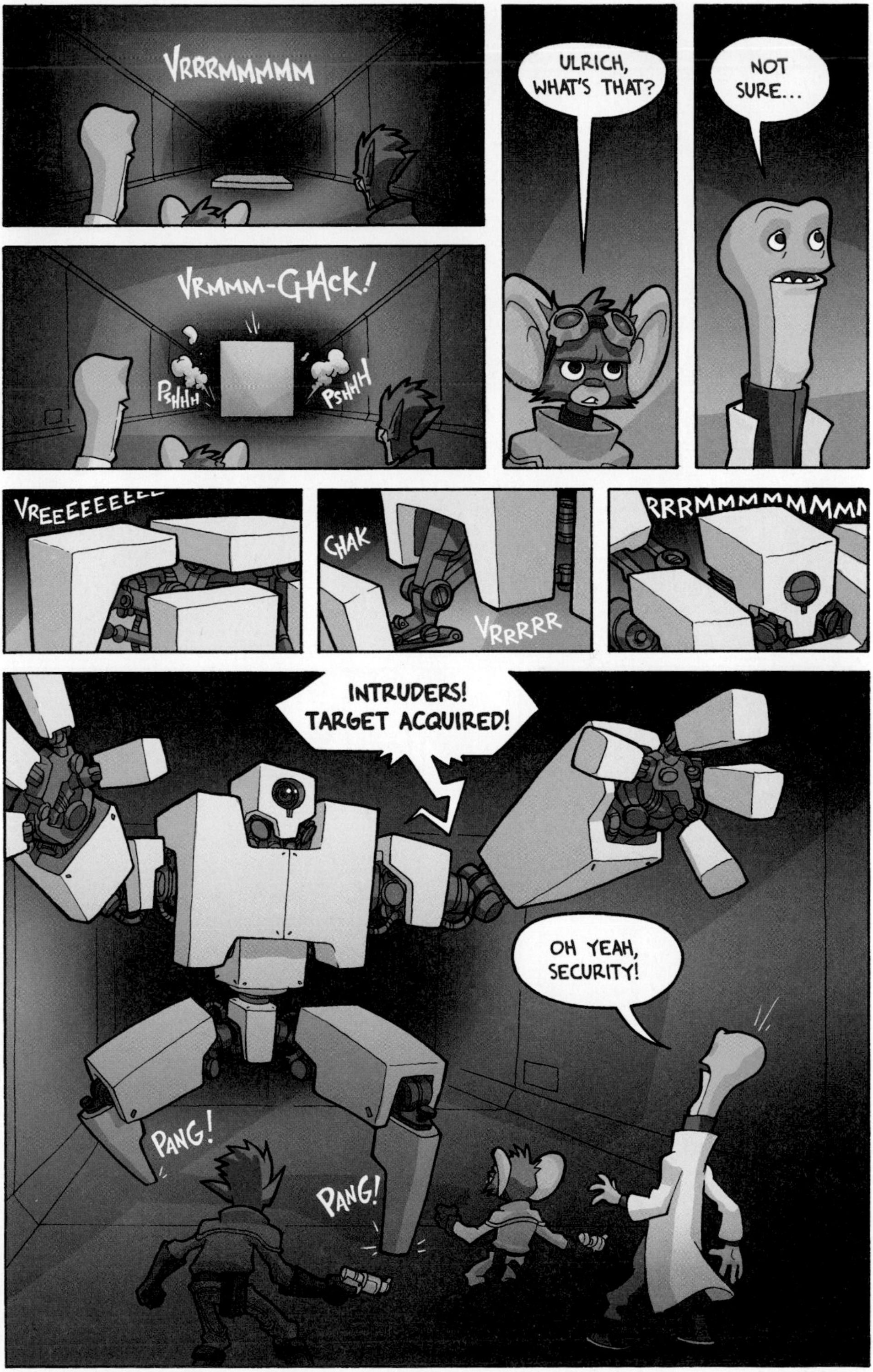
VRRRMMMMM
ULRICH, WHAT'S THAT?
NOT SURE...
VRMMM-CHACK!
PSHHH
PSHHH
VREEEEEEEEE
CHAK
VRRRRR
RRRMMMMMMMM
INTRUDERS! TARGET ACQUIRED!
OH YEAH, SECURITY!
PANG!
PANG!

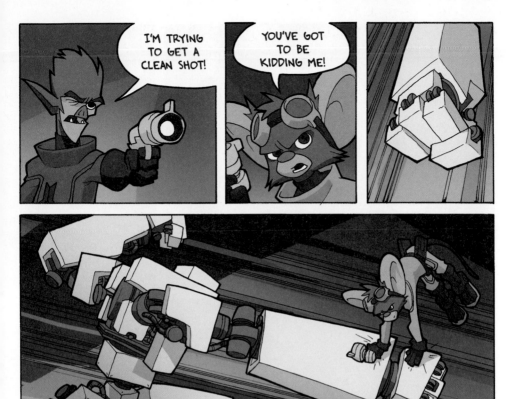

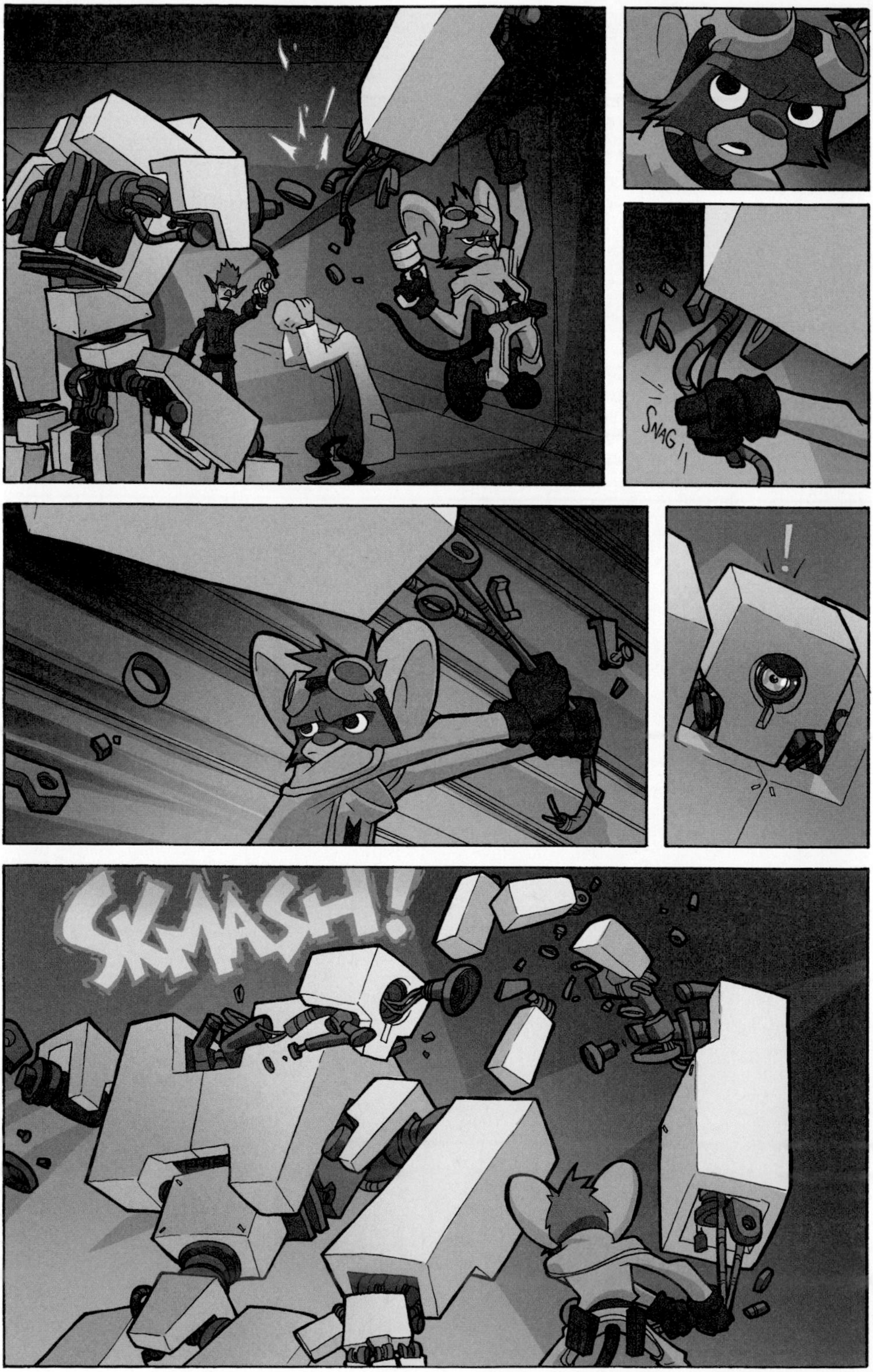
SNAG
!
SKMASH!

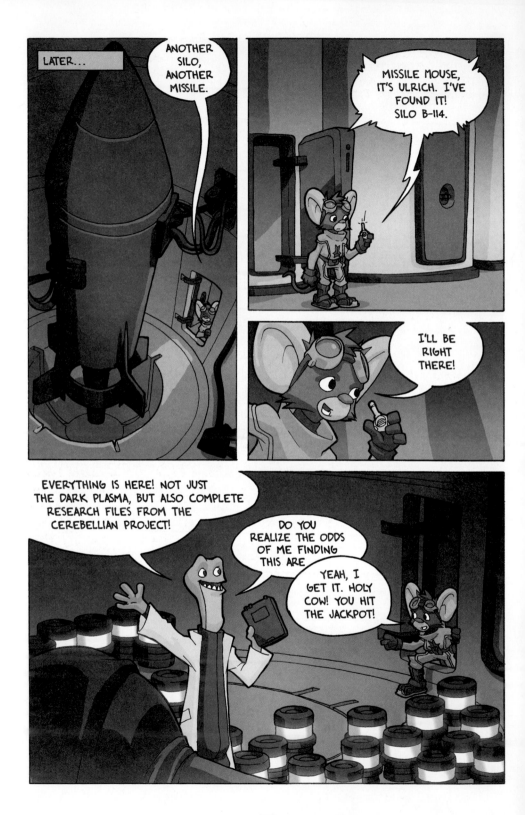

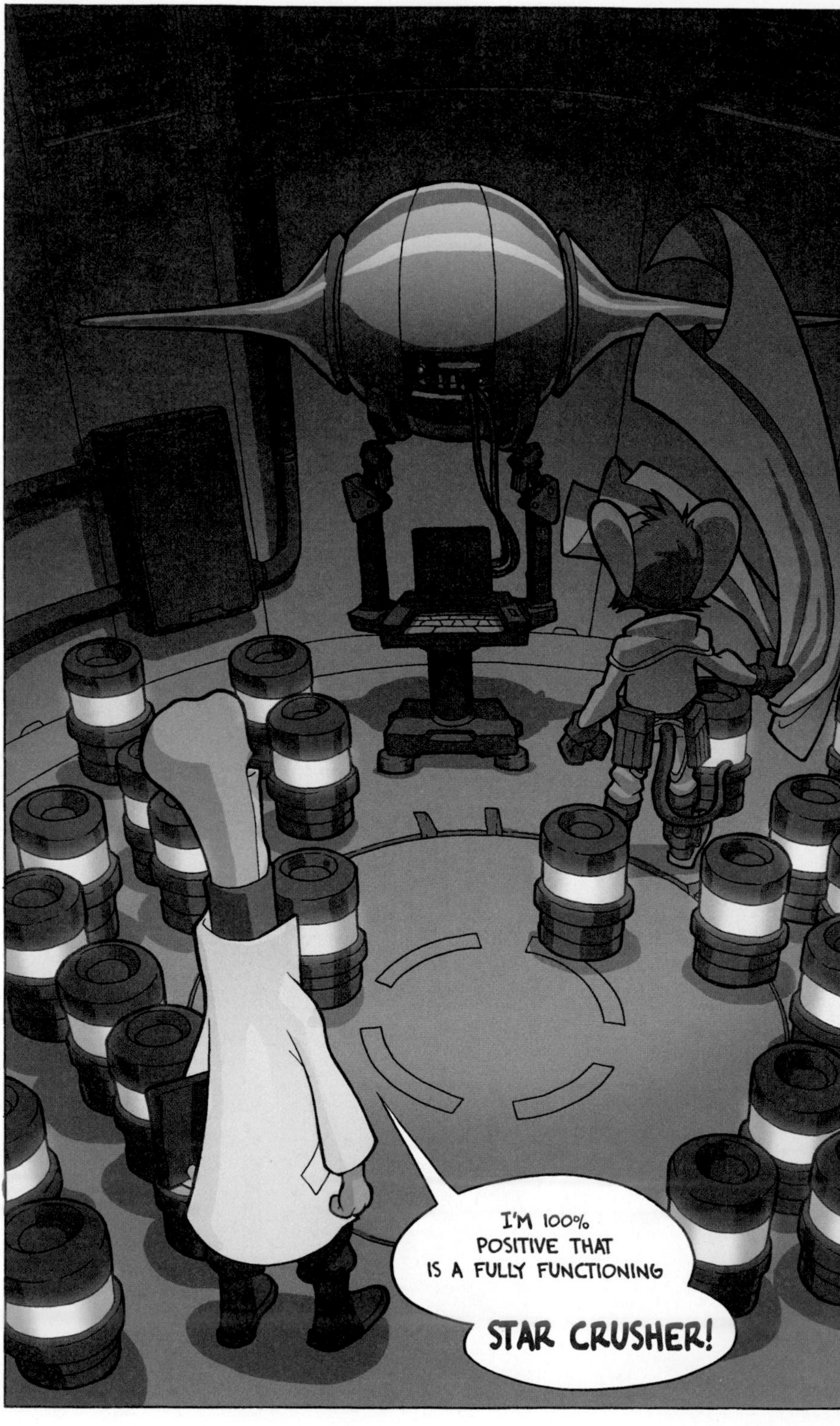
I'M 100% POSITIVE THAT IS A FULLY FUNCTIONING
STAR CRUSHER!

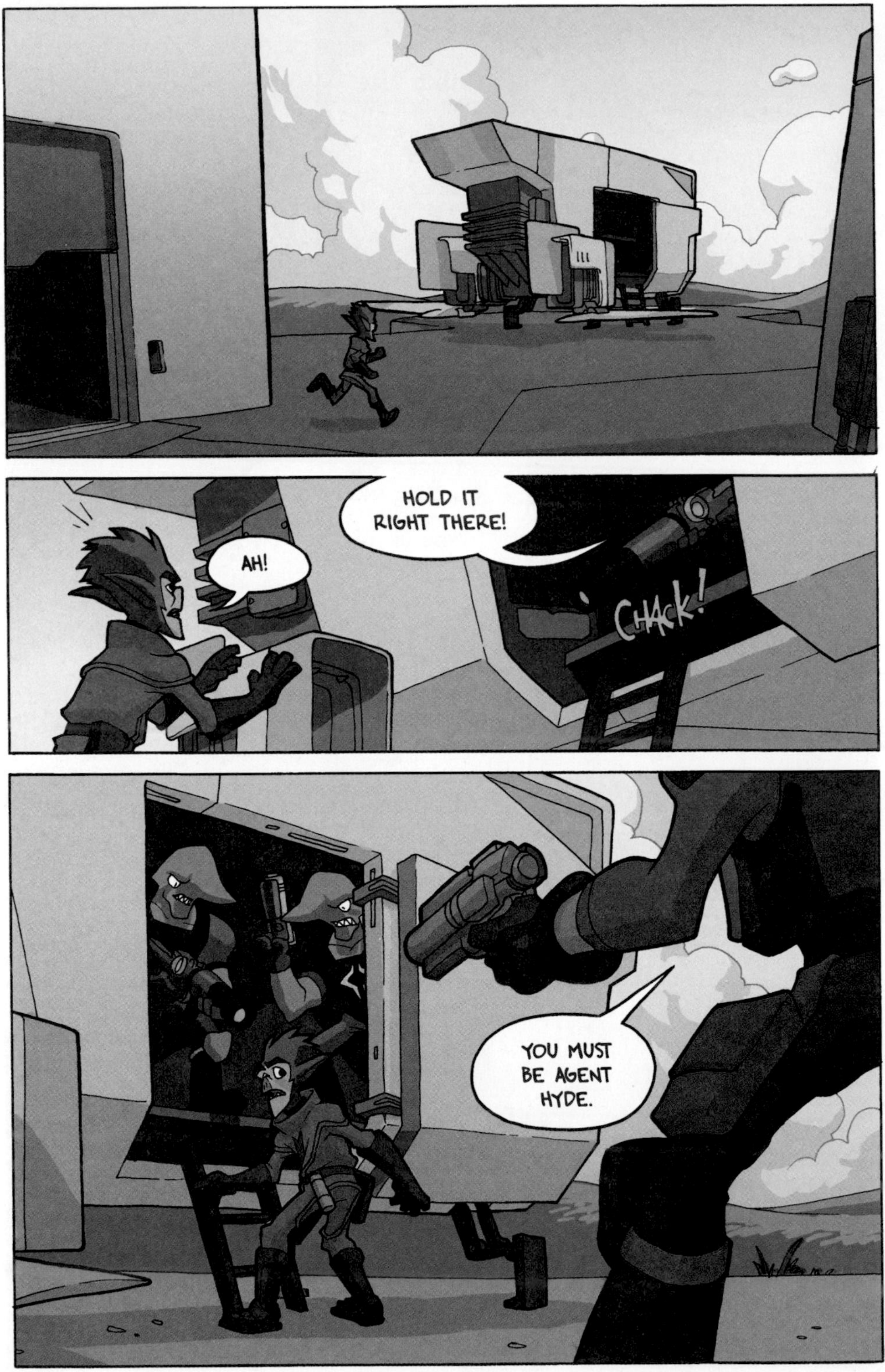
HOLD IT RIGHT THERE!
AH!
CHACK!
YOU MUST BE AGENT HYDE.

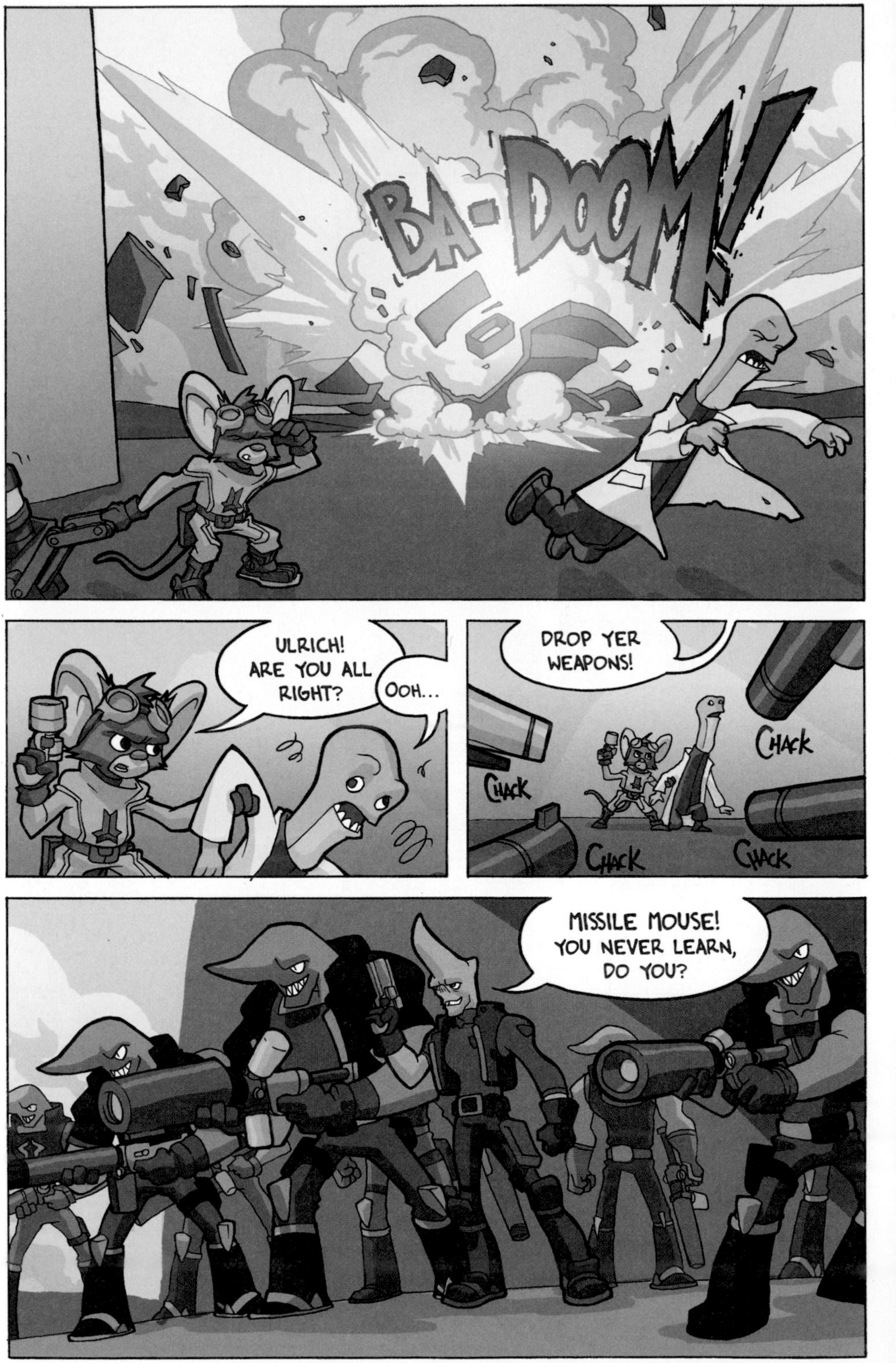
BA-DOOM!
ULRICH! ARE YOU ALL RIGHT?
OOH...
DROP YER WEAPONS!
CHACK
CHACK
CHACK
CHACK
MISSILE MOUSE! YOU NEVER LEARN, DO YOU?

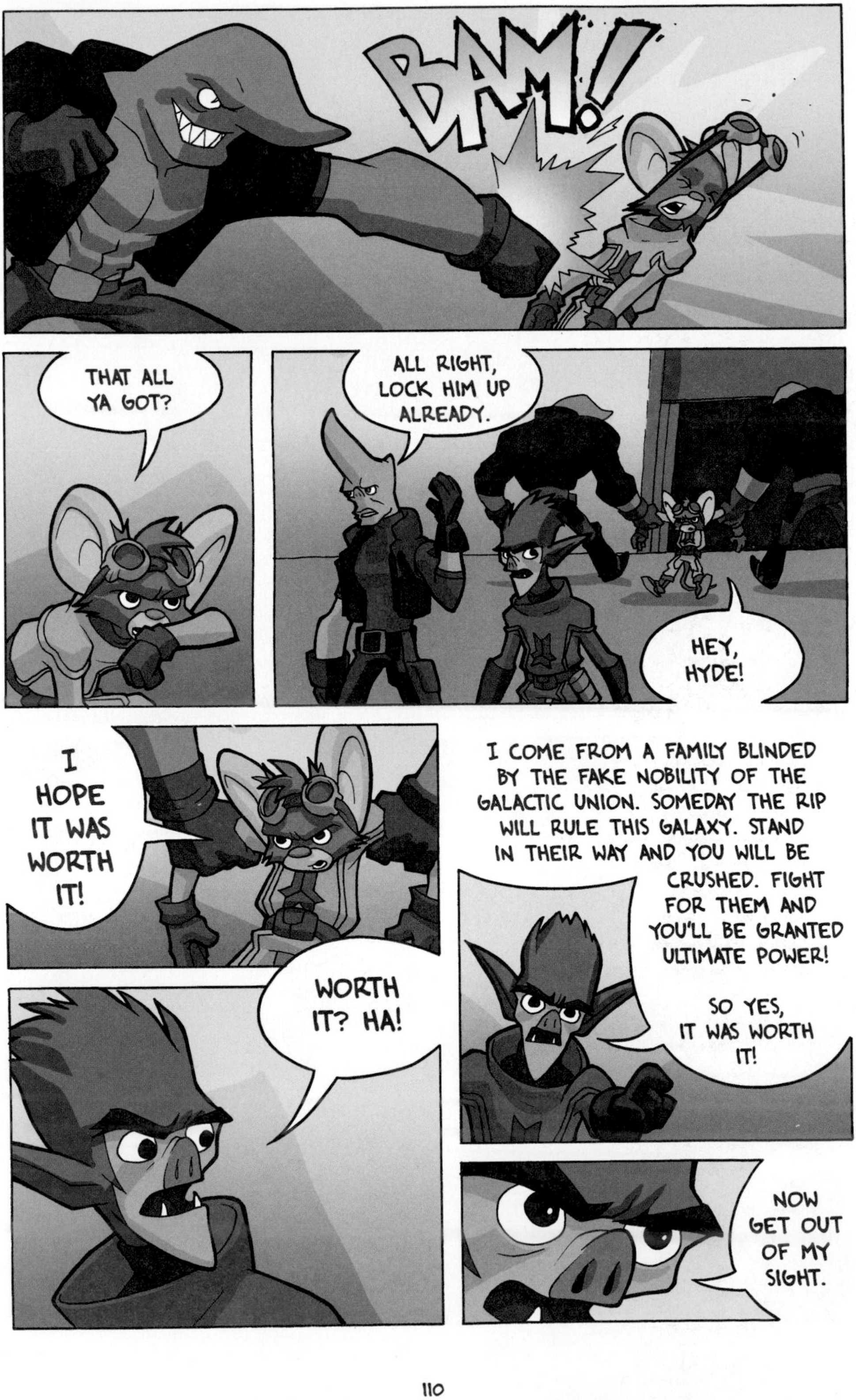
BAM!
THAT ALL YA GOT?
ALL RIGHT, LOCK HIM UP ALREADY.
HEY, HYDE!
I HOPE IT WAS WORTH IT!
WORTH IT? HA!
I COME FROM A FAMILY BLINDED BY THE FAKE NOBILITY OF THE GALACTIC UNION. SOMEDAY THE RIP WILL RULE THIS GALAXY. STAND IN THEIR WAY AND YOU WILL BE CRUSHED. FIGHT FOR THEM AND YOU'LL BE GRANTED ULTIMATE POWER!
SO YES, IT WAS WORTH IT!
NOW GET OUT OF MY SIGHT.

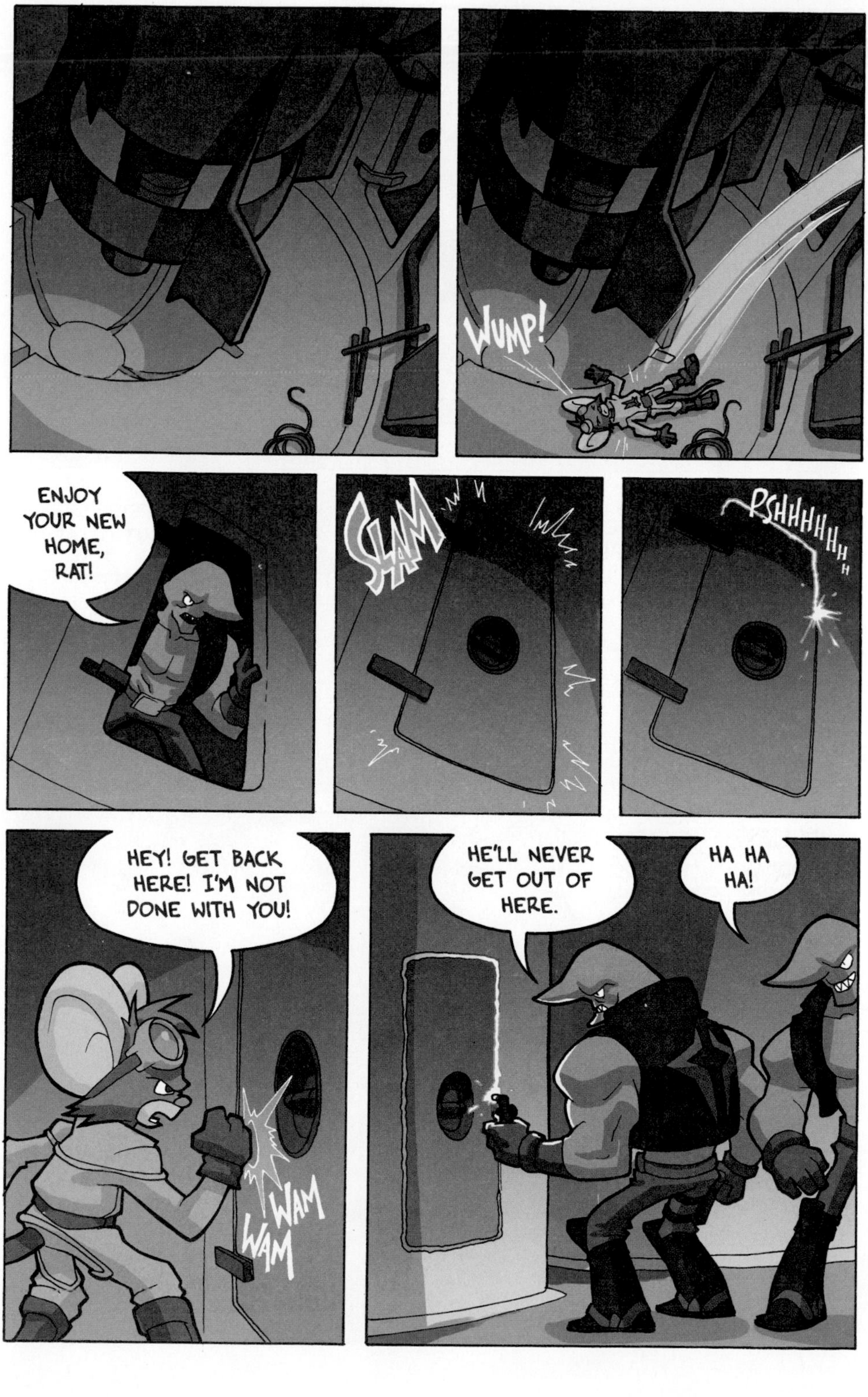
WUMP!
ENJOY YOUR NEW HOME, RAT!
SLAM
PSHHHHHHH
HEY! GET BACK HERE! I'M NOT DONE WITH YOU!
WAM WAM
HE'LL NEVER GET OUT OF HERE.
HA HA HA!

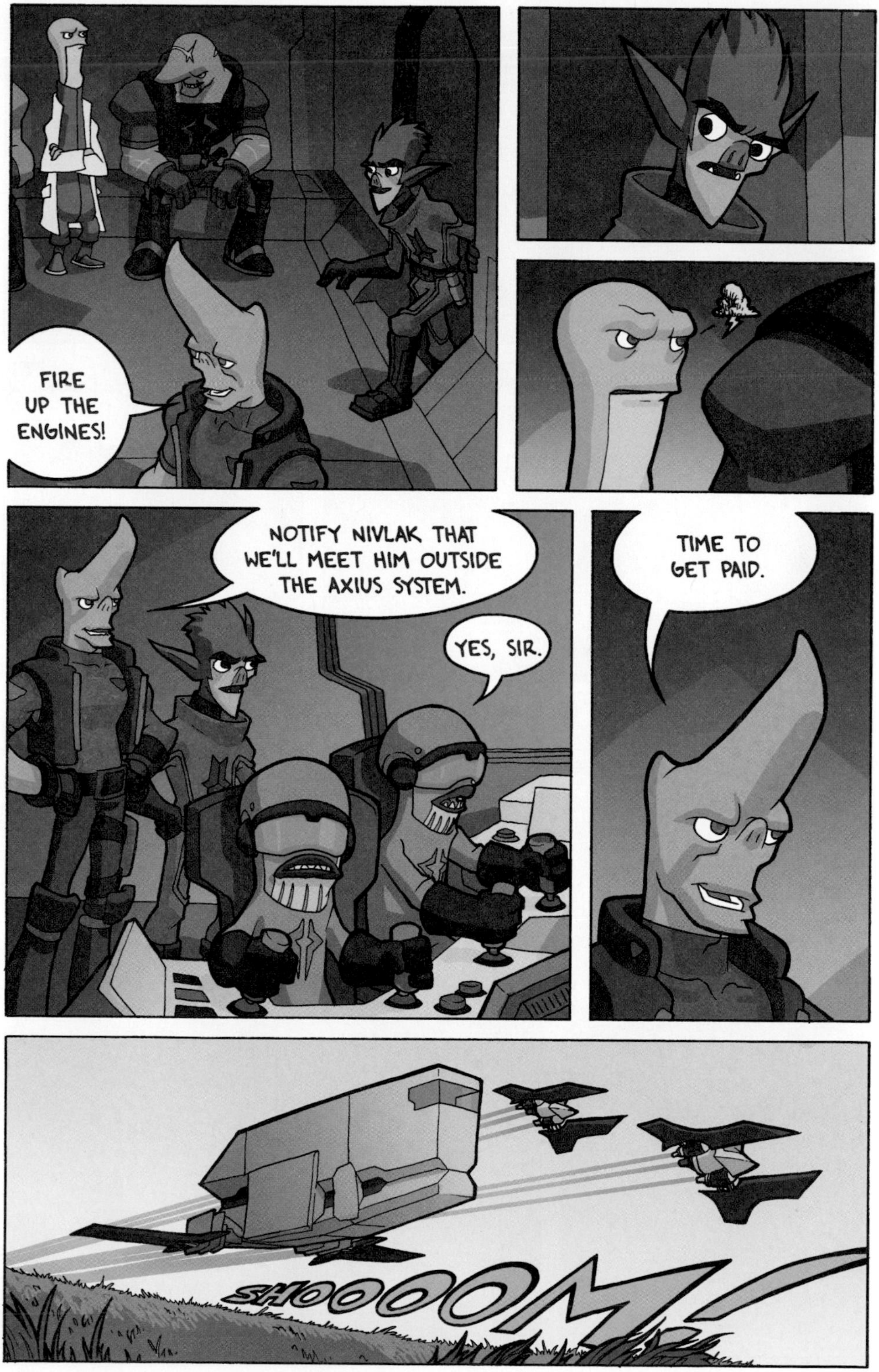
FIRE UP THE ENGINES!
NOTIFY NIVLAK THAT WE'LL MEET HIM OUTSIDE THE AXIUS SYSTEM.
YES, SIR.
TIME TO GET PAID.
SHOOOOOM!

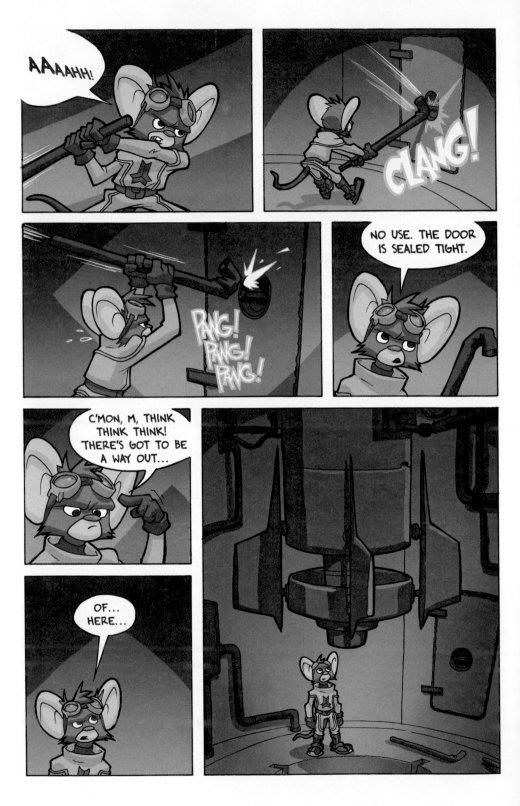

MUNCH
MUNCH
MUNCH MUNCH
RRUMMMBLERUM BBLE RUMM
RRRUMMMBBBBBLERRUMMMBBLERRRRUMMMBBBLERRRUMMB
BLAST!
EEEEEEEEEEEE

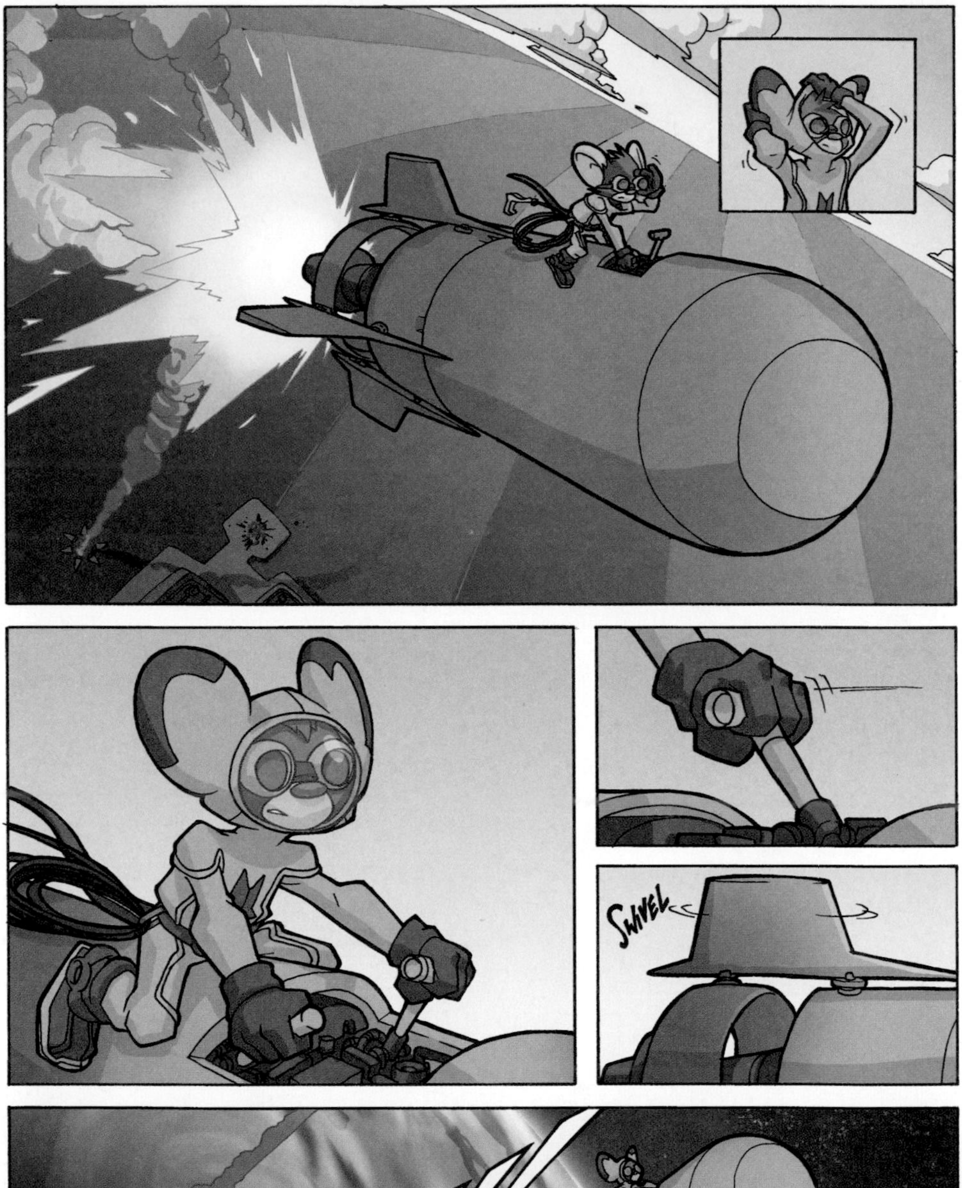
SWIVEL
FWOOOOOSH!

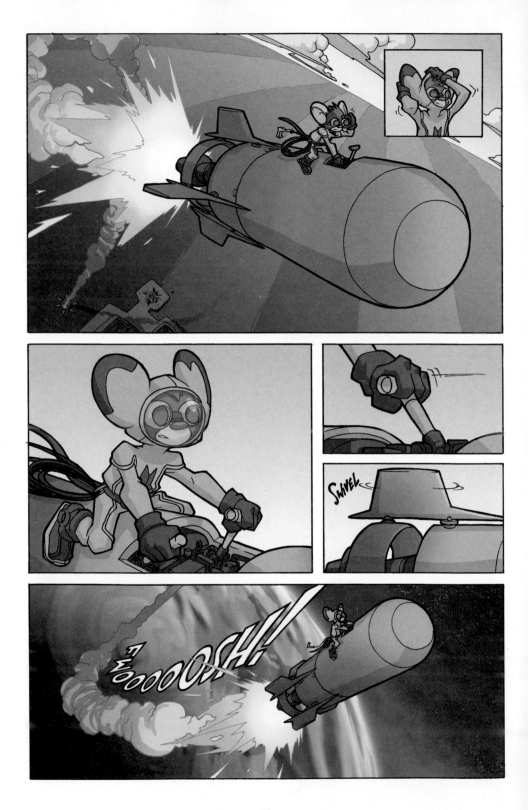

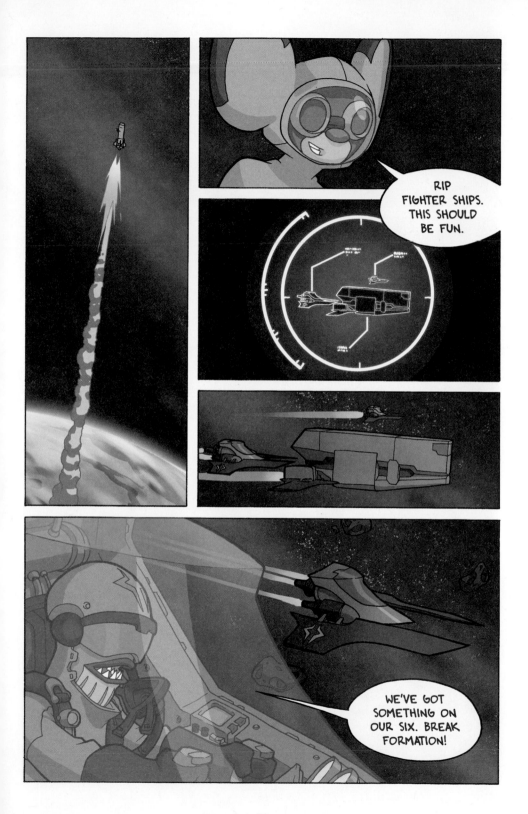

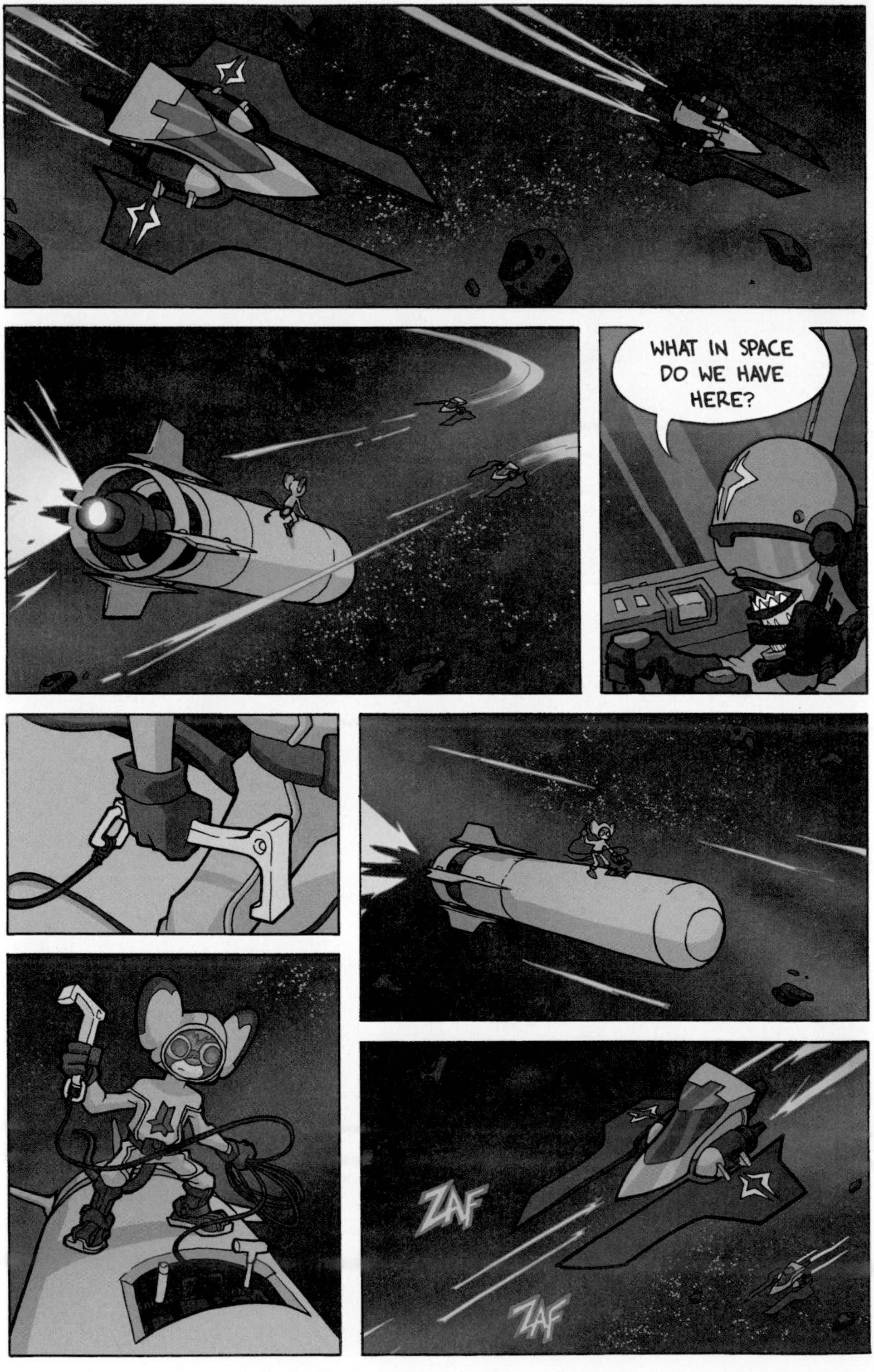
WHAT IN SPACE DO WE HAVE HERE?
ZAF
ZAF

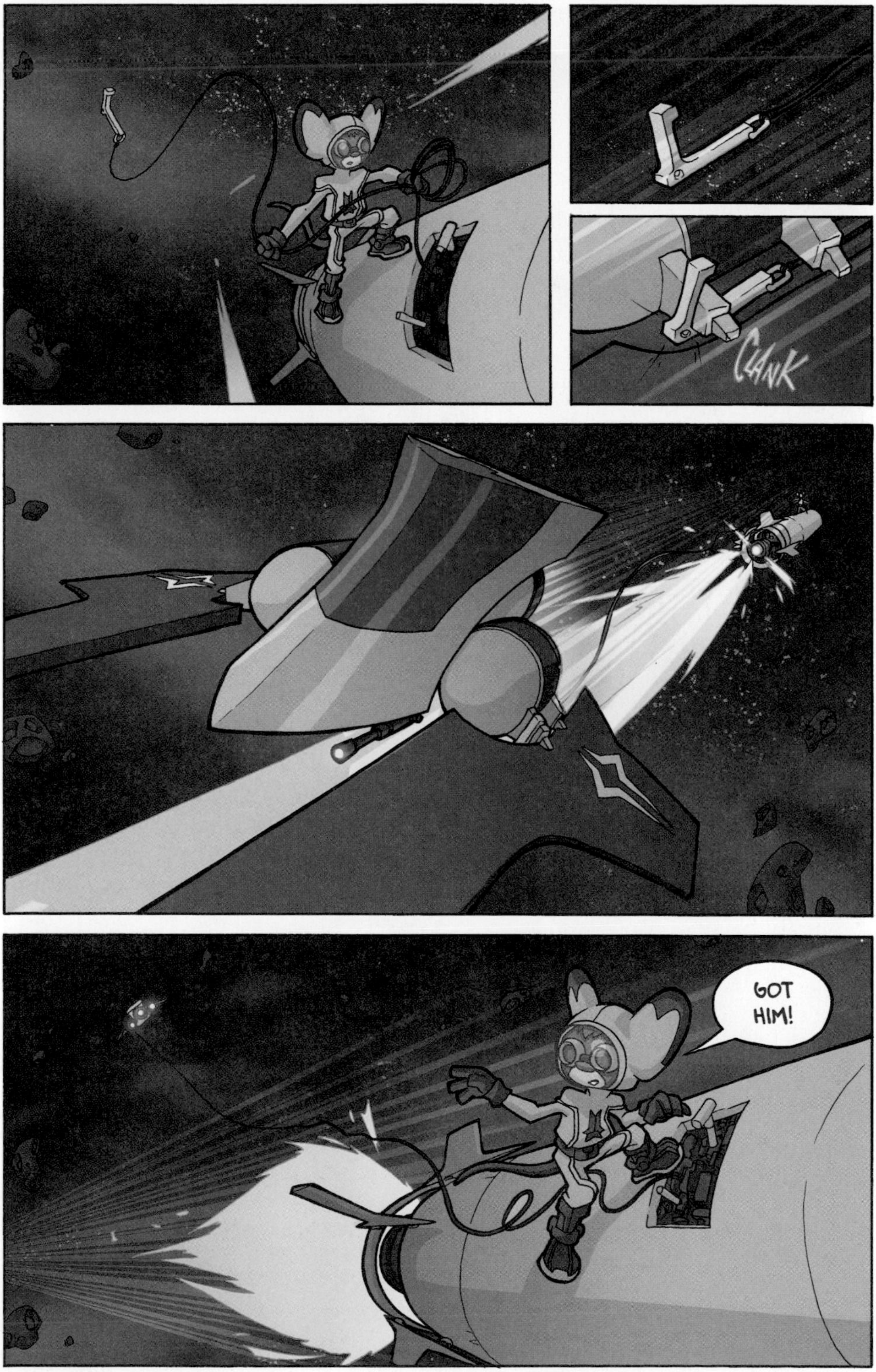
CLANK
GOT HIM!

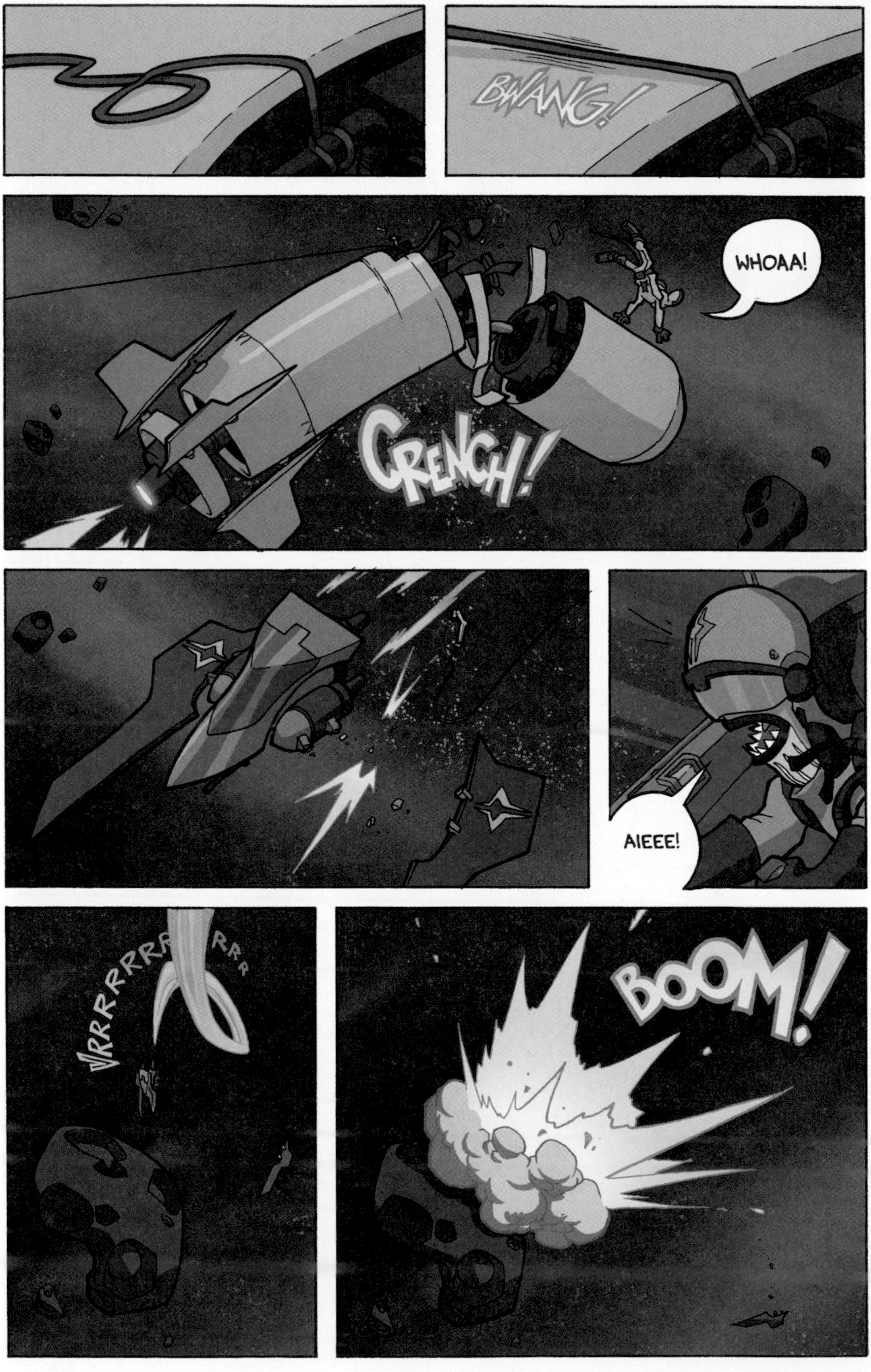
BWANG!
WHOAA!
CRENCH!
AIEEE!
VRRRRRRRRRR
BOOM!

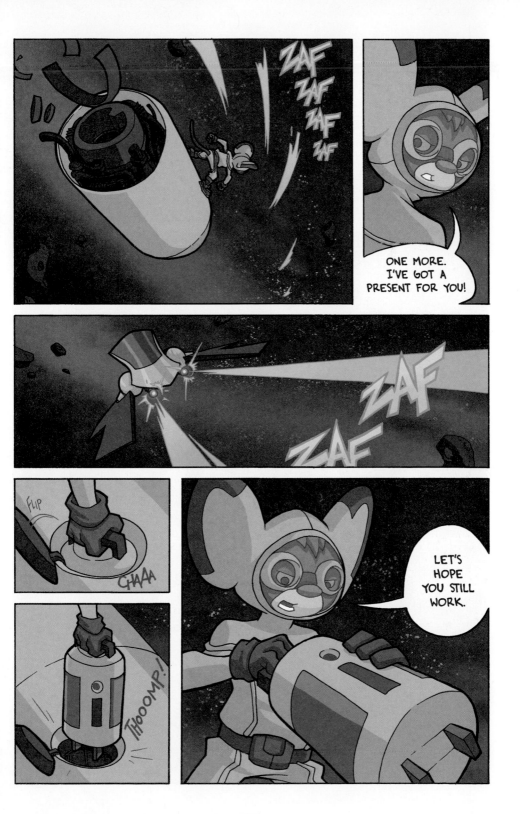

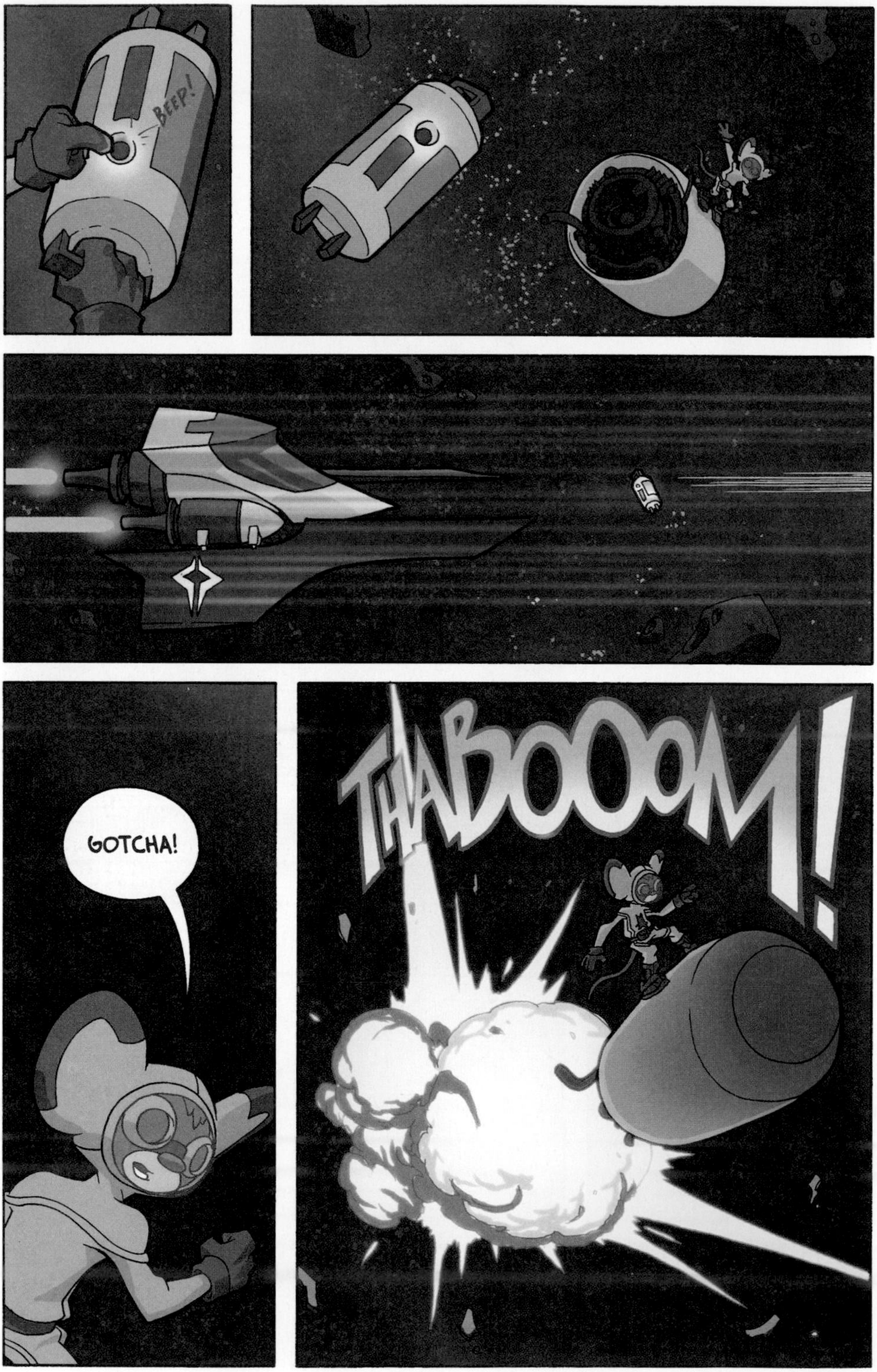
BEEP!
GOTCHA!
THABOOOM!

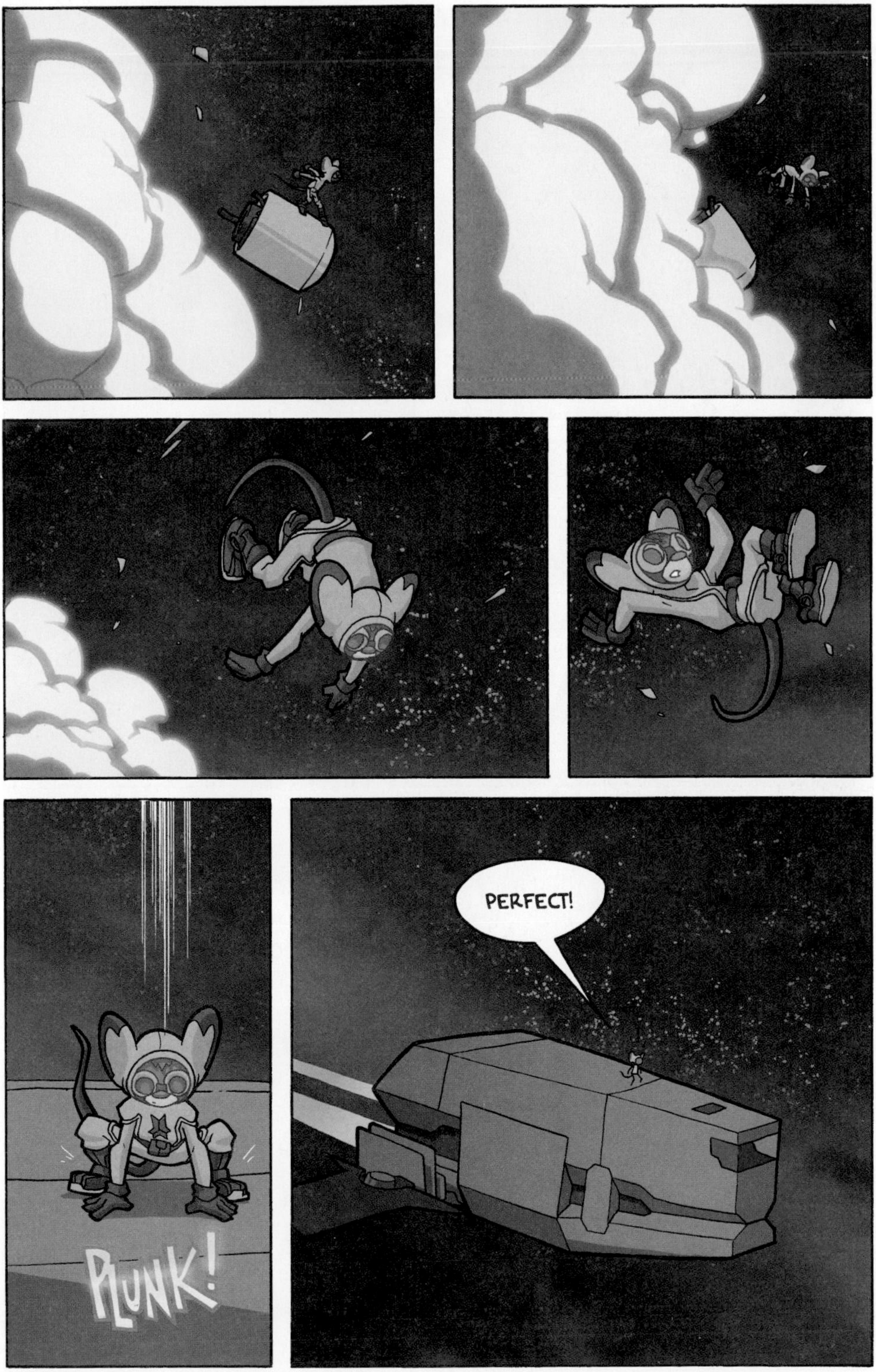
PLUNK!
PERFECT!

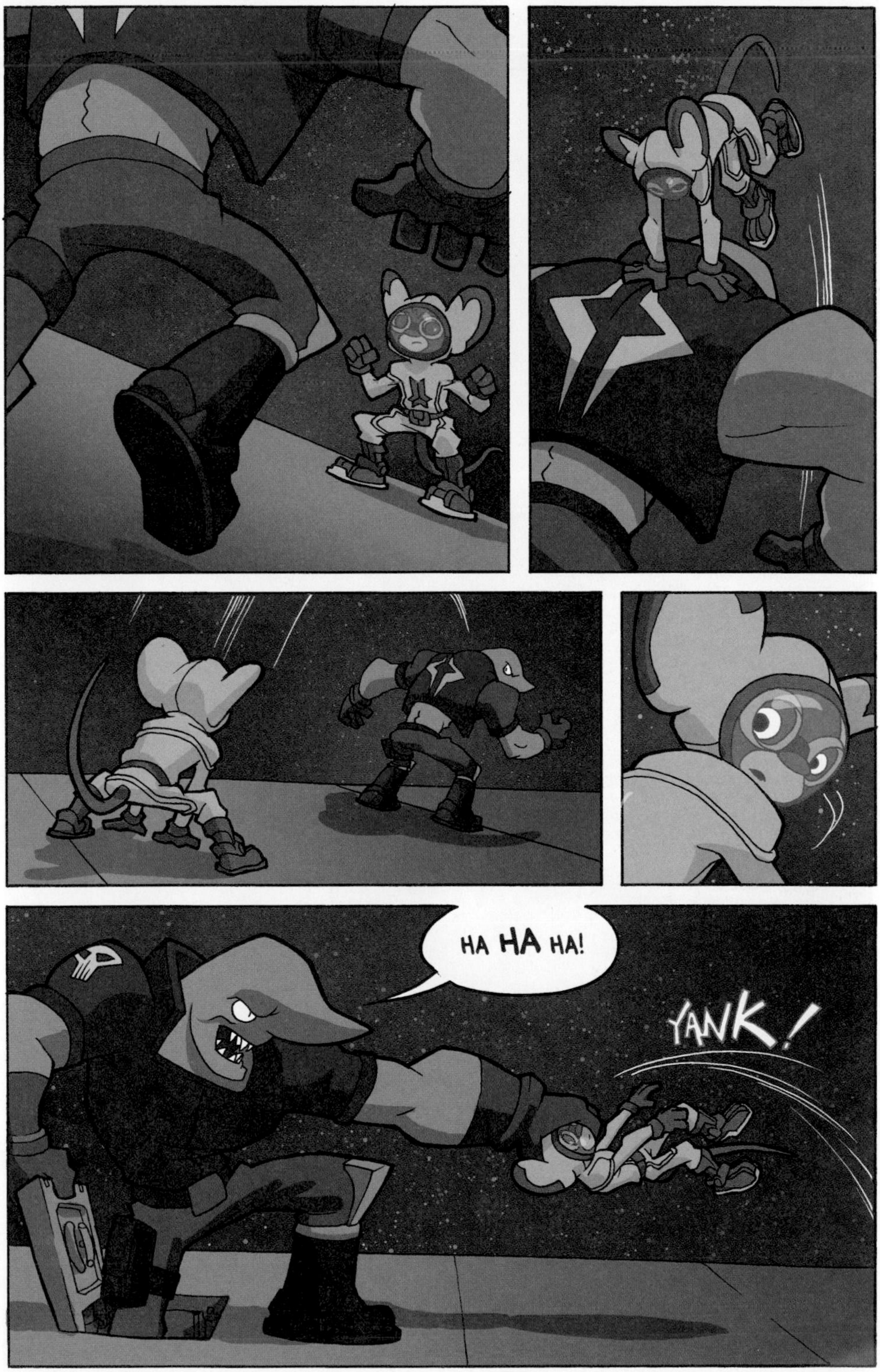
HA HA HA!
YANK!

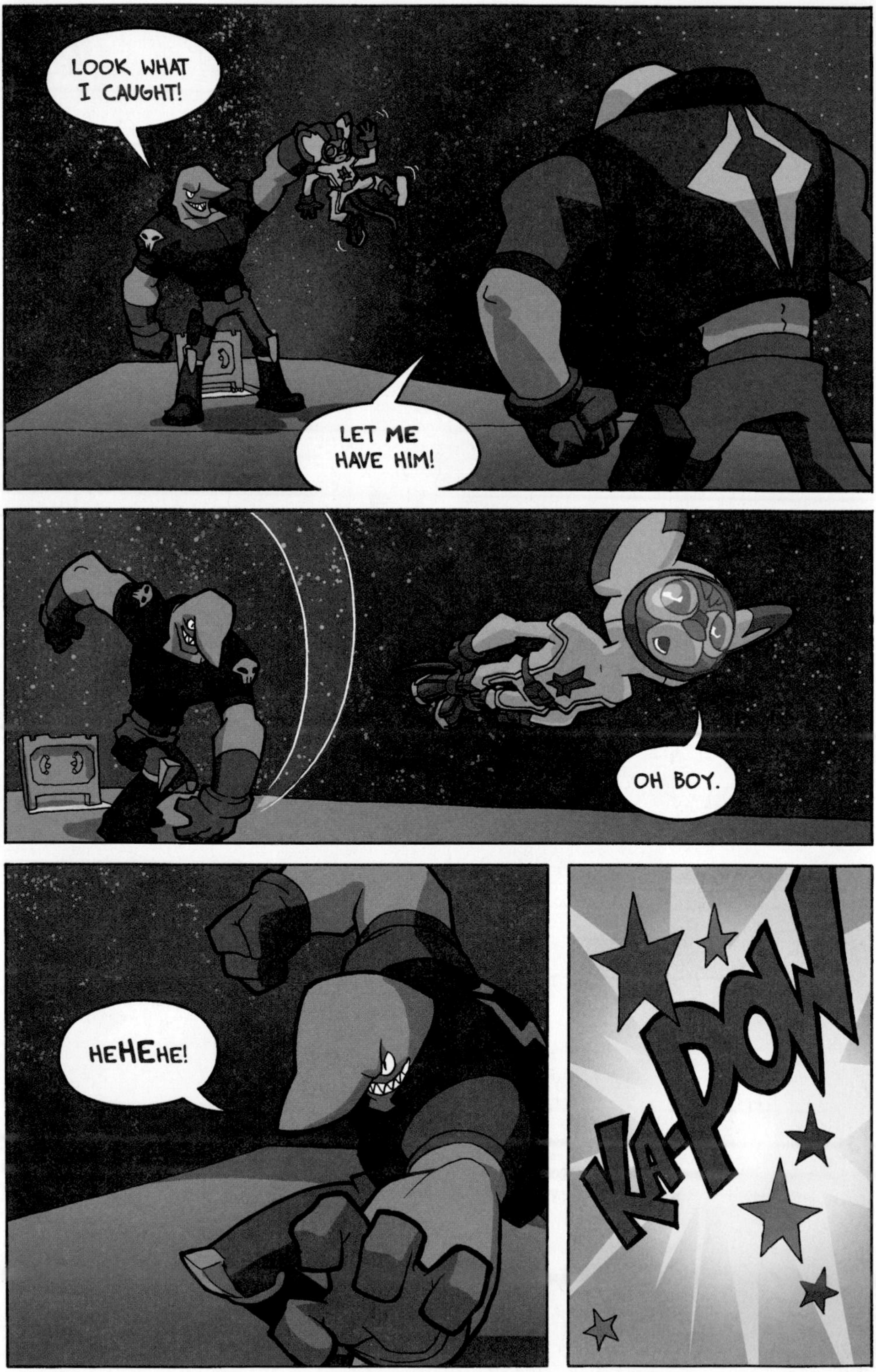
LOOK WHAT I CAUGHT!
LET ME HAVE HIM!
OH BOY.
HEHEHE!
KA-POW

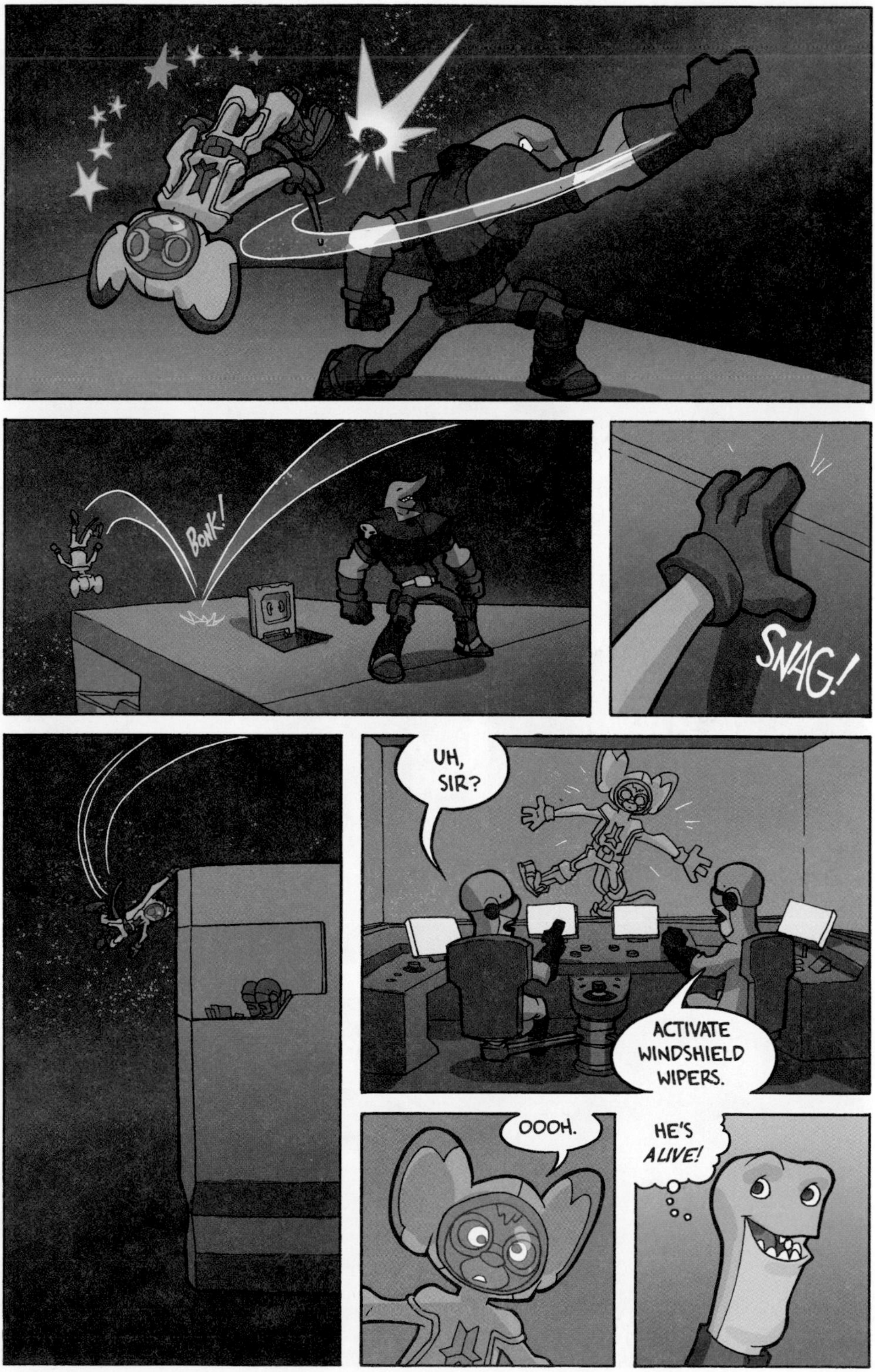
BONK!
SNAG!
UH, SIR?
ACTIVATE WINDSHIELD WIPERS.
OOOH.
HE'S ALIVE!

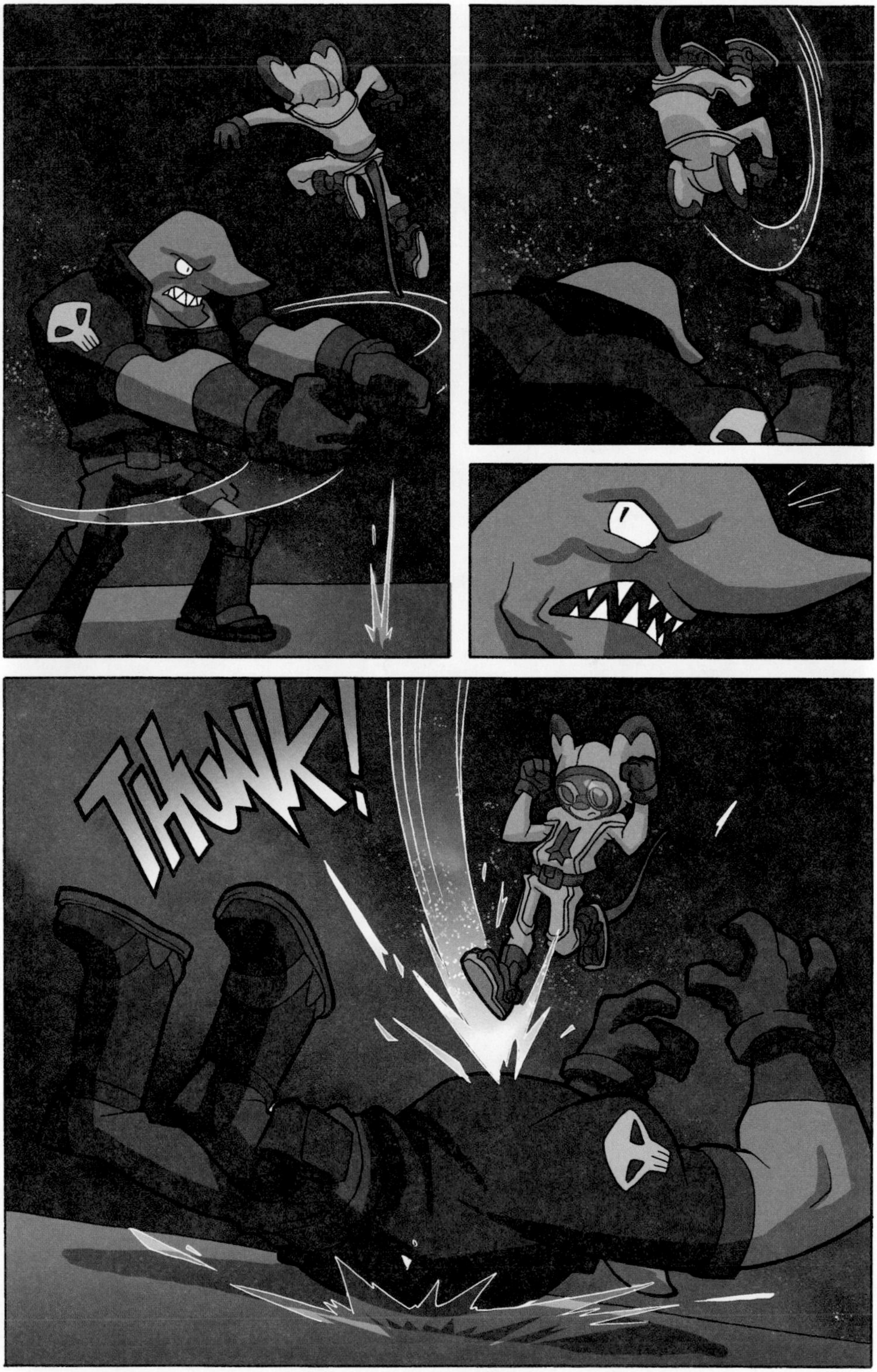
THUNK!

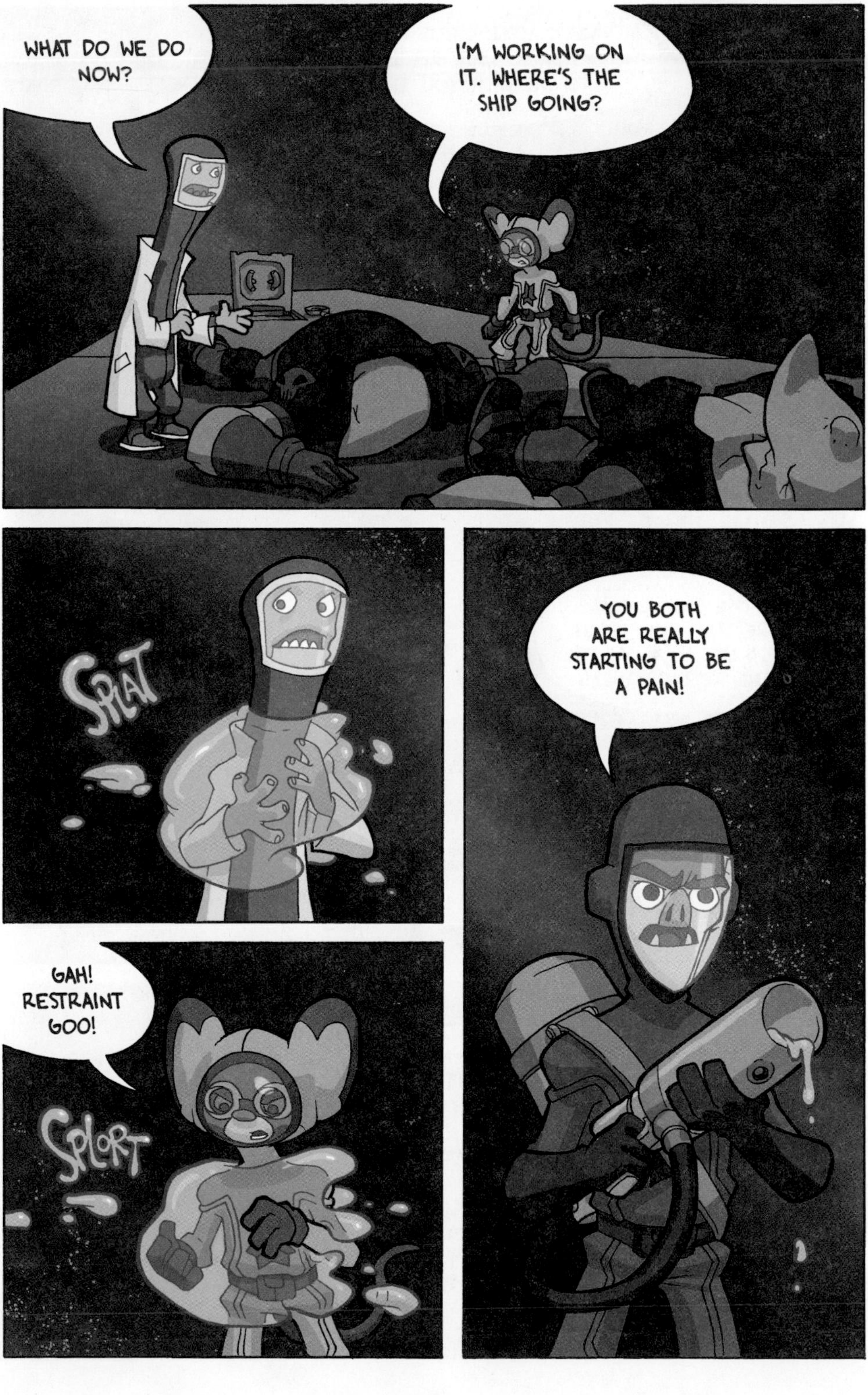
WHAT DO WE DO NOW?
I'M WORKING ON IT. WHERE'S THE SHIP GOING?
SPLAT
YOU BOTH ARE REALLY STARTING TO BE A PAIN!
GAH! RESTRAINT GOO!
SPLORT

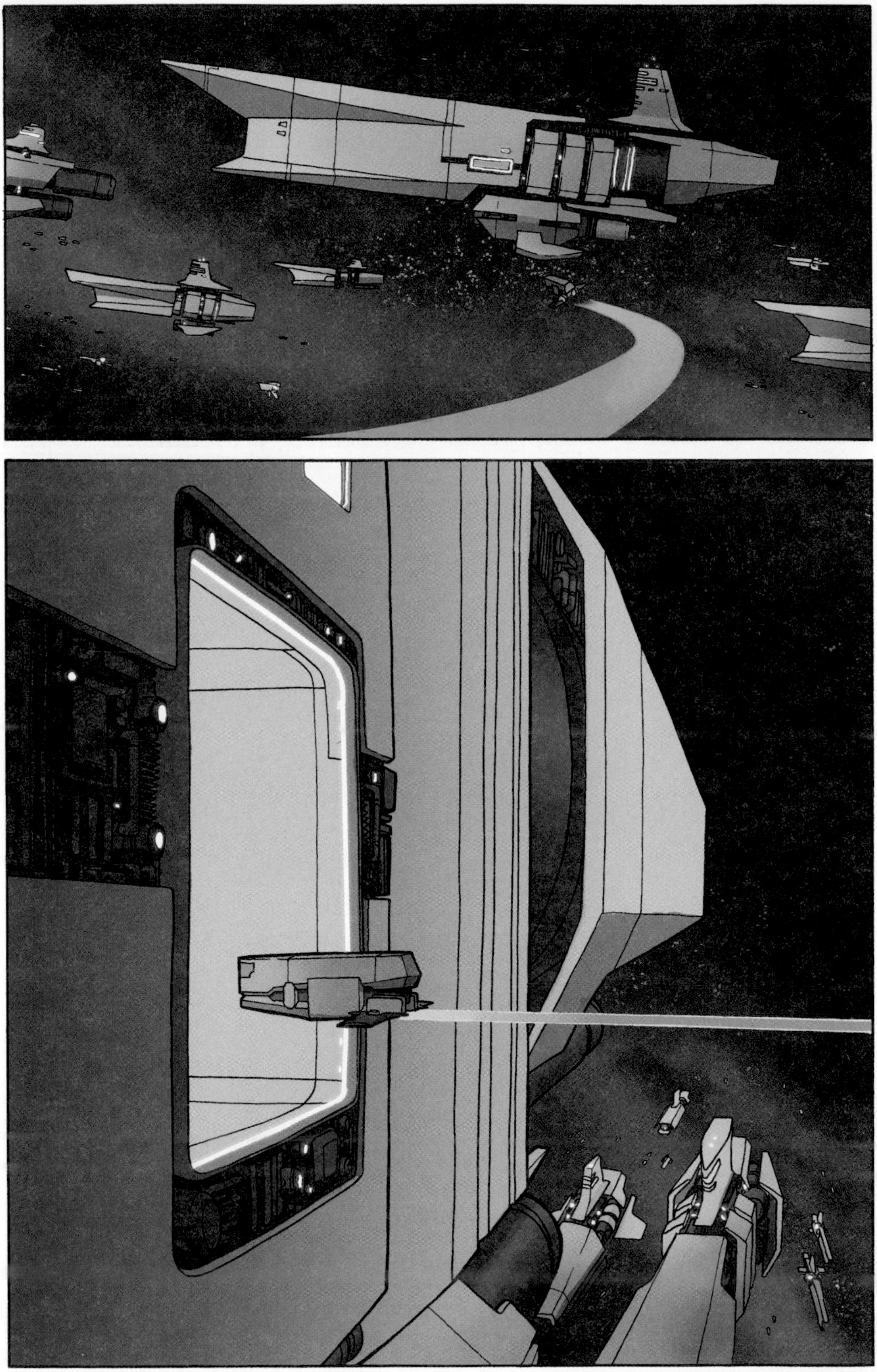

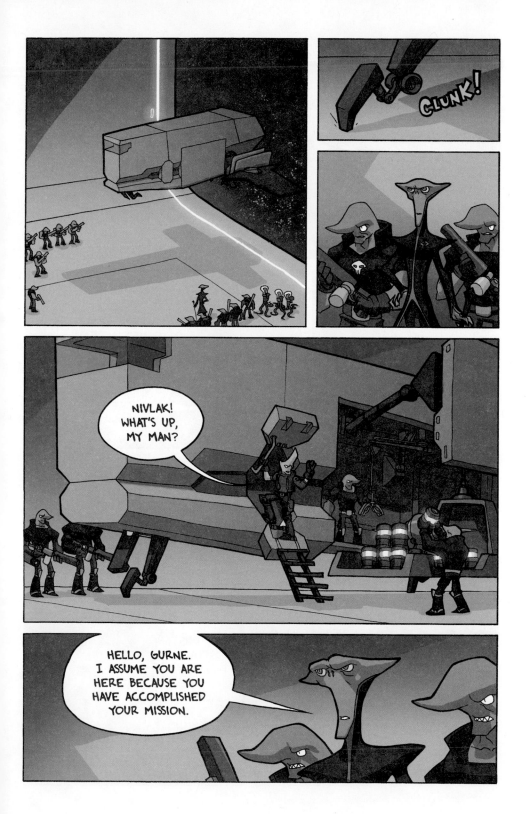

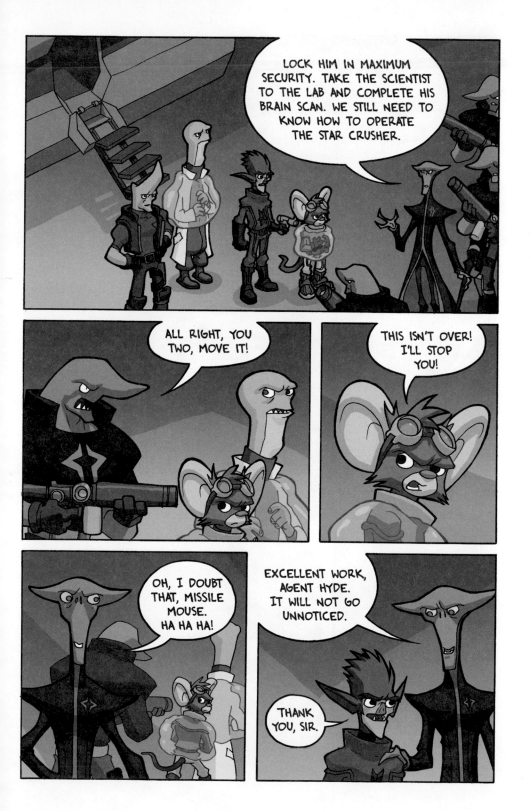

137

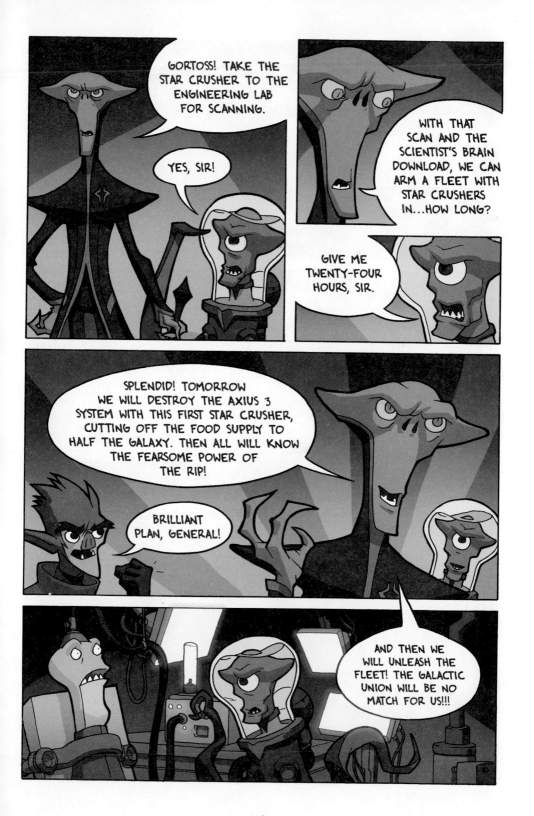

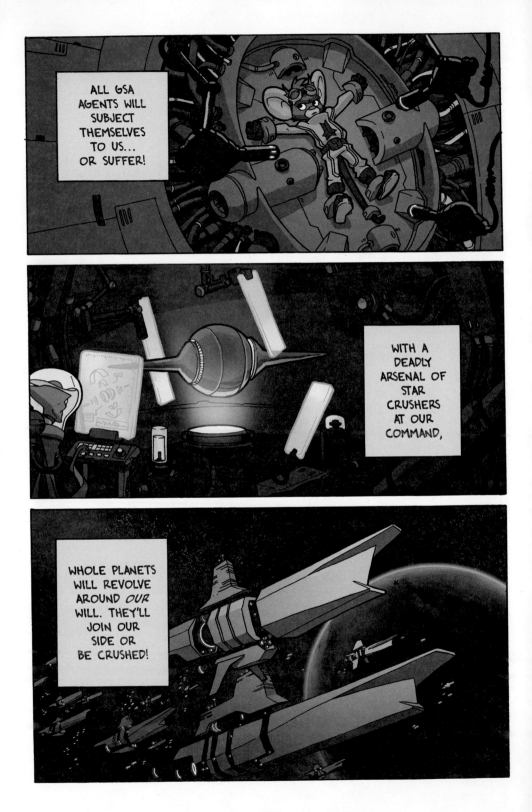

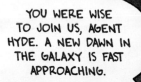

YOU WERE WISE TO JOIN US, AGENT HYDE. A NEW DAWN IN THE GALAXY IS FAST APPROACHING.

NOW, GO REST UP...

WE'VE GOT A SOLAR SYSTEM TO CRUSH TOMORROW.

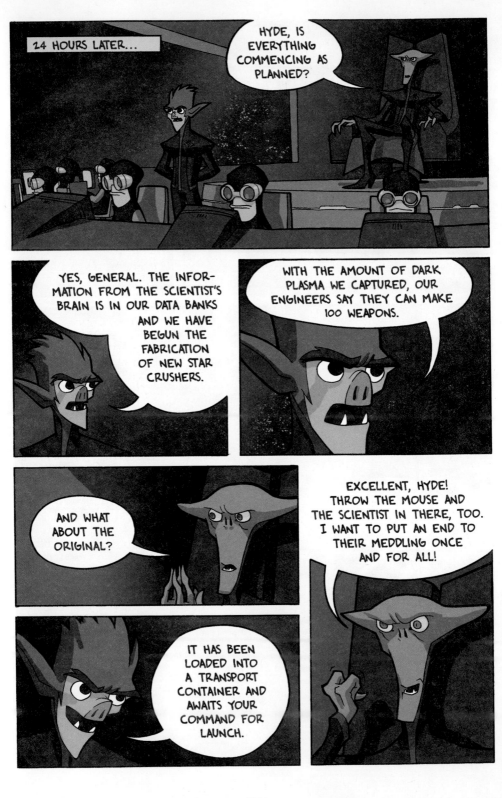

147

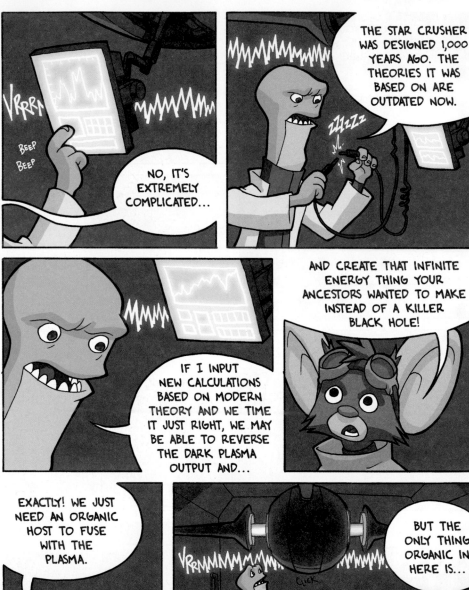

150

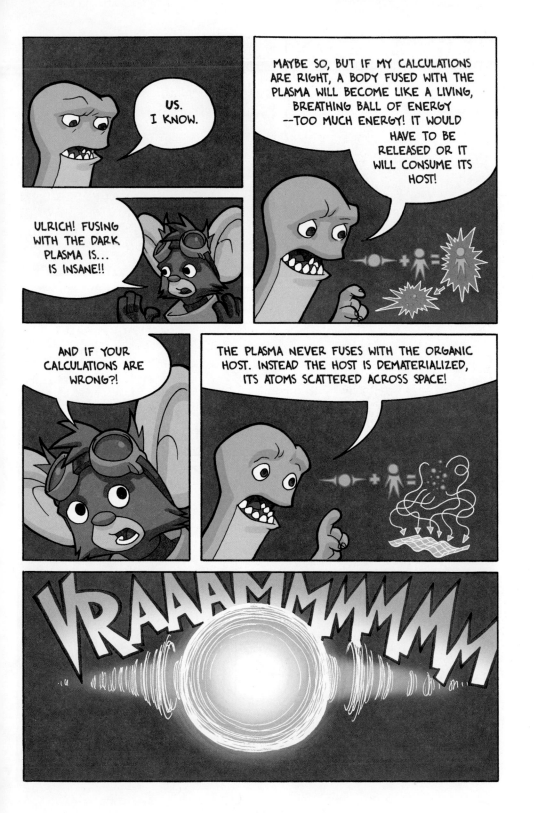

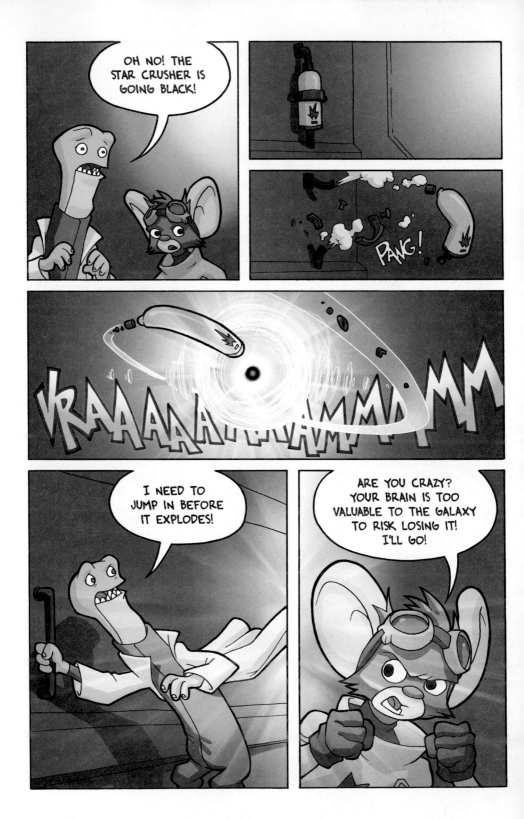

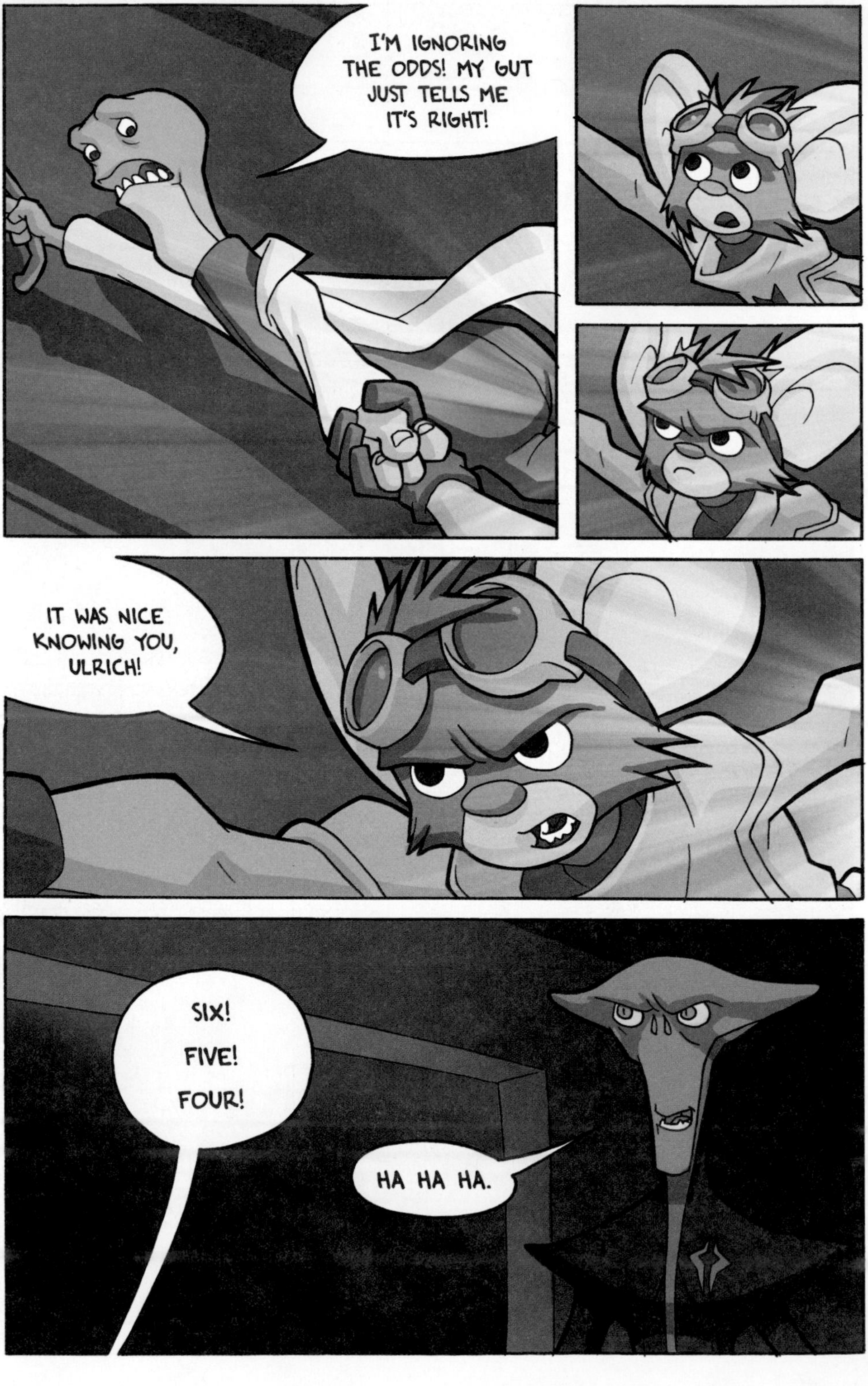
I'M IGNORING THE ODDS! MY GUT JUST TELLS ME IT'S RIGHT!
IT WAS NICE KNOWING YOU, ULRICH!
SIX! FIVE! FOUR!
HA HA HA.

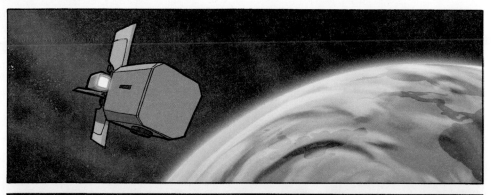

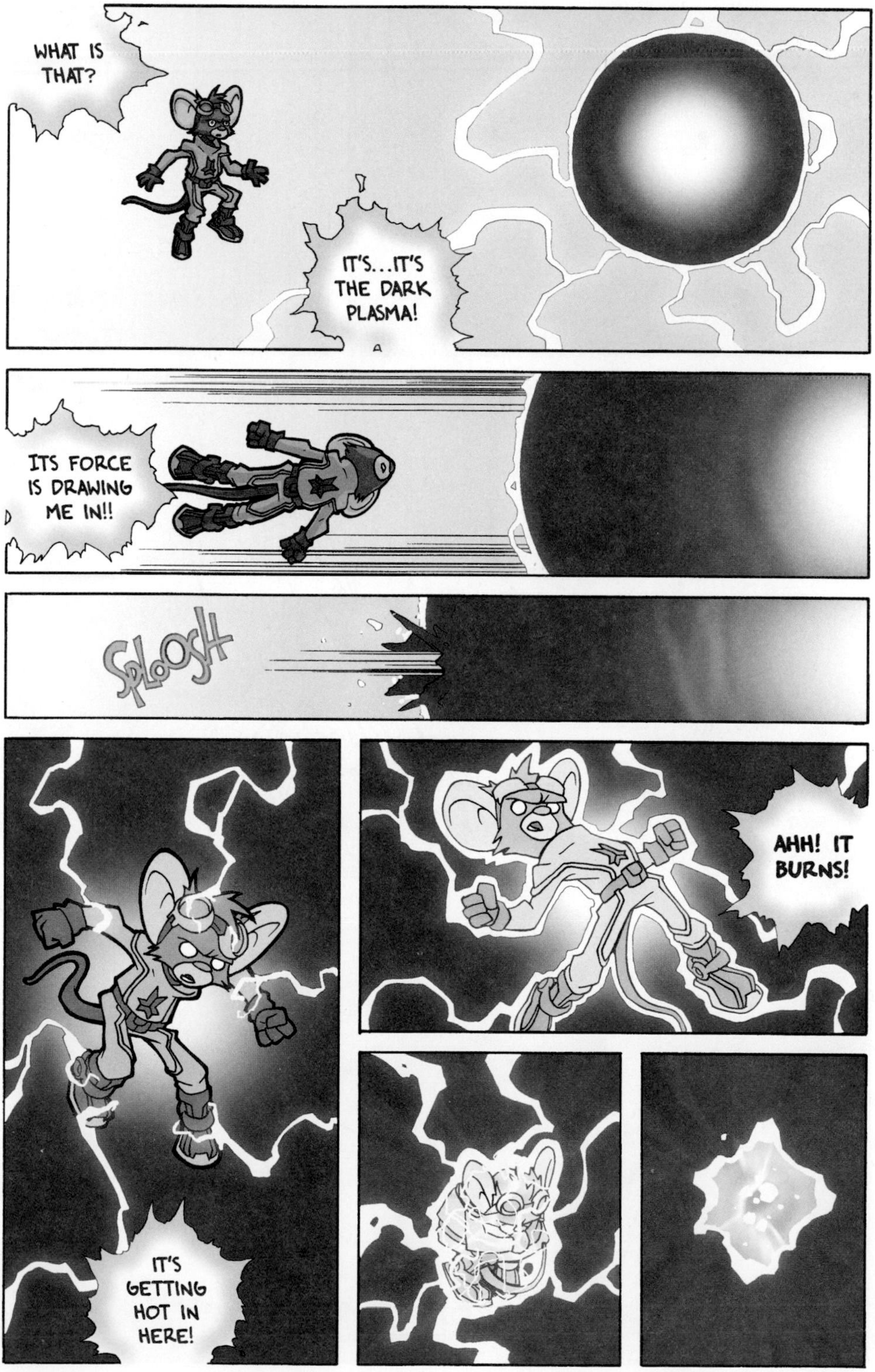
WHAT IS THAT?
IT'S...IT'S THE DARK PLASMA!
ITS FORCE IS DRAWING ME IN!!
SPLOOSH
IT'S GETTING HOT IN HERE!
AHH! IT BURNS!

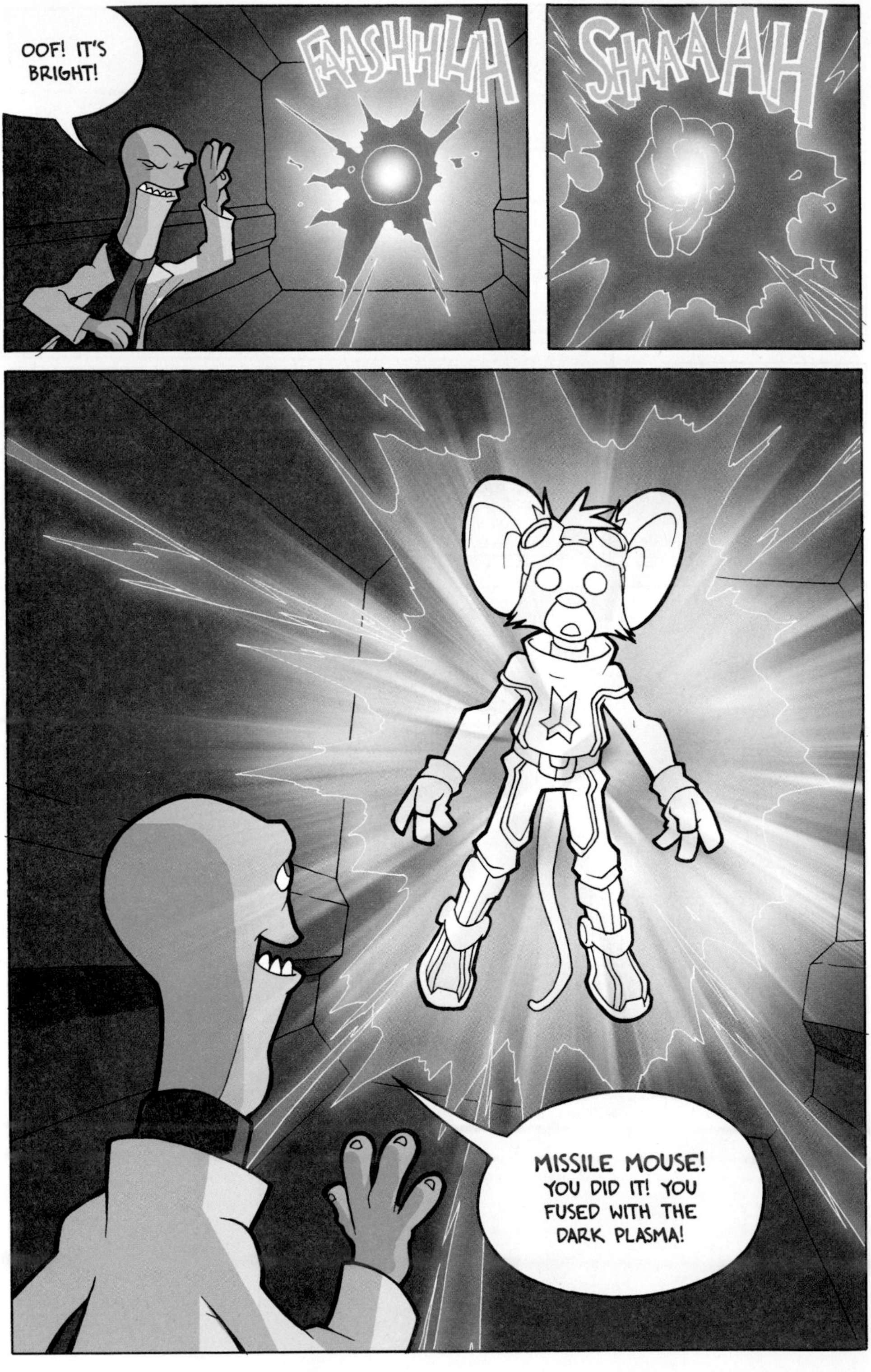
OOF! IT'S BRIGHT!
FAASHHLLH
SHAAAAH
MISSILE MOUSE! YOU DID IT! YOU FUSED WITH THE DARK PLASMA!

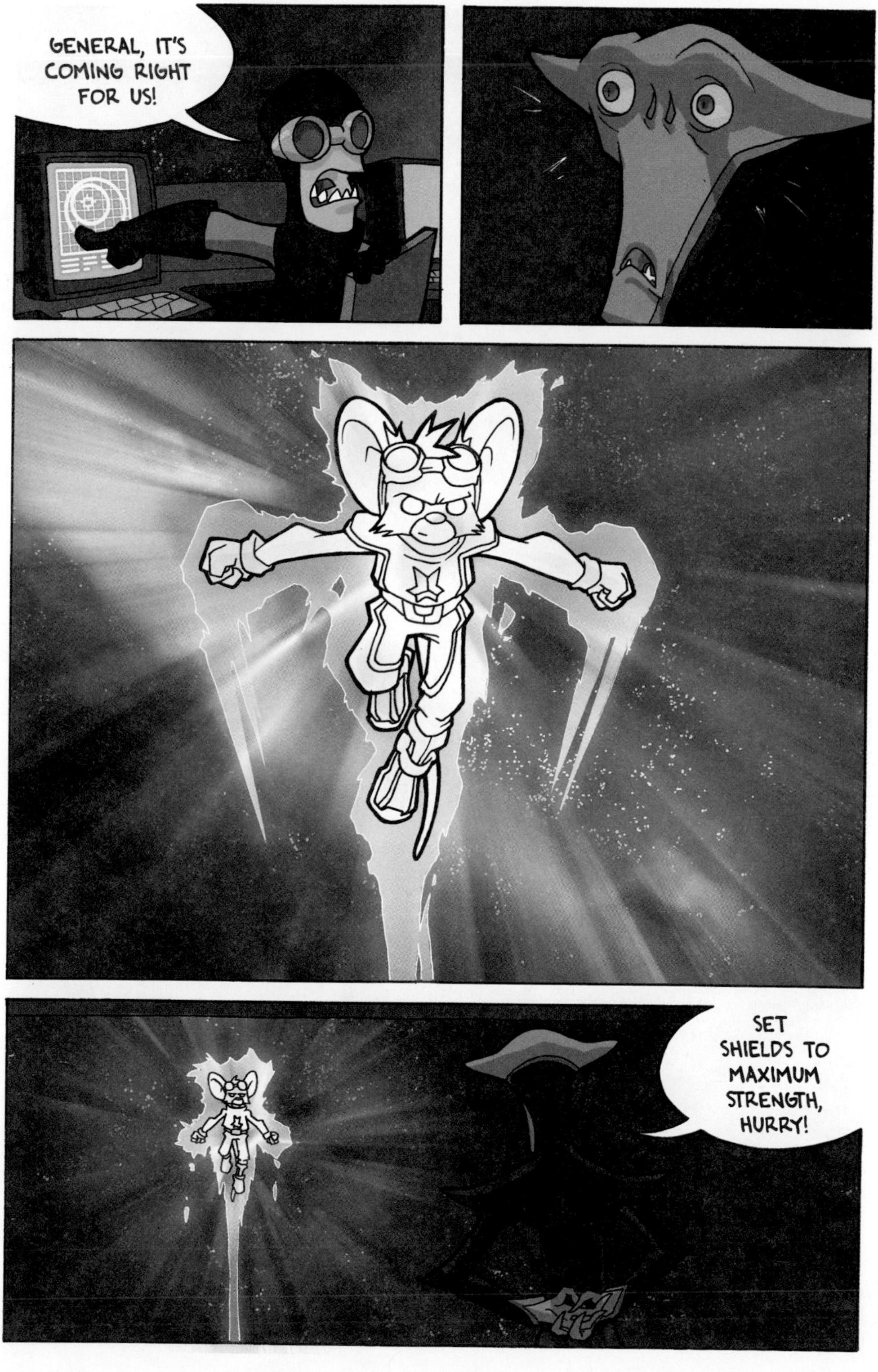
GENERAL, IT'S COMING RIGHT FOR US!
SET SHIELDS TO MAXIMUM STRENGTH, HURRY!

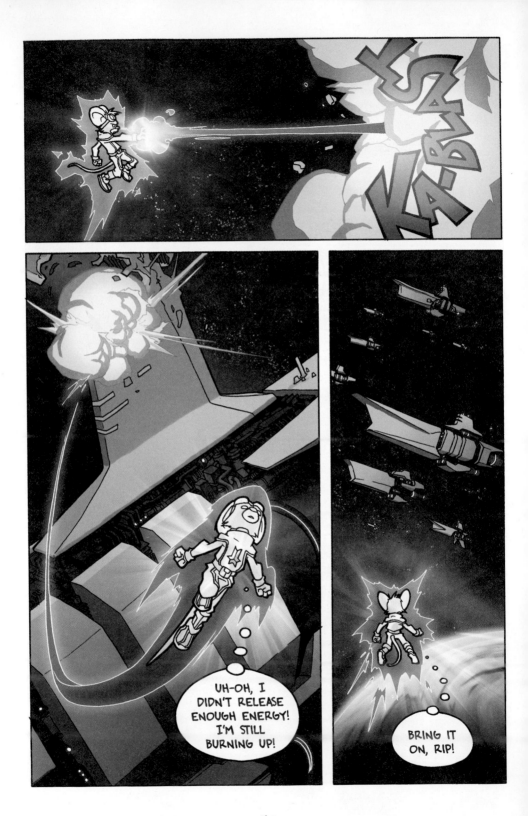

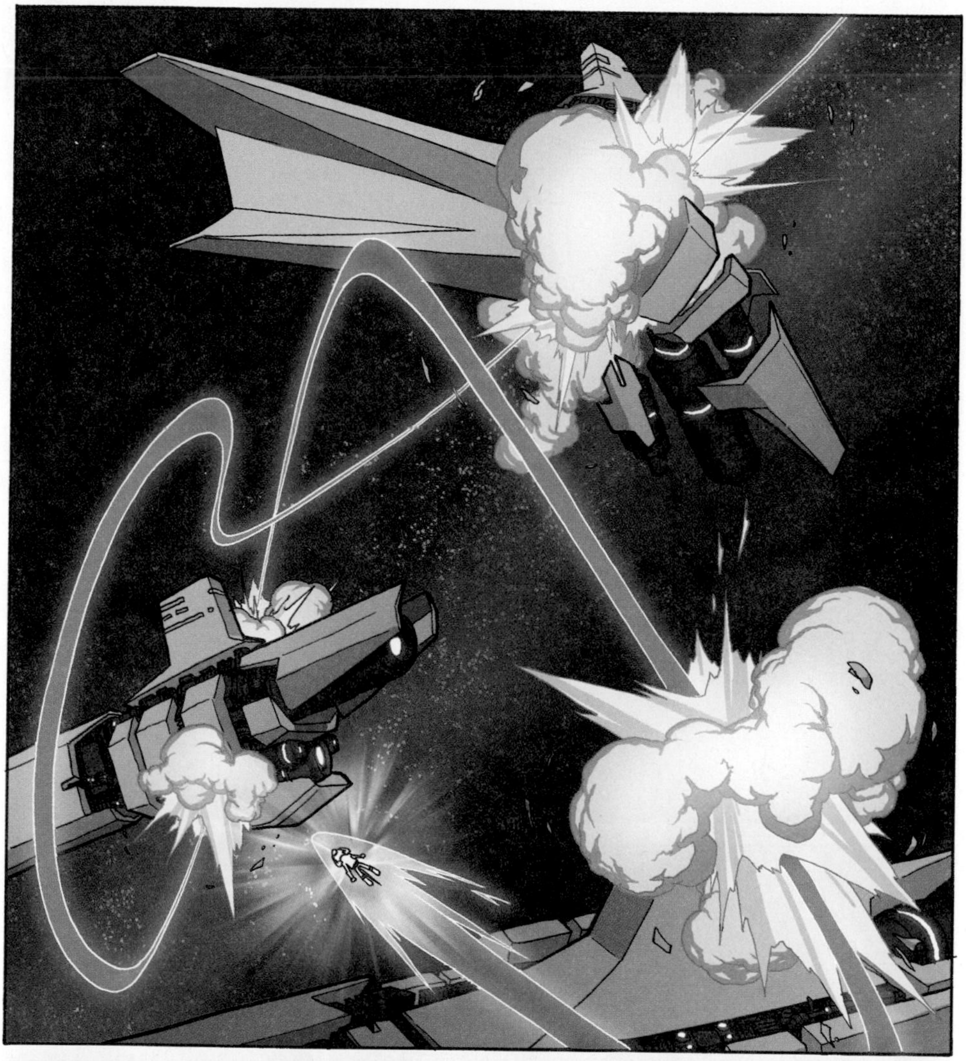

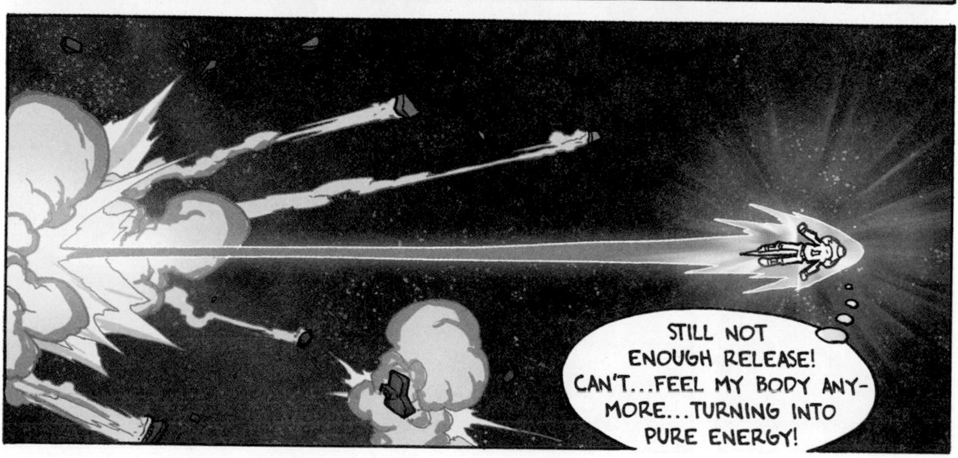
STILL NOT ENOUGH RELEASE! CAN'T...FEEL MY BODY ANY-MORE...TURNING INTO PURE ENERGY!

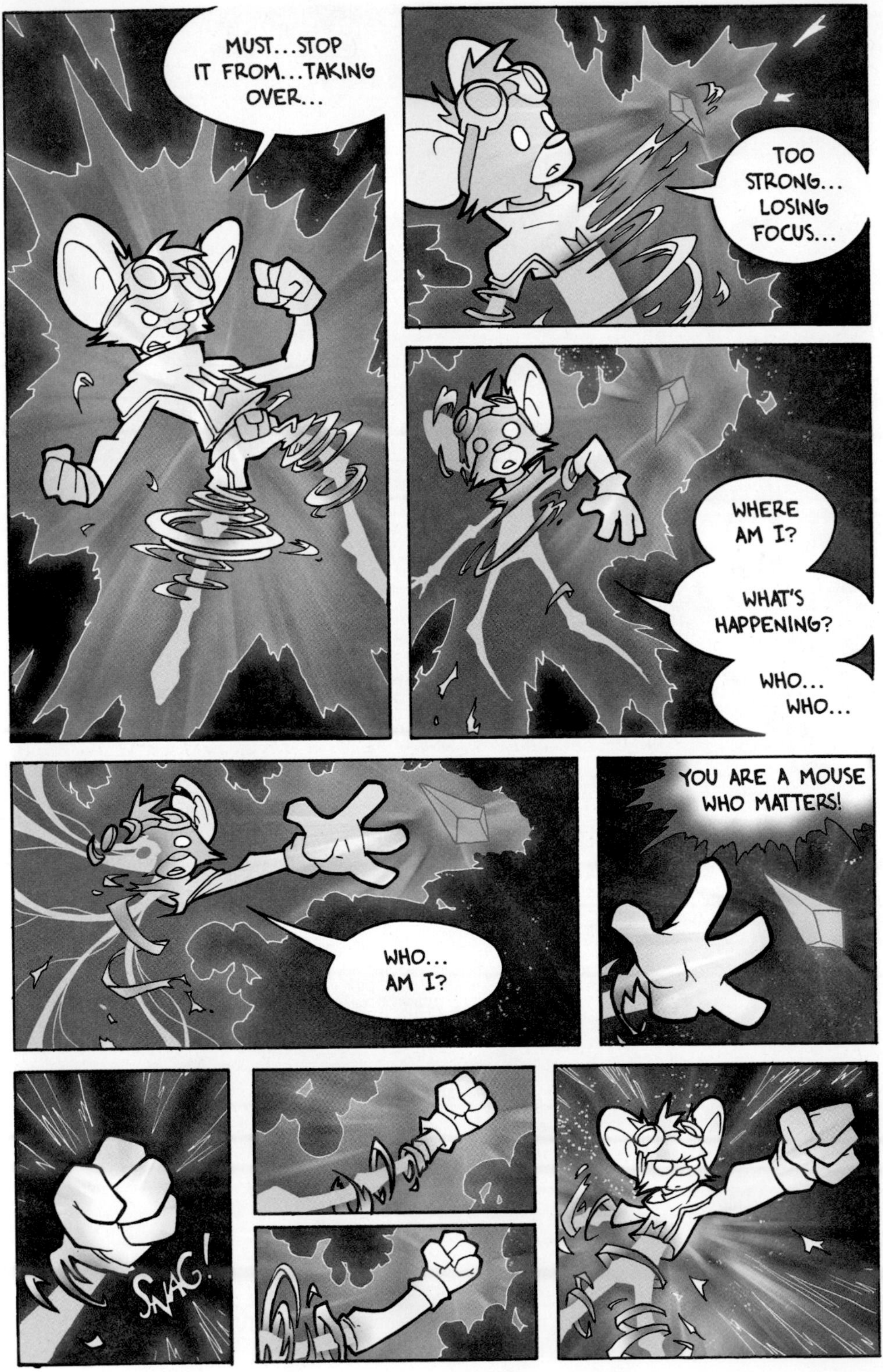
MUST...STOP IT FROM...TAKING OVER...
TOO STRONG... LOSING FOCUS...
WHERE AM I?
WHAT'S HAPPENING?
WHO... WHO...
WHO... AM I?
YOU ARE A MOUSE WHO MATTERS!
SNAG!

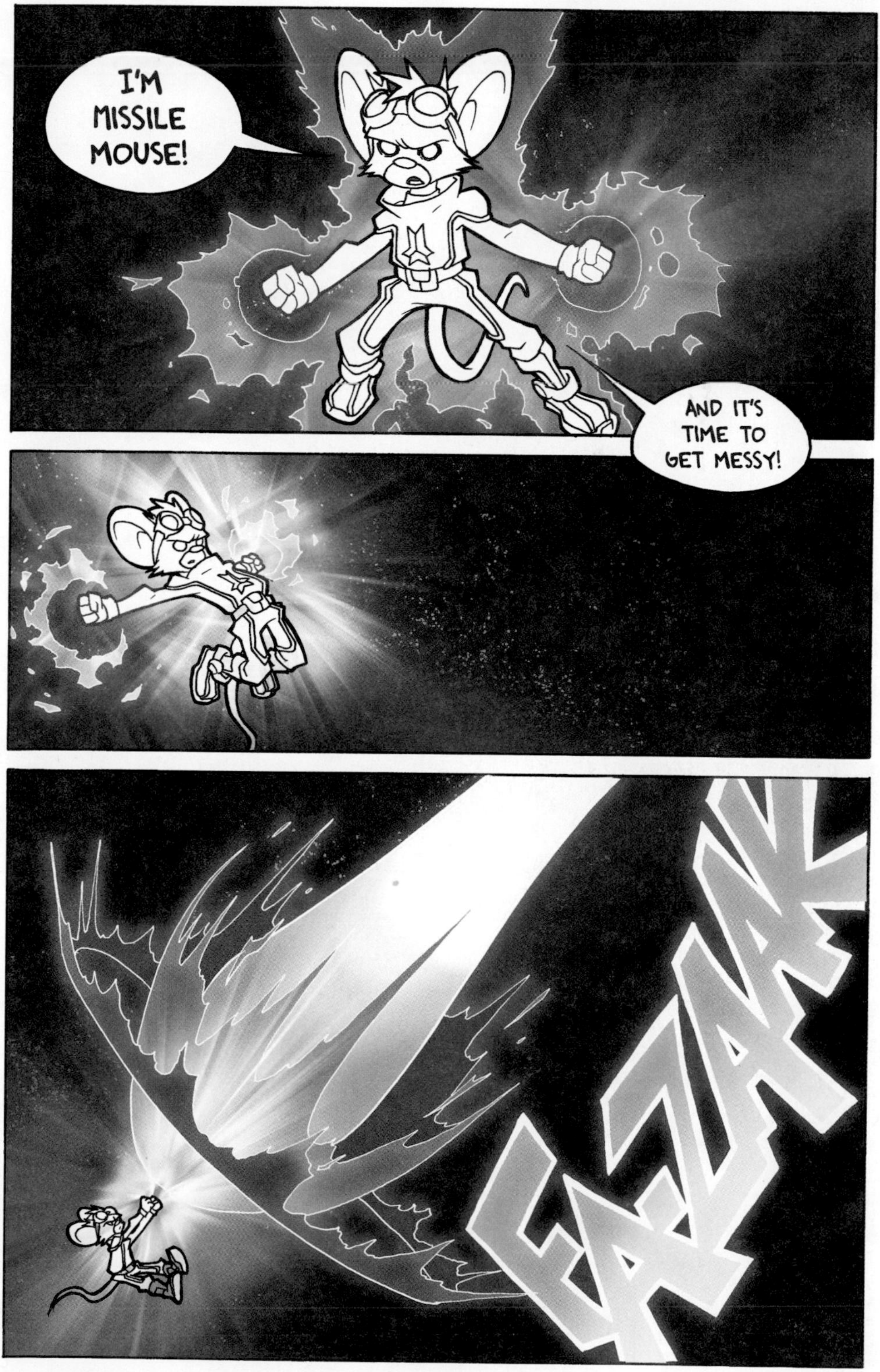
I'M MISSILE MOUSE!
AND IT'S TIME TO GET MESSY!
FAZAK

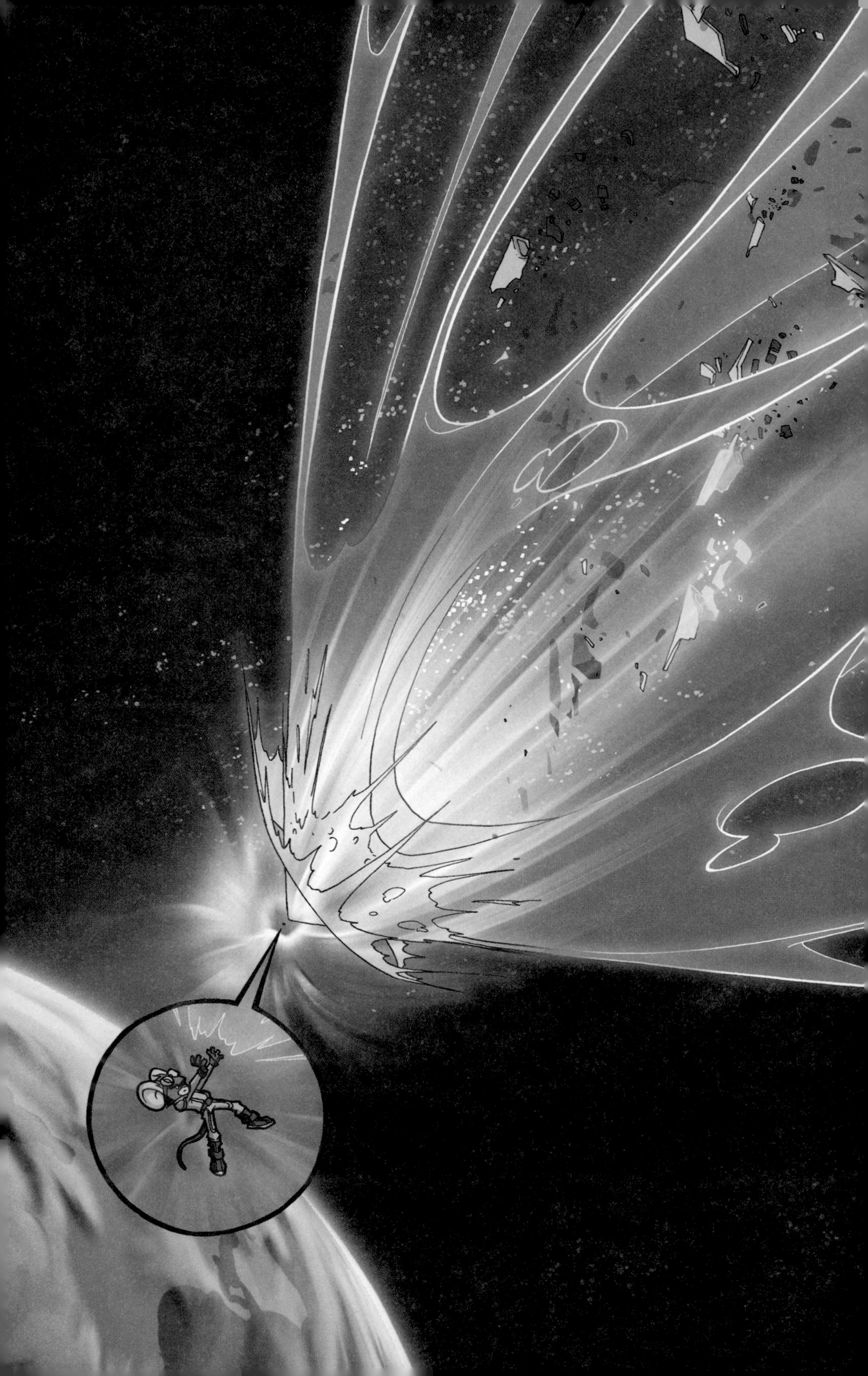

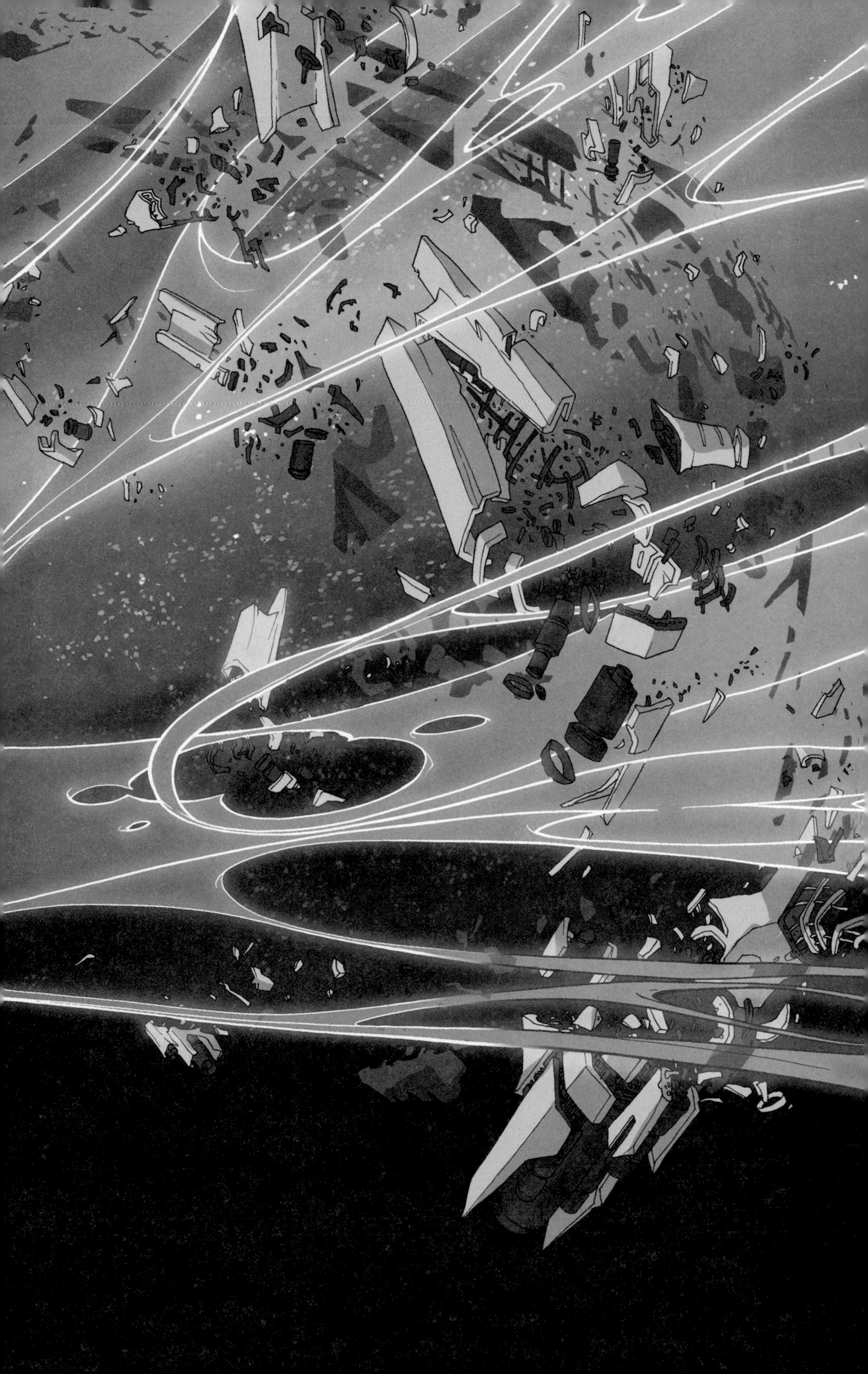

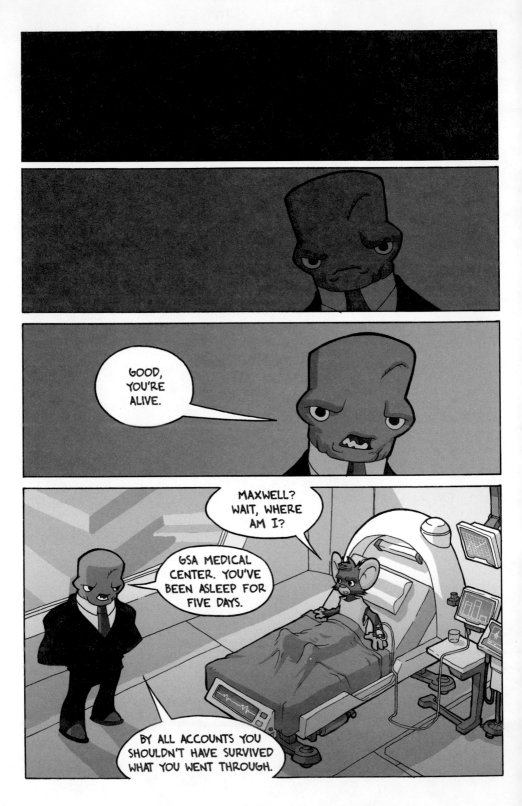

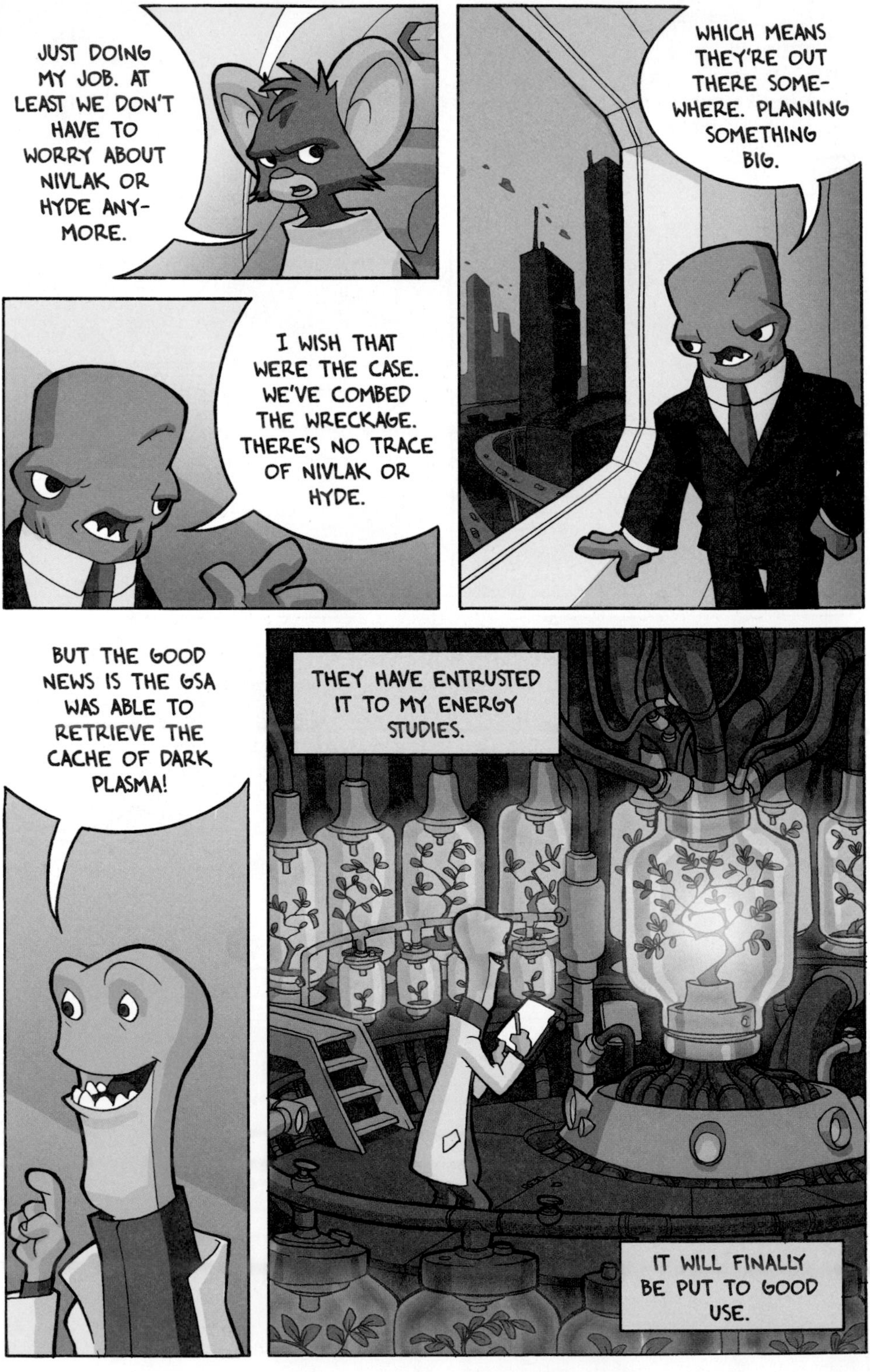
JUST DOING MY JOB. AT LEAST WE DON'T HAVE TO WORRY ABOUT NIVLAK OR HYDE ANY-MORE.
WHICH MEANS THEY'RE OUT THERE SOME-WHERE. PLANNING SOMETHING BIG.
I WISH THAT WERE THE CASE. WE'VE COMBED THE WRECKAGE. THERE'S NO TRACE OF NIVLAK OR HYDE.
BUT THE GOOD NEWS IS THE GSA WAS ABLE TO RETRIEVE THE CACHE OF DARK PLASMA!
THEY HAVE ENTRUSTED IT TO MY ENERGY STUDIES.
IT WILL FINALLY BE PUT TO GOOD USE.

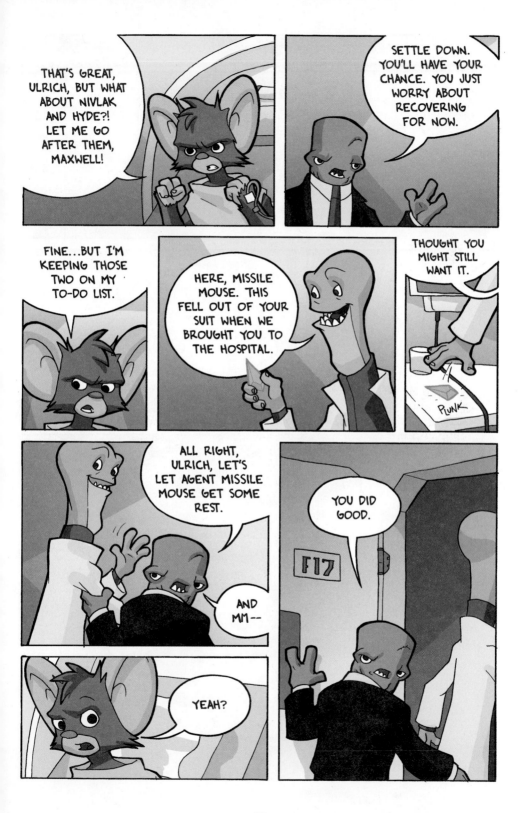

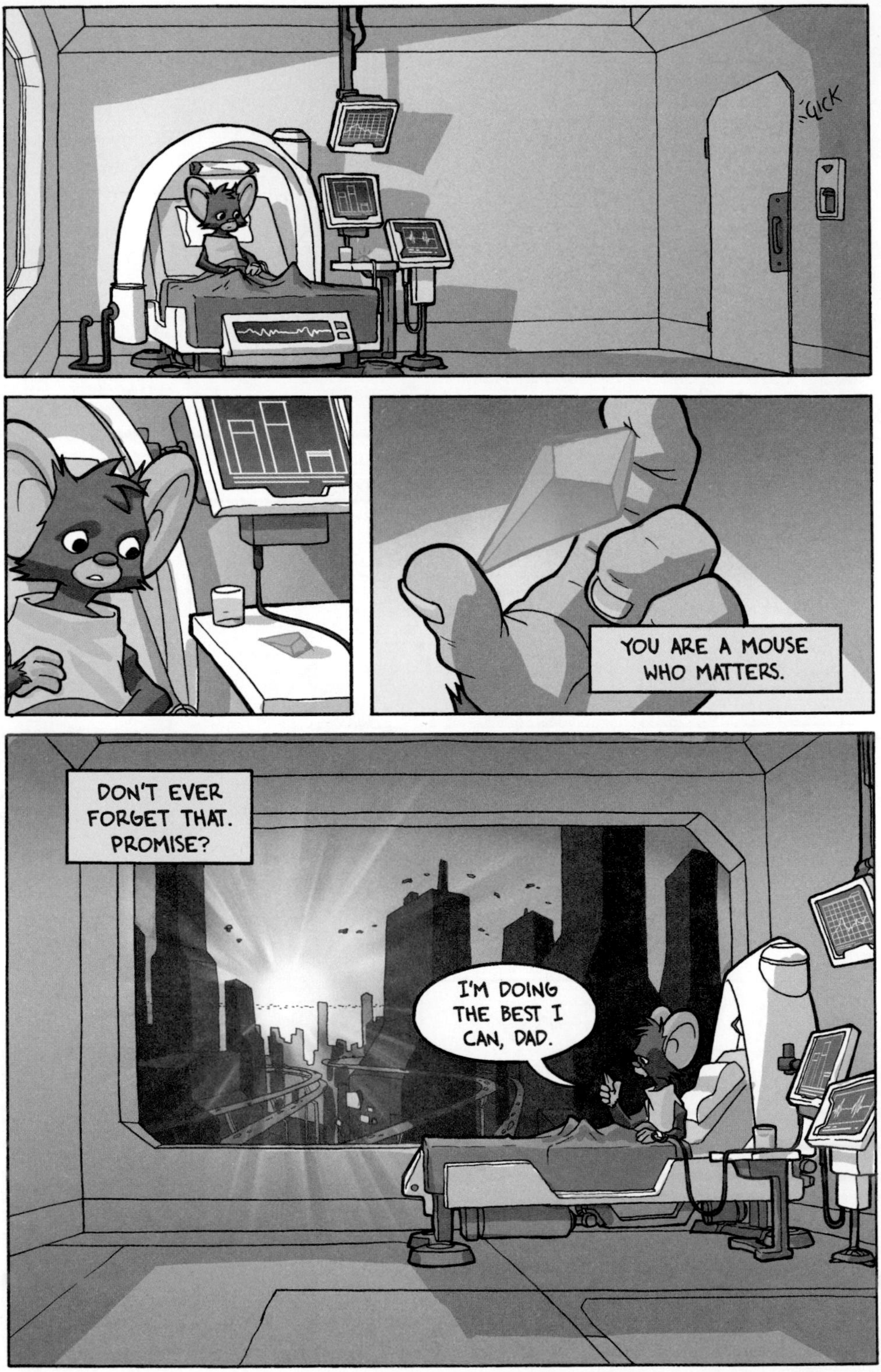
CLICK
YOU ARE A MOUSE WHO MATTERS.
DON'T EVER FORGET THAT. PROMISE?
I'M DOING THE BEST I CAN, DAD.

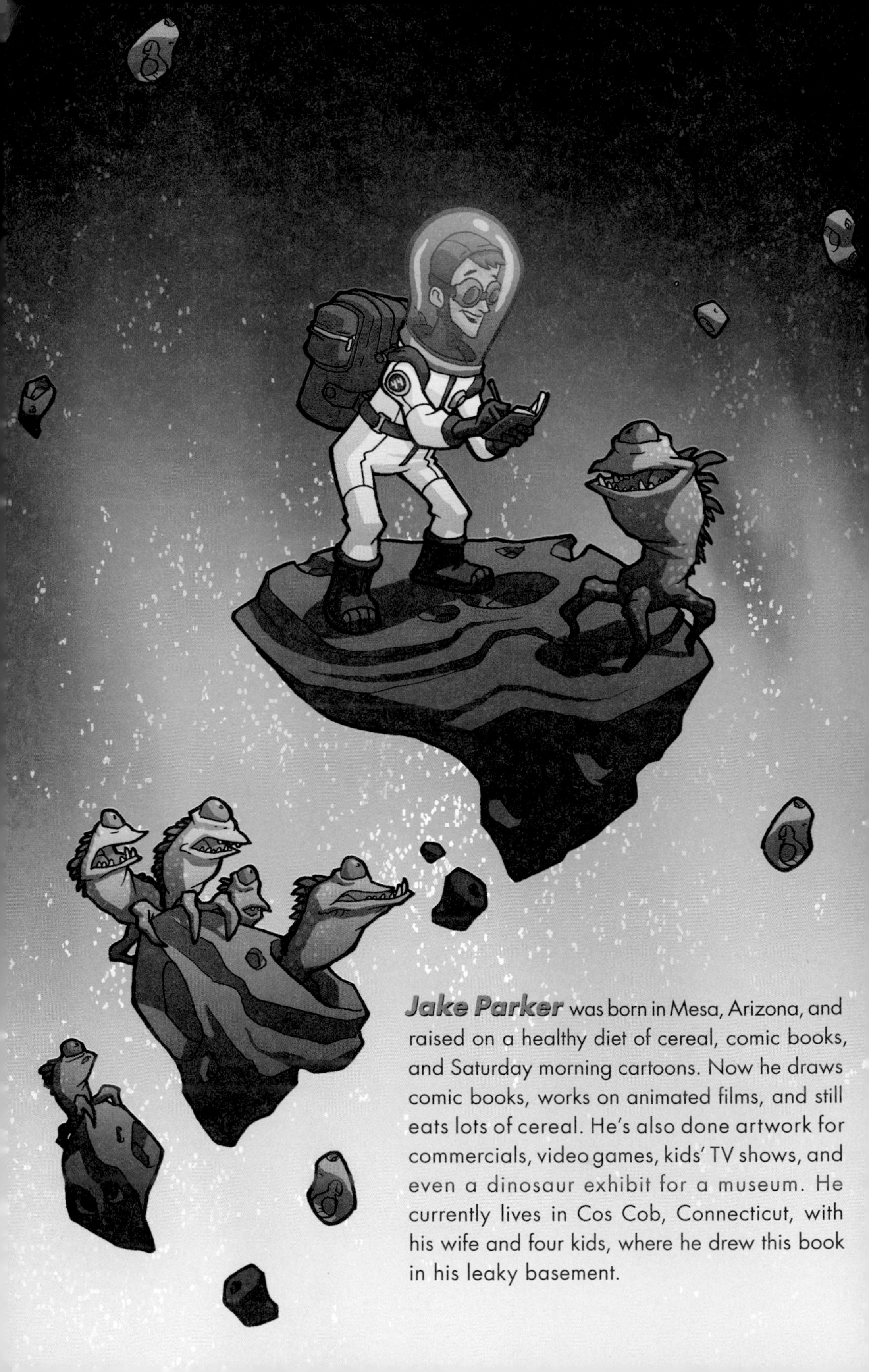

Jake Parker was born in Mesa, Arizona, and raised on a healthy diet of cereal, comic books, and Saturday morning cartoons. Now he draws comic books, works on animated films, and still eats lots of cereal. He's also done artwork for commercials, video games, kids' TV shows, and even a dinosaur exhibit for a museum. He currently lives in Cos Cob, Connecticut, with his wife and four kids, where he drew this book in his leaky basement.